Q.R.F.

By Craig DiLouie

Q.R.F.

©2023 Craig DiLouie. All rights reserved.

This is a work of fiction. All people, places, things, and events portrayed in this novel are either fictitious or used fictitiously.

Cover by Jackie Druga. Interior layout by Brent Nichols. Special thanks to Scott Wolf, who reviewed this work for accuracy in all things military.

Scripture quotations are from the Holy Bible, New Living Translation, copyright © 1996, 2004, 2015 by Tyndale House Foundation. Used by permission of Tyndale House Publishers, Inc., Carol Stream, Illinois 60188. All rights reserved.

Published by ZING Communications, Inc.

www.CraigDiLouie.com

I forsake not—

my country

my mission

my comrades

my sacred duty.

I am relentless.

I am always there,

now and forever.

—from the Infantryman's Creed

Red

Jim Cooper had plenty experience doing the right thing for the wrong reason. Which was why he tensed for action but otherwise stayed put when he spotted the dude storming across the club toward Candygram.

Candygram, whose real name was Pam, catwalked up the lighted stage in her trademark thigh-high striped socks. The regulars hooted loud enough to hear over Aerosmith's "Rag Doll" blasting from the sound systems.

Tossing her hair and casting a mischievous smile at a customer she recognized, Pam raised a leg to demurely peel one of her socks off. The crowd cheered. Offstage, Coop found her a little abrasive, like honey coating tin foil, but she was a hell of a performer.

The dude reached the stage, his mouth moving. From his usual position by the front doors, Coop watched him, watched her reaction.

Pam froze and gave a little headshake before sliding back into her routine. The dude appeared ready to burst but found an empty chair and plopped down, his knee pumping as he waited.

Coop relaxed a little.

Overall, he liked working here as a bouncer. He was up late anyway. He could often spot trouble before it happened, and he looked the part. Tall and toned thanks to daily physical training, which he'd hated in the Army but had kept up ever since, his formidable presence alone offered a deterrent to trouble.

His awareness returned to its usual constant yellow threat level. His eyes swept the guys ogling the mingling women, who sized up the men.

A scantily clad server approached him. Wanda. The women here generally fell into one of three categories: damaged, working stiff, or transitioning to something else. Wanda was the last type. Working her way through nursing school.

"What's up?" he said as she neared. He kept one eye on the stage, where Pam shot worried glances at the dude now giving her the stink-eye.

"Big John told me he wants to see you."

"In the office?"

"Yeah. You need anything to drink while I'm here?"

"No, I'm good, thanks."

"I was thinking something with alcohol." She smiled. "You look especially uptight tonight."

"I assure you it's intentional," he said.

Wanda snorted. "Whatever."

After she left, Coop didn't move. He'd see the boss after the drama between Pam and the anxious dude, probably a lovestruck customer, played itself out.

Her songs ended. She gathered her clothes, gave the audience a final little shimmy, and left the stage while the DJ asked the crowd to *give it up for the lovely Candygram!* Moments later, she emerged from a door next to the stage in her costume and marched straight up to the anxious dude, who jumped to his feet.

Coop couldn't hear them arguing over Ariana Grande, but he read their body language easily enough. Pam chopped the air with her hand. The dude gazed back in disbelief until his face hardened to a determine scowl.

Then he grabbed her arm to yank her toward the door.

Coop surged forward, his threat awareness jumping past orange straight to red.

Red: ready to fight.

Pam yanked her arm away. They were yelling now. The dude tried to grab her again.

His hand never made it.

Snatching the dude's wrist, Coop wrenched his arm. His other hand gripped the back of the man's neck, shoving his head down.

"Time to go home," Coop said, frogmarching him to the doors.

Bursting outside into the cold fall air, he released the dude with a final shove to emphasize he wasn't getting back inside. The usual small crowd of smokers looked over with surprised expressions that quickly morphed into smirks.

Hands shoved at him from behind. He wheeled to see Pam glaring in her sexy candy striper smock. The combination struck him as almost comedic.

"ASSHOLE," she screamed.

She pushed past him to chase after the dude, who stormed off to his car and got in. After some more yelling, he unlocked it so she could climb in.

The door slammed shut, and the car revved and sped out of the parking lot. One of the smokers whistled at the free show.

"If she wanted to go home with me, *I* wouldn't lock her out," he said.

"Yeah," his friend chuckled. "But that's one big if."

Coop shrugged and went back inside. This was his circus, but these were not his monkeys. He resumed his post at the door. Controlling his breathing and using his mindfulness practice, he slowly brought his awareness back down to yellow.

For a moment, he wondered if he went at the dude too hard. Coop had a weakness for protecting people who couldn't defend themselves, though recalling Pam's shove, he was probably wrong about that one part.

In the end, he decided he'd deescalated and removed an unpleasant situation from the club with minimal force.

He spotted Wanda heading his way again in her cute server outfit and raised his hands. "Okay, okay, I'm going."

In the office, Big John sat behind his desk, his large hands resting on his considerable paunch. Wearing a collared shirt half-mooned with sweat at the armpits, he swiveled from his security monitors and the TV permanently set to CNN to take in Coop standing at parade rest.

"Coop," he said in his labored, gravelly voice.

"You wanted to see me, chief?"

"Yeah. I did. What the hell's going on with you?"

Coop frowned. "Chief?"

"I had three girls come in here telling me you went kung fu out on the floor."

"A customer grabbed Pam and was pulling her toward the exit. I removed him from your establishment, which is what you pay me for."

Big John sighed as if fitting the last piece into a frustrating puzzle.

"That wasn't a customer," he said. "That was her boyfriend. They have a kid together. He wanted her to come home to watch their little girl because he got called into a night shift that he didn't have an option to say no to."

"Ah," Coop said.

He should have known the gods wouldn't allow his one good deed for the day to go unpunished.

"I don't give a shit about Pam's boyfriend," said Big John. "I *do* that you didn't follow my protocol. We use force only if we got no other choice."

"I misread the situation," Coop admitted.

Then his eyes widened. The TV. CNN.

What he saw on its flickering screen. Something impossible.

"I hired you out of respect for you as a war vet," Big John growled. "Usually, you're good at deescalating, you show up on time, and you don't try to stick your wick in the—hey, be honest with me. Are you on something tonight?"

Coop blinked. "What?"

"For starters, you aren't listening to a single word."

Coop returned his gaze past his boss's shoulder to the TV.

"I know him," he said.

Big John wheeled to scowl at CNN, which displayed shaky smartphone footage of a husky Black man carrying a bleeding child in his arms over smoking rubble. The program cut to a grave Anderson Cooper talking next to an inset headshot of Staff Sergeant Dante Ramos wearing his U.S. Army Class A uniform.

The caption at the bottom of the screen read: HUMANITARIAN WORKER CAPTURED BY ISIS IN MOSUL.

Big John's eyes widened. "Wait. You *know* that guy? From your time in Iraq?"

"He was my squad leader. During my deployment."

Coop's heart pounded against his ribs. For the first time in years, his hand twitched for the rifle he no longer carried.

"Seriously? ISIS got him. Oh man, I'm sorry."

Coop said nothing. He never talked about the war with Big John, who subsequently imagined the worst.

"Can I offer you any help? Talk it out over a drink or whatever?" The man opened the drawer where he kept a fifth of whiskey and some glasses.

"My problems are mine," Coop answered, still trying to process what he'd seen. "There is one thing you can do, though. Give my next paycheck to Pam."

"You don't have to—" Big John took another look at Coop's grim expression and thought better of finishing. He closed the drawer. "How about you take some time, then. Take the rest of the night off."

Coop crossed his arms. "You wanted to see me earlier."

"I really think—"

"Just tell me what you need."

"All right." The man tapped a stack of cash and a short shopping list hiding in plain sight on his messy desk. "The girls were asking if you could do a run."

"I can." Coop swept the money and paper off the desk and pocketed it.

"Maybe the drive will do you some good, at least. Clear your head."

He grunted in response.

Then found himself in the parking lot with little memory of going there.

A drive.

Yes, a nice, long drive would do him a world of good.

Drive On

He got behind the wheel of his weathered old Dodge Dakota pickup and regarded the parking lot under pole lights and black sky. The bracing air, the truck's familiar smells, and the darkness and solitude calmed him a little.

Under the lights' weak orange glow, Coop unfolded the shopping list and squinted at the looping feminine handwriting. Cigarettes, energy drinks, sandwiches, and one pregnancy test.

The paper trembled against the steering wheel. His right hand inserted the key into the ignition and again jerked away in search of his missing rifle. It had taken him a long time to beat this reflex, the feeling something was missing. Eleven years sober, so to speak, and now he was jonesing to shoot something.

He started the truck, which roared to life and sat idling.

Fuck all this, he thought.

The job, the club, his life as a wandering monk.

Six thousand miles away, the Islamic State of Iraq and Syria had captured Sergeant Ramos, who'd gone back to help the country he'd once patrolled with a weapon. They were going to dress him in an orange jumpsuit and hack his head off on camera.

Coop couldn't do anything about it.

He rested his hands atop his lap and breathed through his nose. In with the good, out with the bad. Focusing entirely on his breath.

He pictured Ramos kneeling barefoot in Iraqi dust in front of a battle cross, and he shoved the memory aside.

Out with the bad, in with the good. Suffering was temporal and therefore illusory. Anything he was feeling, this too would pass.

Sergeant Ramos roared in his ear: *Grenade!*

Coop opened his eyes with a frustrated sigh.

His war had changed him. The human body was designed to survive. The Army taught it to act in a crisis and to kill. Combat taught it to be vigilant and keep the adrenaline and endorphins flowing even when the mind was bored. War taught it to be numb to human pain.

A whole lot of deep cognitive realignment.

They'd sent him home without training him to be a civilian again. He couldn't turn it off. From the minute he handed in his rifle and marched into the cheering crowd waiting at Fort Lewis, normal didn't feel quite normal anymore.

His mind had gradually adjusted, but his body said, *I don't work that way* and remained amped. He'd chain smoked and swilled coffee to keep the edge and then drank heavily to blunt it so he could sleep. He'd felt a deep, righteous anger that the world was not as it should be, that someone loved had been betrayed and someone else was behind it, acting with evil indifference.

It had expressed itself as rage over seemingly insignificant things. An old lady cutting him off in traffic. Calling his bank to hassle over a false credit card charge after sitting a half hour on hold. Standing in line at the supermarket facing a wall of celebrity gossip magazines demanding he care about people he didn't even recognize. Hearing yet another guy who couldn't find Iraq on a map thank him for his service and ask him what it was like to kill a human being.

Coop's experiences in Iraq hadn't broken him. He had plenty of bad memories but also good ones, and he had no serious moral regrets about anything he'd done. He didn't consider himself damaged. But yeah, the war had changed him. He came out of Iraq a different man than he entered. It was that simple.

A permanent psychic imprint.

In a way, he'd aged. He felt like he carried the weight of a century on his shoulders. A lot of history to haul around. Forever at the edge of some great epiphany that would never come, some massive and complete wisdom that would make it all make sense. He wanted to believe in something. He settled for Buddhism, the only belief that made sense to him anymore. While it didn't match his method of worshipping God, it offered a practical way to understand reality.

Curiosity led to conviction, and he became a practicing Buddhist, at least a brand of it that worked for him minus most of the Hindu stuff. Practicing as in it was a way of life. Heavy meditation, mindfulness exercises, physical training, following the Four Noble Truths of how to avoid suffering.

Cognitive retraining.

No more smoking, no more drinking, caffeine reduced to one cup of green tea a day. Inserting himself into the moment to keep the anger from spilling into action. Every time the rage boiled up that the world was not as it should be, the Way brought Coop back to the here and now and reminded him: *This too shall pass.*

Only it wasn't working here, now, sitting behind the wheel of his old truck.

One thing would. It always had.

Back in '04, Coop had driven into Mosul, Iraq under a traffic overpass on which a local had graffitied: WELCOME AMERICA! Nearly sixteen months later, he drove out under the same overpass, on which someone had since graffitied in equally bold capitals on the other side: FUCK YOU AMERICA!

His platoon sergeant had given him a hard sell to re-up, as his enlistment had been ending along with his deployment.

Your resume says you can kill at five hundred meters, Dixon had said with a smirk. *Hardly a marketable skill back home. What are you gonna do on the outside, Coop? Flip burgers at McDonald's? Can I take your order, sir? Would you like that supersized, ma'am?*

Dixon had grinned at the comic picture he'd drawn.

Jeez, Sergeant, Coop had replied, pronouncing it "sarnt" in the finest infantry tradition of insolent obedience. *You make the Army sound like prison.*

I'm teaching you something. You're gonna miss all this. You don't think you will, but mark my words: You will miss it. Guaran-frickin'-teed.

Regarding this as more comedy, Coop had laughed.

Go ahead and laugh, kid. You'll be back.

His unit had deployed to Iraq taut and fit and hungry, and they'd returned whittled to this essence. Years later, he remembered two things about his homecoming. The painful joy of seeing his folks and the stunned regret of handing in his rifle, which had felt like losing a mental limb.

You're gonna miss all this.

Dixon hadn't been wrong.

But he'd never re-upped. Instead, he bought a truck and took a drive that never ended. For ten years, he drifted from town to town, life to life, each a pitstop on a great never-ending journey of escape and discovery. Getting out of Iraq really had felt like a prison break, and it would never catch him if he kept on moving.

If only his old recruiter could see him now. If only his platoon sergeant could see how far he'd gone. Dixon would no doubt be disappointed, and his recruiter wouldn't give a flying Foxtrot.

Coop didn't care. The point was to stay free.

He liked Big John, and he'd miss some of the girls like Wanda a little, but it was time to hit the open road again. He'd worked this job since January, long enough to start planting roots, but he'd passed his expiration date. Coop always kept his pack light, his gas tank full. "Semper Paratus" remained a motto for him in civilian life. Always prepared.

After a quick stop at his house to collect his few belongings, he'd drive on.

He had no clue where he'd go next. That was the point. He'd simply go until it was time to stop. He'd roll past the bright lights of big cities and through a dozen little towns, some picturesque as model railroad setups and others slowly dying. Potholed towns all awash in American flags, slowly crumbling but ever prideful places that capitalism deemed unprofitable and government forgot. And everywhere, he'd see the same earnest, patriotic, God-fearing, and hardworking folks, or least people who saw themselves that way enough to try.

Coop knew them well, as he was one of them. They were the tribe he'd come from and the tribe to which he'd returned. So many of the towns he passed through were like mirrors held up to the one he'd escaped by enlisting. Milan, Michigan, pop. 5,000. Every time he hit the open road, it felt like another homecoming.

The drive one long meditation. The drive itself his destination.

Perhaps the longest yet.

They're gonna cut off Ramos's head and post it on the internet.

Another sigh.

His Blackberry buzzed in his pocket. Someone was texting him. Another irritating scam, probably. It occurred to him, however, that a member of his old unit had seen the CNN report and was reaching out to him.

Coop reached into his pocket and checked the messages.

LOAD YOUR NUTS

He stared at it.

"Shit," he said.

Not with anger this time but surprise.

For a moment, he was back in the war room at FOB Marez before a mission to drop a suspected insurgent's house, surrounded by men he trusted, the room's air acrid with the smells of concrete and canvas and sweat and gun oil. He heard bolts sliding into position, the metallic clack of rounds fingered into magazines. Soon, Sergeant Ramos would conduct a pre-combat inspection to make sure his squad was properly manned up, and they'd roll out to their objective.

Wearing full battle rattle, Lieutenant Hudson Stuckey stood next to the platoon sergeant. He looked up from his map board to yell, "Load your nuts, gentlemen!"

Load your nuts.

Man up for action. Put on your war face.

His lieutenant had seen the CNN report and was reaching out to his old platoon. Probably starting with the men who'd known Ramos the best. The next message was a link to the CNN story. And then:

RALLY UP

Following this was an address in New York State. A little township outside Poughkeepsie. Coop could bound east all the way there on the interstates. Around a ten- or eleven-hour drive from Cincinnati, not counting stops.

With his texts, Stuckey had reminded this nomad that he came from a tribe that knew and accepted him, which carried obligations. One of their own was in trouble. Any man who wanted to visit was welcome.

At the lieutenant's house, they'd haul out the booze, rail at President Obama and the generals for not having already rescued Ramos, and reminisce about Ramos and the war. There wasn't much else they could do, but it was important.

The truest heroes of the war were the ones who'd given everything, including their lives. In at least one sense, Ramos had already given his back in '05, and ISIS terrorists would make it permanent.

They'd execute him, and soon.

Cut off his head and post it as a propaganda snuff film.

So yeah, it was important. Almost sacred.

Of course, Coop had a choice. Once a marine, always a marine? With the Army, not so much. Despite the dog tags he still wore and all the distant memories, he was an ex-soldier now. He was long done with it. He had a choice.

He also had no choice at all.

He texted back: *Be there by supper tomorrow, LT.*

Seconds later, the reply arrived:

DRIVE ON

Cavalry slang meaning to keep going, regardless of hardship.

Coop upshifted and put pressure on the gas pedal with his old boot. The truck's tires crunched across the stones as they brought him out of the lot and back onto the road.

"Roger that," he said to the night.

Doc Moody—his old platoon's combat medic and resident intellectual—once told him that wars don't truly end until the last man who fought them dies.

Proving the adage that only the dead saw the end of war, in particular their own.

It was always with him, and Dixon was right. Sometimes, he missed it.

The Game

December 2003.

Nine months after American forces plowed through Iraq and chased Saddam Hussein into a hidey-hole near Tikrit—

Eight since United States Marines and jubilant Iraqis toppled and destroyed the statue of Saddam in Baghdad's Firdos Square—

Seven after President Bush announced the end of major combat operations on the deck of the USS *Abraham Lincoln*—

Two into Coop's deployment with his Stryker Brigade Combat Team as rifleman, Fireteam Alpha, 1st Squad, 2nd Platoon, Charlie Company, known by its callsign *Casino*—

Mere days after Saddam's capture in said hidey-hole—

FOB Marez, Coop's new home. Just west of Camp Diamondback at Mosul's airfield. A little east of MSR Tampa, the main supply route that snaked up Highway 1 all the way from the capital of Baghdad.

At the gate, images of U.S. and Iraq flags waved together on a sign that read:

"WELCOME
To Forward Operating Base
MAREZ
Home of Iraqi Freedom."

A sergeant from General Petraeus's 101st Airborne, which Coop's combat team was relieving, had told him it was the second sign they'd had made and put up. The first had been vaporized in October.

The vaporizer: a vehicle-borne improvised explosive device, or VBIED. Basically, a vehicle turned into a big bomb driven by a suicidal jihadist.

The sergeant had grinned. "You're in for it now, boy!"

That was two months ago. Since then, Coop settled into a routine he still considered vaguely exciting if mind-numbing. Every day, he awoke to face another twelve- to fourteen-hour day of danger and busywork and immediately had two thoughts.

The first being, *Shit, this sucks.* The second: *What an adventure.*

Five days of mounted and dismounted patrolling, counter-mortar missions, night raids, traffic control, and guard duty in the watchtowers—the latter so boring he almost forgot his own name—usually followed by two days off.

He'd bragged about how badly he hoped to be *battle tested* and *get some* until he realized only the privates talked that shit. That Sergeant Ramos let it slide without breaking him down and building him back up on the spot was telling. Since arriving in-country, the painful lessons had become less about general humility and toughness and more about the day-to-day business of soldiering.

Once Coop dropped the hooah talk, the older guys took him under their wings and taught him everything from how to spot roadside bombs to avoid eating the Charms candy in the MRE packets. Charms were bad juju, he was solemnly warned. He should give them instead to the Iraqi kids, whose luck couldn't get any worse.

Instead of the crucible of battle, the Moslawis mostly gave him oranges and tea and the occasional bomb planted on the road. During his off time, he did his laundry and shopped the PX and masturbated in the shitters and got his rationed half hour on the internet and worked out and played Gameboy on his rack.

He wished he had a girlfriend, someone who'd write to him. He awaited care packages from Mom. He grew homesick and then got over it and then grew homesick again. In the dining facility, which everyone called the D-Fac, he followed the news on the mounted TV screens: *We're heroes back home.*

All told, it was hardly the awesome vengeance for 9/11 he'd imagined in his private fantasies, but he still found it wild enough to be awe-inspiring. An incredible amount of American power and money was on constant display. *Nice country, we'll take it.* He was making history here, part of something big.

It'd almost be fun if it weren't for the mortars.

Private First Class Joe Horvath jolted upright on his rack.

"I'm gonna go see the hajji tanks," he said.

Coop fingered his headphones aside. "What?"

"Come with, if you want."

They shared a metal conex shipping container box with the glorified if sterile name of *containerized housing unit*—CHU for short—which functioned as troop quarters. The trailer offered just enough space for two twin-sized beds, lockers, a treasured coffeemaker he'd picked up at the PX, a new carpet that was still off-gassing, and a pair of grunts.

Spartan accommodations, but at least it was air-conditioned.

Given their similar backgrounds as dazed poor kids who had nothing better to do after high school than join the military, Coop had imagined they'd become fast friends and battle buddies. He soon learned most guys you met in the military were more like annoying cousins you had to spend Thanksgiving with than lifelong friends, having yet to learn the friendship would come over time.

As a result, at this point in his deployment, Coop generally tried to avoid Horvath as a rule, hence the CD player and headphones he bought at the PX, which not only isolated him but ensured he didn't have to listen to Horvath playing Olivia Newton John's greatest hits on repeat on his little boombox. He'd once walked in on his roommate dancing alone to "Have You Never Been Mellow," stamping his feet and swaying with arms aloft; they hadn't spoken of it since.

On the other hand, Coop had a rare few hours of personal time with absolutely nothing better to do, and he was so bored that even being bored was boring.

He pressed STOP, cutting off Soundgarden's Chris Cornell mid howl.

"Deal me in," he said.

Coop pulled on his military blouse over his tee, buttoned up, and fitted his patrol cap. Then he looped his M4 carbine over his neck so it hung ready at his side.

Outside, the air was a brisk fifty degrees, the sky thick with cloud cover with the rainy season already well underway. His boots crunched the stones that passed for a front lawn for his little abode. Not far away, one of Marez's numerous concrete bunkers offered shelter when it rained mortar shells.

The hilltop base sprawled all around him, so big he couldn't see the Jersey and Hesco walls and razor wire-topped fencing that formed the security perimeter encircling four thousand people, some three hundred buildings, and countless vehicles. Simply hauling dirty laundry was a major errand across all this ground; busses driven by locals picked up and dropped off soldiers along various circuits.

Outside the wire, Coop knew, Mosul's minarets stood to the north. To the south, the Syrian Desert. To the east, the Zagros Mountains.

They hadn't made it thirty meters when Sergeant Don Murray hailed them coming the other way. "Where do you think you're going, shitbirds?"

Coop jerked his thumb at Horvath. "He wants to see the hajji tanks."

Murray pulled up. "*Why?*"

"Why *not*, Sarnt?" said Horvath.

Murray was leader of Horvath's and Coop's fireteam consisting of four trigger pullers including the sergeant himself. A product of the middle-class suburbs, the man had always loved history and signed up to see it up close and make some himself.

He reported to Staff Sergeant Ramos, who ran his squad of nine shooters and reported to Lieutenant Stuckey, the platoon leader, and his second in command Sergeant First Class Dixon, who was 2nd Platoon sergeant.

Back in basic, the first thing Coop learned was to say *Yes, Drill Sergeant!* The second was the pecking order that made up the chain of command.

The fireteam leader grunted. "Yeah, okay. Hell, I'll go with you."

Marez had once housed Saddam's Republican Guard Fifth Corps headquarters, which included a graveyard of old Iraqi armored vehicles. Like the ruins of the little ancient Christian monastery the base was also rumored to contain, it was something Coop's squad had talked about but had never seen, as it was simply too damned reclusive. Humping dirt to find it carried an air of absurdist comedy.

The next familiar face they ran across on the gravel path was Specialist Hector Reyes, who carried the fireteam's squad automatic weapon or SAW, a light machine gun. The former

Detroit gangbanger stopped and put on a smile, hoping for a little banter.

They marched right past him with added swagger in their step, as if they were on an important mission that abided no pause for idle chitchat.

"Oy!" Reyes hurried to catch up. "Where are you boys going?"

"See the hajji tanks," Horvath said.

"Okay. Sure. Why?"

"Where were you coming from?" Murray asked him.

"Checking out the hajji shops. Lookit." The SAW gunner showed off a postcard with Saddam Hussein grinning on it and a bootlegged DVD of *Full Metal Jacket*. "They're showing *Master and Commander* at the MWR tonight." The Morale, Welfare, and Recreation Center, which played movies at 2000 hours.

"Seen it," Horvath said.

"Is it any good?" Realizing his mistake, Reyes went on before the man could start piling spoilers on him. "Are you really going to see the hajji tanks?"

"Yup."

Reyes snorted. "Big waste of time."

"Yup."

"*And* you're taking the long way. Follow me, we'll cut through here."

They approached an outdoor beach-style volleyball court. Shirtless, heavily tattooed soldiers battered the ball back and forth on the sand while others sat on jersey barriers ringing the court, awaiting their turn to play.

Murray watched them with an envious stare. "That's what we should be doing today. It looks like fun."

"Why are we looking for tanks, again?" Coop asked.

No one answered. They passed the court and left it behind. Waste of time or not, they had a mission, and it had become all-important because of the simple fact that it was their mission.

After more marching, they finally topped a short rise and gazed down upon a cluster of peeling and broken-down armored vehicles on a large field of dirt.

Coop spotted a made-in-China armored personnel carrier and the armored towing vehicle that had dragged it here. The rest of the machines were hulking Soviet T54 and T55 tanks likely dating back to the First Gulf War.

"Sweet," Horvath said and dashed off.

"Yeah, wow," Coop deadpanned.

"I guess he really likes tanks," Murray said in wonder.

The private stood in front of the Iraqi armor, raised his M4 over his head, and howled, "WOLVERINES!"

The men chuckled at the sight.

His little *Red Dawn* re-enactment over, Horvath jogged back.

"Mission accomplished," he said.

They sat on the ground and stared at the dead Iraqi armor. Murray threw a pebble at one of the tanks, which fell short and started a little competition to see who could score a direct hit on the Republican Guard.

Coop looked up at the cloud cover. "Have you noticed we haven't gotten mortared for the last three nights?"

When he'd come to Iraq, he'd feared everything as he hadn't yet learned what he should be afraid of. After a while, he'd whittled it down mostly to mortars.

The insurgents would lob shells into the base at random intervals, sometimes during the day but usually at night. Signs posted around the base advised him, *In case of mortar, stay calm and stay low.* The first time, he'd leaped out of his rack and did a runner in Kevlar, body armor, and skivvy shorts to the nearest culvert-pipe bomb shelter. Fueled by terror, he'd nearly bowled over a corporal.

Coop served in an American infantry rifle platoon packing enough punch to make it the most lethally powerful unit of its size in history, even without the ability to dial in enough air and artillery support to set entire cities ablaze. None of it mattered when it came to the mortar attacks.

Sure, anyplace else, satellites would pinpoint place of origin, the kill chain would clack until targeting and a deadpanned go order, and a single return salvo from one of Marez's big, beautiful guns would turn the insurgents into a pink mist.

But not here. They couldn't shoot that kind of ordnance into the civilian areas the insurgents fired from without risking a sizable massacre. Instead, a ready platoon on a counter mortar mission would race out to the scene, only to find no one.

The whole thing felt like a game. The Purple Heart lottery, a cute if savage little poke and chase game the Americans played with the insurgents.

After a while, the whole thing kind of got into Coop's head.

Where and when the shells fell was utterly random, and it rendered life and death random with it. Maybe he'd spend an extra minute in the shitter, break into a jog to catch up with a buddy, or stop to catch a cigarette break, and that one little choice might end up being how he'd get hit.

He started to get phobic about it, which he wisely kept to himself.

Coop comforted himself by taking a hard look at the favorable odds he'd never be in the wrong place at the wrong time. A solitary round would fall, maybe a few at most, rarely a sustained barrage; by the time he reacted, it was usually over. Plus Marez was huge in terms of real estate, and he occupied only a tiny part of it.

Still, Coop hated it. His fear made him feel weak. The older guys had told him fear was okay. Everyone felt fear. You allowed it to humble you. But you never let it own you. You never let fear win. That was the great mind trick.

"Way to jinx it, dog," Horvath complained. "Now they're going to call off their hajji vacation and get back to work. We'll get hit tonight for sure now."

"Imagine that's your job," Reyes said. "Mortarman on the night shift. No pay, but the benefits are great."

Murray snorted. "Probably the same guys waving at us and yelling *Guhd bless Judge Boosh* when we're out patrolling."

Reyes scowled into the distance. "Just once, I want to catch the *pendejos* when we're on counter mortar. Catch them right in the act and light them up."

Horvath hauled himself to his feet.

"If you want to catch them," he said, "you have to know how they think."

"And *you* know, Private."

"Here we go," Coop sighed.

"That's right, hotshot," Horvath said. "I know exactly how they think."

"They shoot, they scoot," said Murray. "That's it."

"That's what they want you to think." The kid tapped his head. "You got to think like a ninja, dog. I think like a ninja, which is how I know how they do it."

Murray smirked. "Do share, Private."

Horvath stood and mimed lugging a mortar tube in exaggerated quick strides across the dust, stage-whispering, *"Allah akbar."* He cupped his hands as if setting the tube down and then dropping a round into it. *"Allah* akbar.*"* Planting his fingers in his ears, his looked up at the clouds with goggled eyes before breaking into a frantic celebratory jig, flapping his arms. *"Allah akbar, Allah akbar!"*

Then he packed it up to exit with the same exaggerated bowlegged walk.

The men howled with laughter. Coop chortled through his nose. Not just for the performance but because the whole thing—the giant costly base abutting the airfield, the insurgents, the mortars—struck him at the root as kinda ridiculous. The whole war had its own air of absurdist comedy simply because it existed.

"You obviously have deep insight into the insurgent mind," Coop said.

"Thank you," said Horvath.

Still chuckling, Murray stood and dusted his pants. "Well, okay then. We might as well head back if we want our chow." He eyed Horvath. "Last chance to yell *Wolverines* if you need to get one more in before we go."

"Naw, I'm good, Sarnt," Horvath said.

They started back along the same circuitous route weaving down avenues cutting through conexes, tents, and Quonset huts and across brown open spaces in the shadow of water towers painted with resident unit designations. A large crowd still occupied the volleyball court, though the teams had changed.

Reyes cupped his hand under his nose and said on the down low, "Heads up. Sergeant Ramos on our two o'clock, Gimp coming up on our six."

"Keep going," Murray said. "Don't make eye contact. We're all ninjas now."

"Hey," a nasal voice called out behind them. "Hey, guys! Did you hear?"

Murray kept waking. "No, Private Thompson, we did not."

Thompson was in 1st Squad's Bravo Fireteam. Short and rangy, he wore a perpetual smile that weirded everyone out as it struck them as needy yet somehow predatory. This was a guy who gave the impression he'd hump you for a mile if you gave him an inch. The squad sometimes argued over whether he'd been put together wrong in the womb or had simply been dropped on his head.

"Where were you guys?"

"We went to see the hajji tanks," Horvath said.

Thompson's head bobbed in an enthusiastic nod. "Aren't they awesome?"

Coop laughed. "Great minds…"

"Anyway, see those big ol' lights up there?" The kid's finger jerked toward massive floodlights mounted on poles, four all told. "Word is they're gonna turn them on tonight and light this bitch up so we can play night volleyball. Hooah?"

"Make a nice target for the hajji mortars to sight on," Coop groused.

"Hajji can eat my dick." Thompson puffed out his chest. "Who's with me?"

The men looked at each other as if he'd suggested they play Russian roulette. That this time, the Gimp had well and truly lost his marbles to even conceive they'd be interested in this poor example of his spastic schemes.

The looks slowly turned into egging smiles.

"All right, *ese*," said Reyes. "We're in."

Coop had heard the adage that war is ninety-nine percent boredom and one percent bowel-liquefying terror, ten percent hurry and ninety percent wait. What they didn't tell him was half the boring wait itself had two parts.

One was keeping an eye out and doing mindless chores like scrubbing rounds so they didn't jam a weapon. The other was dreaming up dumb things like touring broken-down Iraqi tanks and playing night volleyball within shooting range of a city that wanted to kill them.

It all served a purpose.

Coop thought about standing under these bright lights tonight and felt the same old phobic dread. He didn't want to take the risk. On the other hand, he couldn't back down in front of his team.

He put on his game face. Ramos always said facing your fears was how you leveled up your manhood. Tonight, he'd do it. He'd spike the ball, flip the bird at the insurgents, and laugh in death's hairy face all in one go.

And if the court did get shelled, well, Coop had come to Iraq to be tested with interesting experiences. *Inshallah*, as the Iraqis said. If God wills it. Welcome to Iraq. *You're in for it now, boy.* Some things weren't in this control.

"I'm in too," he said.

Just in case, his eyes roamed around until they'd spotted and marked the nearest concrete bomb shelter.

"Zip your lip," Murray said. "We're about to pass the sergeant."

As if he had a bat's hearing or eyes in the back of his head, Ramos twisted in his seat on one of the Jersey barriers and regarded his errant boys.

"'Afternoon, 1st Squad."

Along with his comrades, Coop stiffened. "'Afternoon, Sergeant."

"Did I hear you boys correctly about playing here tonight? While the dumb lights make it a nice fat target? Because if you're that suicidal, I could always take you back to those Iraqi tanks and shoot you now."

Coop almost whistled in admiration. The man truly missed nothing.

"We're not gonna play here tonight," Murray assured him. "That's crazy."

"Are you sure? Look, I'm trying to be nice. I hate to see you in any suffering. It'd be far less messy if I just put a hole in you quick and clean. Your families would still get the four hundred K in Serviceman's Group Life Insurance."

"We were only talking, Sergeant."

"Well, that's fine, I guess. Let me know if you change your minds. Drive on."

The boys beat a hasty exit from his amused smirk. Trickling flop sweat, they waited until they were out of eyeshot to start elbowing each other.

"Did you shit your pants, *ese*?" Reyes asked Thompson.

"What?" The kid blustered. "He ain't scary."

"You can make fun of me all you want," Coop said. "I do not mind saying it. The sarge puts the fear of God in my heart."

No one made fun of him.

"Four hundred thousand if I buy the farm?" Thompson said thoughtfully.

Reyes snorted. "Did you read *any* of that paper you signed when you joined?"

"I've just never seen that much money before."

"And you never will, kid," Murray said. "Because you'll be up there in the clouds, saluting the angels."

At the big white-canvas dining tent, they cleared their weapons and washed their hands at the soap and water dispenser barrels. Inside the D-Fac, servicemen, civilian contractors, and Iraqi National Guard in training ate at long tables neatly arrayed in rows by salad and pasta bars on the gray concrete floor. TVs set to the Armed Forces Network covered infantrymen handing out donated toys to Iraqi kids in a Baghdad hospital.

Coop and his comrades grabbed cans of Pepsi with Arabic writing and loaded warm trays with chicken fingers and burgers that either the climate or the cooks had sucked all the moisture out of until ready to be served as flavorful, edible leather. They sat near Doc, the platoon's combat medic, who as usual chewed his supper with his nose buried in a book.

Eating in silence, they all thought about the volleyball court and how fun it would be to play there under bright lights at night, hours they were usually fooling with their Gameboys in their CHUs or hanging out at the MWR or rereading the same worn paperbacks. They thought about how everyone else would be playing while they stewed. Now that their squad leader had warned them off it, it had become a rare and precious jewel just out of their reach.

"I'll bet 2nd Squad will be playing tonight," Murray grumbled.

"I'm, like, the king of volleyball," said Thompson. "We so would have won."

"He didn't order us *not* to do it," Reyes ventured.

Coop chimed in. "They wouldn't have installed the lights if it wasn't safe."

"You're going to get blown up," Doc said without looking up from his book.

"Shut up, Doc," Murray said. "All right, that's it. Who's in?"

The boys grinned. Coop nodded, even though he'd now be facing not one but two major fears tonight. The mortars *and* Sergeant Ramos. For sure, he didn't want to lose face, but it was more than that driving him to agree.

It was the game. The game of Iraq.

After dinner, Murray, now grumbling he was a *goddamn team leader* and could play *goddamn volleyball* if he *goddamn well pleased*, showed leadership by setting a rally point and time. This done, they returned to their CHUs to await sundown.

A game was already in progress by the time 1st Squad swaggered back to the court wearing their black shorts and gray tees. The novelty of nocturnal games lent the place the same kind of excited atmosphere one found at a professional sporting event back in the real world. The spectators now actively cheered instead of shouting taunts while waiting their turn.

They grinned at each other. Yes, they were here, and this was good. They'd made the right call.

Murray got them on the list. Coop looked up into the blinding glare of one of the massive floodlights and gave all his fears the finger.

When it was 1st Squad's turn to play, they stepped onto the sand to stadium roar. Reyes played to the amped-up crowd, pounding his chest and pumping his fist.

"Are you not *entertained?*" Horvath yelled, going full *Gladiator*.

They were up against some guys in 1st Platoon's Weapons Squad, who snarled and pounded fists into palms and pawed the sand with their feet as theatrically as possible.

The world exploded.

A brief breathless whistle, like a kettle's shrill played backwards, followed by a blinding flash of light and heat.

The deafening bang sucked the air from Coop's lungs and sent him flying in a twirl of limbs to land hard on his side, his mouth filled with sand.

Something burned along his back.

"Wasp bit me," he groaned, though he heard nothing except muted shouting over the blasting ring in his ears.

He spat a wad of sand. "Help. Medic."

Another heart-stopping bang sounded near the court. The ground trembled under him. More shouts, and then the lights extinguished.

A man almost crawled past him and then stopped. "Coop? Coop, is that you?"

Murray's worried voice.

Another man dropped to his knees next to him. A penlight flicked on. Fingers probed along the fire stabbing at his back.

"Hey, Coop. It's me, Doc. I got you."

Coop spat another wad of sand and grimaced. "I think I'm hit."

The light switched off, plunging him back into blindness.

"Yup," Doc said. "A peppering wound. You're okay. Hold tight for me. Stay here and don't freaking move."

The medic jumped back to his feet to treat another casualty.

"Shit," Murray was saying. "Holy shit, I'm sorry, man."

Boots stomped the ground and stopped in front of his face. A man crouched to have a look at him. His hand appeared, and Coop took it. The hand squeezed to reassure him he wasn't alone, the man wasn't going to leave him.

"Hell of a way to earn a Purple Heart, kid," said Sergeant Ramos.

Homecoming

Normally, Coop would follow the road wherever it took him next, but this time, he had a mission and an objective. After so many years of wandering, it felt good to know where he was going.

A few hours into the drive, he rolled into a rest stop to stretch out for a few hours of rack time. The next morning, he meditated in front of a tree and did fifty push-ups. Then he drove on until spotting a small town called Clearfield. Liking the name, he left the interstate again to tank up at a Kwik Fill and get some chow.

Passing the attendant a twenty, Coop headed into the convenience store. A few other early birds poured themselves coffee. His daily mug of green tea wasn't on tap today, so he grabbed a black coffee to go. Subconsciously, he inventoried the entrances and exits, the location of each customer and what he had in his hands.

The door jingled, and a bright-eyed, clean-cut teenager in a camouflage Army combat uniform walked in with a heavyset, middle-aged woman that was likely the boy's mom. Big ears protruded from under his patrol cap.

The kid got his own coffee for the road along with a few snacks and headed to the register. Coop guessed leave was over and he was en route back to base.

The woman behind the counter thanked him for his service, rang up the snacks, and told him the coffee was on the house. The man behind him also thanked him—tragically, as if saying, *Hey man sorry you have to die for some bullshit we can't ever seem to get rid of*. The soldier turned to thank him for saying so.

He wasn't answering for himself but for all who served before him, so he said it with the proper amount of humility. Standing by the door, his mom gazed on with a proud smile and eyes watery with worry.

The soldier caught Coop staring at him with a fierce expression and raised his chin as if to say, *What are you looking at, pal?* Understanding crossed the boyish, acned face, and his eyes widened a little with a respectful nod, the look a member of the tribe gives when he recognizes one of his own.

Coop imagined the kid saying, *I got this, pops.* No doubt seeing him as an old man at just thirty-two. War was always started by old men over power and money, but the young owned it. *It's my turn. I'll take it from here.*

He paid for his coffee and breakfast sandwich and returned to his truck. The teenaged soldier was gone. Seeing him had been like looking in a mirror through a time warp. Before the World Trade Center came tumbling down, Coop had been just another dumb, pot-smoking high school kid in a hurry to go nowhere fast. The military offered a *somewhere*, a way up and out.

Army of One.

Be all that you can be.

The slogans hadn't gotten him to sign the enlistment papers. What did was the lure of grand purpose. A chance to connect to something far bigger than himself.

Get payback for 9/11. Protect America from terrorism and Saddam's weapons of mass destruction. Liberate an oppressed people from a brutal tyrant.

An opportunity to make history.

When he graduated, Coop told his recruiter he wanted to be in the infantry. He wanted to be tested. This was his generation's war, and he wasn't missing it.

If he was going to fight it, it'd be on the front lines.

He got his wish. The recruiter gave him the 11X enlistment option, resulting in fourteen weeks of brutal basic and advanced individual training at Fort Benning, Georgia. When it was over, he earned 11 Bravo.

He became an infantryman.

And soon enough, he deployed to Iraq.

He'd learned by then to fear it, but this had only made him more excited to experience its dangers for himself. Back then, he still thought of himself as immortal. The star of his own personal movie. He figured he'd get some combat experience, earn his stories, and go home more interesting.

Be all you can be. Coop just wanted to be *anything*.

Someone else. The man he wanted to be.

In the end, the only thing about the war that turned out not to be utter bullshit for him was these Army slogans. Three years after signing up, Coop left Iraq and the military a different man burdened by heavier gravity, true, but in many ways, he was a better man. He'd gained self-respect and learned about himself.

And even after the story of the war unraveled—no connection to 9/11, no WMDs, and Al-Qaeda openly operating in Iraq only *after* the invasion—he nonetheless held onto an immense and valuable if narrower sense of purpose. That purpose becoming loyalty to the men he served with and helping them get home alive.

So yeah, he'd gained self-respect and purpose, only it had one particular cost he hadn't counted on.

Back home, the earnest Americans who seemed familiar wherever Coop went also now felt alien to him. In the red states, they gushed at him with something like worship. In the blue states, they offered basic respect coupled with indifference. At bars, every now and then some drunk guy would work on his insecurities by trying to test "soldier boy" in a fight, but that was about as difficult things got.

By the time Coop flew home, a majority of Americans no longer approved of the war and many outright hated it, but none saw the soldiers as responsible for the hot mess. After being raised on myths of Vietnam veterans being spat on and called baby killers, he hadn't known what to expect. The indifference irritated him, but the glowing praise oddly proved far more grating.

People thanking him. Announcing they would pray for him, eyes moony with hero worship. He was the closest many Americans would come to the war in the flesh, and they wanted that connection to be meaningful and memorable. That was fine, but he couldn't help but feel some used him to feel good about themselves and reinforce their beliefs. That they wanted to rewrite his story as theirs.

After a while, he simply stopped telling anyone he was an Operation Iraqi Freedom vet, unless it was on a job application or to get a discount at a patriotic retail chain or to get out of a *you ain't from around here* moment with a local cop. He quit wearing his OIF ballcap everywhere.

Serving in uniform and being in the shit had given him a sense of superiority over his countrymen, and even after he matured enough to let go of this swollen pride, he still didn't understand them. Like some kind of *Twilight Zone* episode, he'd gone to war hoping to become special and arrived home only to discover he preferred to be anonymous.

Not today.

Where he was going, he'd be neither. He was returning to his people. The men he called his tribe. The lieutenant would be there and maybe others from his old outfit. Maybe guys from his squad.

Murray was wheelchair-bound after a drunken car crash back in '09 and lived in Hawaii, so it was doubtful he'd show. Reyes had blown his brains out in 2012. Horvath had stayed in the military and was still serving. Coop hadn't received much word about anyone else. So these guys were out, but maybe others would come. He remembered liking some of those guys enough to become buddies, others he could barely stand the sight of them, and a few he avoided as outright psychos. But they were all kin.

Good or bad, they understood him. He could talk to them.

After eleven long years, it might be good to talk. Really talk at last.

With Ramos facing certain death, it might be necessary.

Even on this long drive, the usual meditation didn't cut it. The memories flooded back to drag him into the past like a weird form of time travel. Waking dreams of firefights and body parts in the D-Fac and mass graves outside Mosul.

Coop found himself in it so deep he almost missed his exit in Newburgh.

He drove north along the Hudson River past beautiful homes and manicured lawns dimming into twilight as the short, crisp day ended. This wasn't the usual snapshot of rundown Americana. These people were making it.

Coop slowed as he neared a driveway leading up to a big two-story Cape Cod-style house. Yard floodlights softly illuminated the board and batten siding and large dormer windows flanking the central gable.

This was the place.

A woman flitted past one of the bright main floor windows. The lieutenant's wife? Coop smiled at the warmth the home radiated.

Someday, he thought.

One day, he might have a woman and a home like this, when he was ready.

Then he noticed the man standing by the mailbox.

Coop parked on the side of the road and cut the engine, which immediately set to ticking as it cooled. He climbed out and paused for a quick stretch.

"Advance and be recognized," the man said with a lopsided smile.

Coop grinned back.

"Doc? Is that you? Long time."

Specialist Kyle Moody had served with Lieutenant Stuckey's rifle platoon as its combat medic. In the weak, gloomy light, Coop sensed the man's height and automatically filled the rest of the details from memory.

Tall and rangy, boyish face, blond hair. Ready sigh for dumb soldiers doing dumb things like getting mortared while playing on a brightly illuminated volleyball court at night. Big lunging steps to hurl himself skidding onto his knees to aid someone who'd been hit.

Coop closed the distance with his hand outstretched, while Doc spread his arms wide. After a few feints and false starts, they finally got on the same page and grabbed each other for an equally awkward bear hug.

"*Habibi*," Doc said, addressing him as *friend* in Arabic.

"You gained a few," Coop said.

Doc was no longer the same tall, skinny kid wearing regulation prescription glasses so ugly they were colorfully nicknamed birth control glasses. His cropped hair had grown out near his shoulders, covering up the scar he'd received at the D-Fac bombing. Under his unzipped fall jacket, his body had gone to flab. He'd upgraded the ugly glasses to designer eyewear.

The decade swirled past in an instant, leaving Coop with a sense of vertigo. Yet another form of time travel in action.

Doc patted his belly. "Still getting my fill of peacetime. And you—hell, you look even better than you did when we were dumbass kids. You jerk."

"It's damn good to see you."

"You too, brother."

"So what's the process here? We just walk up and ring the doorbell?"

"The LT said to text him when I got—"

"Aieyah," another familiar voice called out from near the hedges ringing the house. "Welcome to my humble abode, Gamblers."

Coop grinned again at hearing his armored cavalry regiment's war cry and his platoon's old nickname. Upon arriving in Kuwait to await the long drive across the desert into Iraq, Sergeant First Class Dixon gave a speech about how every day they'd be gambling with their lives and the lives of the men next to them.

At Casino Company, we turn the odds on the house, the platoon sergeant said. *We count cards and keep an ace up our sleeve. Eyes out, bootlaces tied, weapons clean, cover and armor on at all times, shit squared every minute of every day.*

That's how we beat the house, you gamblers. That's how we win it all.

The boys loved it. They'd been the Gamblers ever since, a name that combined a sharp edge with a morbid sense of humor. To prove it, most of the guys had gotten a tattoo on their biceps of a skull with the ace of spades stamped on its forehead grinning over a pair of dice.

Coop had one himself. Everyone got to choose his own number on the dice roll, and he'd picked out a hard eight. He just liked the solid, unbreakable symmetry of it.

"Get your asses up here," Lieutenant Stuckey added. "We're going to the guest house out back."

"Roger that," Doc called back and pulled a face at Coop. "*Guest* house. Well, well."

Coop responded with a low whistle. Their old lieutenant was living large.

They followed Stuckey along a side path to the lighted porch of a small brick ranch house set back on the property against thickening trees.

Reaching the door, the platoon leader turned to offer a welcoming smile. He still had the same fierce blue eyes, though he'd gotten a little paunchy over the years, and his eyes had the tired glaze of a father of small children.

He wore an olive green sweater with shoulder and elbow pads that lent it a military look. His hands were sunk into the pockets of khaki chinos.

He withdrew one and offered it to Doc. "Welcome, Doc. Long time."

"I wish it was under better circumstances, LT." Again calling him by the abbreviation for his rank, pronounced "El Tee."

They warmly shook hands. Stuckey gave Coop a quick onceover.

"Man, look at you. What's your secret?"

"Wholesome living on the righteous path, sir."

Stuckey's hand took his in its firm grip.

"The only time I hear 'sir' these days is when I'm saying it to my father-in-law," he said. "It's just Hud now, Coop. Hud or Hudson, your choice."

"Roger that."

"And at ease, troop. You're my guest."

Without realizing it, Coop had been standing in a posture approximating parade rest, hands behind his back and legs braced.

Doc chuckled. "You can take some guys out of the Army…"

Coop offered a sheepish smile. His body had even stronger memories than his mind. Maybe there was no such thing as ex-soldiers either.

"Come on in, gentlemen," Stuckey said. "I'm happy you made it."

Coop followed him and Doc into the small house and pulled up short at the sight of a balding, heavily muscled man glowering on the couch, nursing a beer and a smoldering cigarette.

"You'd better call your mom," Horvath said.

Coop blinked. "What?"

"So you can tell her I'm with you tonight and won't be dropping by."

There it was. The same rough deployment humor served up with the same old smirk. Like Doc and the lieutenant, Horvath was the nineteen-year-old kid Coop once knew, but he also wasn't.

Reunion

Horvath took Coop's hand in his crushing grip.

"Look at you, Specialist," he said. "My little boy's all grown up."

"Are you on leave, or did you get out?"

Resuming his seat, Horvath regarded his beer. "Got out. It was time. The War on Terror is just about quits." He blew a raspberry.

Coop shook his head not because his comrade left the Army but because it had taken so damn long. It was hard to imagine the Horvath he knew re-upping, much less moving up to the rank of staff sergeant, one of the stalwart centurions of the modern imperial legion. He'd heard through the vine that Horvath deployed to Iraq again during the surge and also went to Afghanistan on two deployments.

This guy used to brag about how many Article 15s he'd gotten for underage drinking, sleeping on duty, mouthing off to higher-ups, you name it. He made an art of shamming, so skilled at avoiding work the boys started calling him "Ghost" because he disappeared into thin air whenever a superior needed a volunteer.

Staff Sergeant Horvath. It had the ring of a joke that had written itself. Coop found it weird to think that over the years various boys likely looked up to Horvath the way he and Coop used to with Ramos, regarding their squad leader as indestructible and inhuman and cool as a cucumber fired from an M203 thumper.

"Whew," Coop said, feeling the years. "It's been a long time."

"Grab a drink, gentlemen," Stuckey put in. "Me and Joe here have a head start imbibing our way down memory lane. You'll need to catch up."

Doc was already at the fully stocked bar and examining the liquors on display. He scooped up a bottle with a satisfied sigh. Ice clinked into a glass.

Coop took a look around the little living room. Wood paneling adorned with unit memorabilia, photos of Iraq, and a glass case filled with medals, including the Silver Star Stuckey earned at Yarmouk Traffic Circle. Framed by the couch and easy chairs, the coffee table was filling up with Horvath's empties.

And in the corner, out of the way, a TV stood with the sound off, set to CNN. Wolf Blitzer had on some talking head to discuss Donald Trump's surprise electoral victory the week before. Nothing about Ramos.

The house struck Coop as a clubhouse devoted to a favorite sports team, only that team happened to be the U.S. Army and its experience in Iraq. His old lieutenant appeared to use it as a mancave where he stored his memories, with a PlayStation at the ready in case anyone from the old outfit wanted to drop in.

"Coop?" Doc stared at him. "I asked what you're drinking."

He hesitated. He hadn't had a drink in years, and he wasn't sure he wanted one now. He couldn't help but feel tense, surrounded as he was now by men from his old platoon and the lieutenant's memorabilia.

Imbibing our way down memory lane, Stuckey put it. Once the booze started flowing, they'd start reminiscing, and Coop wasn't sure he wanted to go there.

"I'll have a beer," he said.

He'd once trusted these guys with his life. He found he still did. They understood him. Maybe they were the only men who did. Wherever the conversation went, he could talk here.

"What's it been like for you?" Horvath asked him. "Life after the Army."

Coop popped the cap off his Stella Artois and took a long, bitter swallow. "I'll be sure to let you know as soon as I figure that out."

"That's our Coop. Always the deep thinker."

Doc poured vodka over ice. "What have you been up to, though?"

"This and that, mostly," Coop replied. "I just quit a job as a bouncer at a stripper club so I could come here."

Doc raised his glass to Stuckey. "See that, LT? That's unit loyalty right there."

The lieutenant responded with an amused snort.

"I can just see it," Horvath said with a wicked grin. "Ol' Coop telling the girls about how bad he had it over there, how haunted he is after looking death in the eye in combat so America's babies can sleep safe in their cribs at night. He'd have them gushing support for the troops in about five minutes."

Coop smiled and regarded his beer. "It wasn't like that."

The men regarded him with bright-eyed expectation. They considered his revelation he worked at a stripper club to be high comedy ripe for a titillating story to break the ice. Coop had nothing to offer, though. It had been a solid job, another stepping stone to wherever he was headed, and that was it.

When he got home from Iraq, he hadn't been above telling the various lonely women he hit on at bars that he was a war veteran. They'd ask him what it was like, and after a few stories, if her eyes went soft with pity, he knew he was in. But then he'd remember that sad look on her face once he'd sobered up the next morning, and it'd piss him off. So he stopped telling women he served in the Iraq War.

The men grinned at his embarrassed expression.

"He's holding out on us," Stuckey said. "Look at him."

"Get a few more beers in him, and he'll open right up," Horvath said.

"What did you do before that job?" Doc asked.

Coop sat on one of the easy chairs and shrugged. "Like I said, this and that. I've been all over, Midwest mostly. I can't tell you how many towns I've lived in and jobs I've had. I guess I'm still looking for the right place to settle down."

"You're taking the whole Army of One thing a little literally," Stuckey said.

"You sound like David Carradine in that old show *Kung Fu*." Doc chuckled. "What's his name. Caine. Wandering from town to town, protecting the helpless, righting wrongs."

"Sure," Coop agreed. "If every time Caine tried to help, it blew up in his face and he made everything ten times worse."

His comrades laughed at this admission and its sad ring of truth.

His beer was going down fine, rolling over his tongue like a cool sip of water on a hot day. He told them the story of Candygram and her hapless boyfriend, how things turned out. Like many things in his life, it made a better story than when it happened.

The men roared again with laughter. This part reminded him of the war, where a solid tale passed as a form of currency in the field. It didn't exactly break the ice, but everyone was starting to get good and thawed.

Already half sloshed, Horvath gazed at him proudly, as if thinking, *There's my buddy. Welcome to the party.* Doc threw him the kind of look where a rare animal recognizes its own breed. They hadn't known each other all that well back in the day, but Coop understood Doc had a similar drive to help people, on top of another similar trait of probably being too singular for the military.

"Mostly, I just try to keep my head down and mind my own business." Coop turned to Stuckey. "What about you, sir? Hud? What have you been up to?"

The lieutenant poured out a gin and tonic and settled onto the couch near Horvath. "I worked at an investment banking firm down in New York for a few years, bought a lot of real estate in Poughkeepsie, had a second kid." He shrugged. "Not as interesting as you, but I have no complaints. I'm doing very well."

"I thought you would have stayed in and become a lifer," Horvath said. "You'd be major by now for sure, on the fast track to general."

"Jeremy was already on the way when I was over there. When my time was up, Carol said I had to choose my family or the Army."

"You made the right choice," Doc said.

Coop had to agree; the lieutenant seemed to have built a very nice life for himself here, plenty interesting as far as he was concerned. He didn't say this aloud. It was still weird to relate to his old platoon leader like this. Back in Iraq, he'd had two modes when dealing with superiors, obedience and snark.

"You have any pictures?" he finally said.

Stuckey smiled and produced one from his wallet. In the photo, two tow-headed boys flanked a smiling blonde.

"She is smokin'—" Horvath caught himself, remembering where he was and to whom he was talking. "She's a beautiful lady, LT."

"She sure is," Stuckey said. "This one's Jeremy. And that's little Doug."

"They're your mission," said Coop, who understand the value of purpose.

"Yeah, I suppose they are." The man's smile turned bittersweet. "Anyway, enough about me. Your turn now, Doc. Fill us in."

Doc finished his vodka and rose to pour another splash over the ice. "I had a tough time after the Army. I managed to hold down a job as an EMT working the night shift. Then a year ago, I met a woman who found out I was an OIF vet and gave me an earful about the war being a quagmire. Said the war only benefited the defense contractors, KBR, the merc companies like Blackwater, and Iran."

Horvath snorted. "Some antiwar college fag, I'll bet. They can say whatever they want. They can thank me for the right."

Doc swirled the vodka in his glass. "Yeah, well, now I'm one of them. It turned out Marjorie's also a vet and volunteers with Iraq Veterans Against the War. We started dating. She really straightened me out. I'm going back to school next year, finally put the GI Bill I joined up for to work. I'm going to become a doctor."

Horvath's face darkened. He bent his head to light a fresh cigarette, producing a cloud of silver smoke.

"That's great for you, Doc," Coop said to fill the awkward silence.

The medic's revelation didn't surprise him. Doc had been too smart for the Army. The Army had a lot of smart guys in it, actually, but Doc had always been too much of a thinker, the sort who always asked *why*. Always the one with some *we're only making shit worse* remark that got everyone depressed.

"Of course you joined the antiwar crowd," Horvath finally answered Doc. "Because you always were an overthinking pussy. The war would have turned out just fine if the generals hadn't sold us out. All that COIN bullshit."

COIN, the counterinsurgency strategy that turned the Army into hearts-and-minds winning nation builders, which many soldiers thought was insane as no amount of blood and treasure was going to culturally transform Afghanistan and Iraq into mini Americas.

He added: "We fought that war with one hand tied behind our backs. We cared more about ungrateful civilians who hated us than we did our own guys."

"McChrystal math," Doc muttered. "All we did was make terrorists."

Coop had heard of this famous idea attributed to General Stanley McChrystal, whose team concluded that every civilian casualty created ten insurgents, what he called *insurgent math*. As a result, he'd issued very strict rules of engagement in Afghanistan to minimize civilian casualties, which had put him at odds with his own soldiers who were ordered to hold their fire when in doubt.

"Here's some math." Horvath took a quick drag and blew an angry smoke cloud. "A thousand hajjis weren't worth even one of my boys getting hit."

Feeling the heat rise in the room, Stuckey raised his hands.

"Gentlemen, let's leave the politics alone," he said. "Can we all agree we executed our mission with honor and integrity and to the best of our ability?"

No one objected.

"Goddamn right," Horvath said. "We served with pride."

Cooper finished his beer and opened another bottle. Following his rule about keeping his head down, he'd stayed out of the debate. Intellectually, his default position was close to Horvath's, though his gut told him Doc was onto something. No matter what they did in Iraq, the insurgency only seemed to grow.

Stuckey rose to pour himself his own refill.

Swirling his gin and tonic in its glass, he added, "I don't know what it all meant. All that was above my paygrade. I can tell you I discovered the best me I could be in Iraq. Leading you men into combat." He raised his glass. "Gentlemen, I'd like to propose a toast. To Staff Sergeant Dante Ramos."

Horvath stabbed out his cigarette in his ashtray on the coffee table and grabbed his bottle. The men drank in a respectful moment of silence.

"So what do we know?" Coop asked.

"Ramos was working with a volunteer group called the Knightingale Commandos," Stuckey replied. "They go into war zones and hand out food, embed with frontline units as combat medics, that sort of thing. What sets them apart is they're mostly former soldiers and they carry weapons for self defense when they're in the field. Ramos was in Mosul when ISIS apparently grabbed him."

Doc cleared his throat. "Do we know if he's, uh, still alive?"

"Last I checked, there's nothing reported in the media about it. The only way to know for sure would be to tune into ISIS's snuff channel."

Coop winced at the idea. The Islamic State regarded murder and destruction as a tool of religious purification. A matter of social hygiene. A way to get God's attention and approval. They'd set up an entire propaganda agency, Amaq, to brag about it. Their website featured hundreds of videos of victims being shot, burned alive, crushed by tanks, blown apart by munitions, and beheaded.

"Maybe we could reach out in the military," he suggested. "See if anybody is working on a rescue."

"There ain't no rescue," Horvath said. "Obama ain't gonna do anything."

"What about the Iraqi Army?"

"They're probably thinking they have bigger fish to fry."

Coop shot a look at Stuckey, who frowned and nodded, confirming it as fact.

The room fell silent again. He tossed back the last swallow of his second beer and went to the bar for something stronger.

Doc let out a surprising chuckle.

"I remember when we were stationed at Fort Lewis," he said. "This one night, a buddy from Weapons and I headed up to Tacoma on a weekend pass and found a karaoke bar. He was old enough to drink and would buy for us, so I was set for the night. So, who happens to walk up onto the stage? Sergeant Ramos."

Coop exchanged a bemused glance with Horvath. "Say what?"

"He sang, 'Let's Get It On,' I shit you not. He had a hell of a voice. He sounded just like Marvin Gaye."

Horvath's surprise turned into a guffaw. "You have to be shitting me."

"It gets even better. I was scared out of my mind he'd catch me underage drinking. I couldn't get up and leave, or he'd see me. I figured my best option was to simply stay put and sneak out after he left the stage."

"Oh, he saw you all right," Stuckey guessed.

Coop had to agree. Ramos never missed a thing.

"After he finished the song, the place went wild," Doc went on. "Apparently, the sarge was a regular. I figured it was time to egress, but who suddenly appears at my table standing like a mountain over me?"

"Sergeant Ramos," everyone said and cracked up.

"Yup. He pointed at his eyes"—Doc acted it out by pointing at his own eyes with his index and middle fingers—"and then pointed at me, ending by placing his finger over his lips. I nodded back at him. He didn't bust me, and I kept my end of the deal. I never told anybody about his singing for thirteen years."

Coop laughed. "You got off easy."

"Oh, it gets better. I felt like I had a strong enough hand to push my luck. I went *back*. In fact, I went to that bar every time I had a weekend pass. Heard Ramos roll through all the Motown hits. Every time he finished, he nodded at me, and I nodded back." The lopsided smile returned. "Man, he could hold a tune."

Coop wagged his head in chuckling disbelief. It was hard to imagine Ramos as anything other than what he'd displayed: a hard-as-nails, tough-love NCO who lived and breathed the Army.

Back when Coop was a teenager in uniform, Ramos had seemed larger than life. Even after all this time, finding out his squad leader was not only human but had a love for karaoke of all things offered an odd thrill.

"When I showed up in Iraq fresh from West Point and all my training, I thought I knew everything," Stuckey put in. "I'd parachuted out of planes at Airborne School, learned patrolling at Ranger School, ran mounted ops at the Mechanical Leader course. Sergeant Dixon set me straight with kid gloves. Sergeant Ramos? Not so much. Like Dixon, he'd been in the show during the invasion in '03 and knew his stuff coming and going. 'Outstanding, truly outstanding, sir,' he'd say when I'd roll out a plan." The men chuckled, as his imitation of Ramos's vaguely Puerto Rican accent was spot on. "'But if you *don't* want to get everybody killed, I'd suggest...'"

"'Wrong answer, Private,'" Coop said, quoting Ramos's standard response to one of his soldier's answers to a question that was more often than not painfully rhetorical. "'You may ponder further while beating your face giving me twenty.' I did so much pondering, I found the Buddha."

Horvath shook his head in admiration. "The man bled green."

Another round of laughs followed, along with more drinks, fresh stories. Soon, they were reminiscing about everyone in the old squad and platoon. They toasted Murray and Reyes and ol' luckless Thompson. The hours rolled into the night and kept going until the night itself seemed to unravel and blur.

Words slurred, sentences trailed off unfinished. Doc went into a sappy ramble about his girlfriend. Horvath told war stories about Ramadi and Afghanistan. At last, he declared he was going to fly over to Iraq and bust Ramos out himself, only to lurch off to empty his bladder. Even the cool lieutenant started to get sloppy, spilling a drink onto the rug and getting up with a shrug to fix himself another.

Coop didn't want it to end. Hanging with these men felt oddly like being home.

The Army made a virtue out of silent suffering. Not silent at all, actually, as it also seemed to run on snark and bitching, but when things got real, you either told it to the chaplain or you shut up. Real hurt was for pussies. Bad morale messed with combat effectiveness and could get soldiers killed, and it could be infectious.

So you manned up. You compartmentalized it. Everything you felt that might add weight and drag you down, you saved it for later.

In its wisdom, however, the military had certain occasions that allowed raw self-expression and emotional catharsis, and mourning was one of those times.

To Coop, it felt like every story strengthened Ramos against his captors, maybe kept the man alive a little longer. If the sergeant could see them now, he'd certainly approve of their drunken vigil.

For the men of the rifle platoon known as the Gamblers, it helped brace them for the worst. If they stopped, if they turned out the lights and slept, they knew they'd likely wake up to hear Ramos was dead.

At last, they talked about the Battle of Mosul back in '04, when they rolled out as a quick reaction force and fought a five-hour pitched battle at Yarmouk Traffic Circle. They had yet to talk about OP Applejack. The nocturnal counter-mortar mission at the lonely observation post on a hill overlooking the Tigris River, where Ramos broke himself and created a debt.

Saving the best for last, only they never got around to it. They didn't have to, as it was always there, even unspoken.

Stuckey was the first to crack. He got up from the couch and immediately bent to rest his hands against his knees. "Whew. I can barely stand up."

"That's how you know it's working, LT," Horvath told him.

"Gentlemen, I am going to turn in before Carol comes out and hunts me down. She's the love of my life and the mother of my children, but…" He wagged his head as if to clear it. "You'll find beds in the bedrooms. Couch right here. Crash wherever. I'll see you bright and early for breakfast."

"Good night, sir," Coop said. "This was good."

"Yeah." Stuckey's eyes glazed over a moment, as if lost in some private memory or a wistful thought. "You know… Yeah. No. It'd be nuts."

"What's that, LT?" Horvath clumsily waved. "Let's hear it."

"I was just thinking you were onto something."

"About what?"

"We *could* go over to Iraq ourselves and try to help get Ramos out. Put the pressure on and make a stink until either our Special Forces or the Iraqis step up. Wouldn't that be something? I…"

Coop and the other men stared at him.

"Never mind." Stuckey smiled. "I'm off to bed, gentlemen. Good night."

After he left, Coop and Doc exchanged a bemused glance.

"He wasn't serious, was he?" Doc said.

"I'm pretty sure it was the alcohol talking," Coop said.

Horvath polished off another Stella and belched. "I think if the LT misses his glory days this much, he should re-up."

Movement to Contact

March 2004.

Two months since American forces gave up searching for weapons of mass destruction after the Bush Administration admitted this rationale for the war was almost entirely wrong—

Five since Coop arrived in the Sandbox—

MSR Tampa, Mosul, Iraq.

Four Stryker infantry carrier vehicles rolled up the highway with a broad dispersion of seventy-five meters in case of IEDs blowing up on the roadside.

These new vehicles were still being thoroughly combat tested. And the troops of Coop's brigade combat team, the first to use them, were the testers.

Riding on eight wheels kept rolling by a 350 HP engine, the Stryker was nine feet tall, twenty-two feet long, and weighed sixteen tons. With no tracks, it moved so quietly they'd heard the locals called Stryker rifle platoons the "ghost riders."

The boys loved the sound of that, only a lot of times they weren't all that quiet with Metallica blasting or the lot of them belting out some hip hop song.

In any case, when it came to urban fighting, they'd rather be in one than a Humvee, particularly with the constant and growing threat of roadside bombs.

The only problem was the Stryker's layered steel, Kevlar, and ceramic-tile armor remained vulnerable to rocket-propelled grenades, which the insurgents also carried in abundance. As a result, the Gamblers' Strykers had received a key retrofit: an ungainly bird cage of slat armor that girdled the vehicles.

It pretty much worked, only the additional five thousand pounds of metal was hell on both maneuverability and the wheels, which had to be checked three times a day and often changed out.

Inside Charlie Victor 12, Ramos and his squad sat on the hard seats, half of them unbuckled as the seatbelts couldn't easily fit around the bigger soldiers when they were in full battle rattle.

The driver wore a helmet on the back of which he'd stenciled, *How's my driving? Call 800-DIE-FDIE.* The truck commander stood in his hatch behind the swivel-mounted fifty-caliber Browning machine gun, a heavy, five-foot-long beast that blasted six-inch rounds joined in steel links. For extra protection, the man had surrounded his hatch with paint cans filled with sand.

Helmets and weapons sticking out of the rear hatches, Coop and Reyes played the role of air guard, eyes out and covering the vehicle's six. As he was outside the wire today, Coop wore the Kevlar helmet that pinched his forehead, chafing ballistic armor that gave him a blocky appearance, camouflage uniform, kneepads, grenades, and ammo magazines stuffed into pouches on his chest.

Shabby two- and three-story apartment blocks, row houses, shops, food stands, and lonely palm trees ground past. Men strolled along either in traditional ankle-length caftan robes and head cloths held in place by cords or Western-style clothing. A few women shopped in abayas worn over dresses.

Reyes angled his SAW toward an Opel car that ventured too close, and the driver wisely backed off. Pushing a traffic control point, shooting a rifle into the air at a wedding, or zooming past Strykers on the road because you were late for work had all proved effective ways for Iraqis to get killed. Coop was happy at least someone had learned the lesson how not to commit suicide by American soldier.

He went back to scanning windows, doors, and roofs, especially the flat roofs that offered good fields of fire and handy perches for dropping grenades.

"This is a bullshit op," Reyes said.

"Tell me about," Coop grumbled.

"By now, we could have nabbed—"

"I meant I already know. I didn't mean actually tell me about it."

Reyes whistled. "Somebody is sure punchy today."

The *what an adventure* honeymoon was over, leaving only Iraq and more Iraq and then still more Iraq with a side of flies. Meanwhile, Iraq was getting harder by the minute, and Coop had faced a choice of getting harder himself or breaking.

He'd grown harder. He needed it today.

At zero dark-thirty, he'd reported to the tactical operations center for a mission. And not just any mission, but finally one that actually sounded like it mattered.

Like every unit, the Gamblers regarded themselves as elite special forces in the Army's never-ending big dick contest. The truth, however, was they were just regular line leg infantry.

Trigger pullers. GIs. Grunts. Bullet magnets.

This time, their fantasies came true. Lieutenant Stuckey announced they were going to take down an IED factory in a night op. As if just to make it all even cooler, some Baathist, a former member of the Revolutionary Command Council and adviser to Saddam Hussein, was reportedly holed up there ripe for capture.

Stuckey showed them how it'd work by drawing it on the sand table, and Coop had been excited and nervous to discover 1st Squad would be going into the building. They spent the afternoon practicing until they had it perfect.

The Baathist's codename was *Sandman*. The radio codeword for mission success was *unforgiven*. Coop pictured a breaching charge blowing the door, storming inside with the violence of action, flashbangs popping as they cleared rooms. Totally high speed, like something out of a Tom Clancy novel.

After four hours waiting in the tactical operations center, with dawn fast approaching, he learned the mission was scrapped for reasons unknown.

Why? Shut up, that's why.

Seeing as they were all dressed up with nowhere to go, they were instead ordered out on a movement-to-contact patrol, basically a search-and-destroy mission. This involved driving around basically waving their wieners at the Iraqis until someone shot at them and they could unload on him.

Their standing order: be alert, get positive ID on the enemy, and light him up.

Reyes waited long enough for comic timing and then went on, "The dude actually had his own playing card in the invasion 'most wanted' deck. A big dog."

Coop growled. "Could somebody please take a shot at us already?"

"Careful what you wish for, troop."

"No, seriously. I actually want somebody to shoot at me."

Most mounted patrols, nothing happened, while on others, you got shot at anytime you stopped moving. Of the two, Coop preferred the latter because A, the insurgents couldn't shoot for shit—the firefights typically being so quick and brief, he was surprised and even a little embarrassed to receive the Combat Infantryman's Badge he'd once hungrily coveted.

And B, because sending hot metal downrange offered a release to the tension.

In the fleeting bits of action he had experienced, Coop discovered that combat was nature's crack cocaine. If a truly realistic war movie were ever made, it'd thrill audiences with around nine thousand hours of torturous boredom and mind-altering inanity, but combat *felt* like a movie.

A few spray-and-pray bursts would be fired their way, and the entire platoon would suddenly lunge into action like a single hungry, predatory organism.

In combat, all the bullshit vanished, leaving only the here and now.

His first time, he'd had the universal thought: *I'm being shot at. They're shooting at* me. Then the training kicked in and he'd been surprised to discover he could think and speak coherently while people tried to murder him. You never knew if you really had what it took to be a soldier until the bullets started flying, and he'd been happy and a little oddly disturbed to find he did.

He hadn't even seen who was trying to kill him. In most firefights, he'd be lucky to catch even a muzzle flash from some far-off rooftop or window. That first time, he'd ended up blazing away at a building Murray told him the bad guys were shooting from.

Nonetheless, it had all assaulted his senses like a heated first-person shooter video game. In the lingua franca of soldiers, he'd *gotten some*. There was a primitive joy to it, and after the combat hangover, he always craved it again.

No such luck today.

Lieutenant Stuckey came on his radio headset.

"Golf Six to all Golf Victors," he said, using the Army phonetic alphabet for *Gamblers vehicles*, with *Six* identifying the commander. "The TOC has seen fit to give us a new tasking. We will provide security for EOD to remote det an IED in the Sinjar district. At Yarmouk Traffic Circle, head east on Bab Sinjar."

TOC: tactical operations center, the guys back at Marez calling the shots.

EOD: Engineer Ordnance Disposal, the guys called in to detonate bombs found around the city.

IED: improvised explosive device said EOD guys would remotely detonate.

Maybe somebody will shoot us at the traffic circle, Coop thought.

The whole area was a hotbed of insurgent activity.

In fact, he had a bad feeling.

The Stryker sped onto the circle's asphalt, using it to swing from north to east between tall buildings. Patrolling standard procedure called for finding different routes to objectives, but Coop had driven this way time and again. The circle was a major hub of arteries cutting through Mosul. In West Mosul, it was hard to avoid it, unless you wanted to drive real slow through a maze of residential streets.

Still sensing danger, he coiled like a steel spring behind his M4, scowling at his sector while in his mind he played out where he might be attacked from and what he was going to do if an attack erupted. He scanned rooftops, windows, corners, and doors, internalizing all of it instantly as situational awareness.

The bad feeling worsened.

First, they'd get hit by an IED, which would disable the lead vehicle and stop the column in a kill zone. After that, small arms and rockets would start blasting from neighboring buildings. What the Army called a *complex ambush*. Finally, Coop would get what he privately craved: a real, honest-to-God firefight.

If things got hot enough, the platoon would call for the quick reaction force. When they arrived, that's when the secondary IED would go off.

Yup, he could see exactly how it would all play out.

Only it didn't.

In fact, nothing happened at all.

Coop's adrenaline drained out of him as the vehicles rolled onto Bab Sinjar. He was starting to feel very loopy. He'd been awake and on alert since 0200, and he'd only gotten two hours of shuteye before that, maybe thirty hours all week.

"You got any Rip Fuel, Rey'?" he asked. "I'm dying here."

Reyes produced a bottle, shook it, and produced two pills, which he handed over in his gloved hand. Coop dry swallowed them and waited for the little cocktail of ephedrine, caffeine, and aspirin to provoke his nervous system.

He pictured a big Army ceremony where his battalion commander handed him a T-shirt saying, *I went to Iraq for a firefight and all I got was this lousy IED.*

"Cowards," Coop growled.

"Huh? Who are you pissed about now, *ese*?"

"The insurgents. They never take us on in a fair fight. It's always pot shots and suicide bombers and drop and pops in the road."

The month before, a vehicle borne IED driven by a Sunni jihadist went to a busy Shia neighborhood, detonated, and killed a hundred people. All that was left of it was a smoking crater. The blast had blown out windows for blocks.

The skinny mushroom cloud had been visible all the way from FOB Marez.

The IED had become the weapon of choice for the insurgency. All it required was a spent mortar or artillery round casing packed with some C-4 and metal scraps, nails, glass, or anything else that hurt, all of which were readily available in today's Iraq. The bomb usually detonated via an electrical charge from a pair of copper wires an insurgent would connect to a battery's leads.

The militants hid them in garbage and piles of rubble. They even packed them into dead animals. Sometimes, they wrapped electrical cord around a few artillery casings and put it out like a present in plain sight, just to bait American ordnance disposal techs into an ambush. Most IEDs were small drop and pops, others buried in the road and sometimes even daisy chained for multiple detonations.

The insurgents were always thinking of new and novel ways to play with Coop's head and put lethal holes in his body. Every day, it seemed, they got a little better at it, pushing both the art and the science. Very quickly, the IED had handily taken over from nocturnal mortar attacks as Coop's personal sword of Damocles.

Reyes surprised him by chuckling.

"Man, look at all the firepower we're packing," he said. "All the training, all the arty and air support on speed dial. There's a Kiowa helo over our heads right now. We got *GPS*, man. Freaking satellites. Our fighting capability extends across the big green machine all the way to *space*. You think *we* fight fair? The hajjis can't go toe to toe with us, and they know it. So they kill us however they can."

"I feel like all I'm doing here is driving around waiting to get blown up."

The SAW gunner shrugged.

"That's the mission," he said.

"Yeah, well, the mission blows the big one."

The mission: find, capture, and destroy non-compliant anti-Coalition, anti-Iraq forces. What it meant: driving around patrolling, trying to stay awake all night at an observation post, or playing cop at a traffic control point, followed by chow hall and a meeting to talk about doing it all over again the next day.

Reyes chuckled. "You listened to your recruiter, didn't you?"

"Of course, I did. He helped me get into the infantry and told me I'd probably deploy here or Afghanistan."

"Yeah, and he was making promises the whole time about how you'd get into the shit, how every day would be high speed over here fighting for freedom…"

Coop bit his lip. "Well…"

"Yeah. Dumbass."

Coop recalled giving Rocky, who was in Bravo team, a similar speech about manning up and the better qualities of humble pie just three days earlier when the rifleman had hit the wall himself. Bursting bubbles was something of a blood sport here, but it was more than that. Whenever someone caught the mopes about the mission, the other guys bounced him straight.

Today, it was his turn to get bounced.

Reyes added, "Your recruiter lied to you, *ese*. Bush lied to me about WMDs. Guess what, it don't matter. We aren't the heroes of this story. We're just in it."

"All right," Coop cried. "I give. Any more straight talk, and I'm gonna desert."

"All good." The SAW gunner gave a sly look. "You know what you need?"

Coop did not like that look. "Whatever it is, no, I do not need it."

"You need a morale boost."

"No, no. Please."

But it had worked already, he was already laughing.

Reyes clenched his non-shooting hand into a fist in front of his mouth and started beat boxing. Coop recognized the song.

"Come on, you got this. LOOK OUT, THE BOYS ARE BAAAAACK."

Coop joined in. "HERE COMES THE FREAKY SNEAK ATTAAAACK."

Inside the Stryker, the squad started singing along.

They reached Al-Sinjar, which looked like most of downtown Mosul—khaki, rundown, and dried out by Iraq's harsh sun. The platoon established comms with the EOD unit and split up to establish traffic control and security at four points surrounding the IED isolated for detonation.

"Imagine what their recruiters told *them*," Reyes said.

"Who?" He already knew what the insurgents were told. *Kill the foreigners, die for Allah, and enter Paradise to claim your virgins.*

"The bomb disposal guys."

Coop thought about it. "'You'll love it. It's the safest job in Iraq.'"

"'Fast track to a post-military career as an astronaut.'" The SAW gunner made an exploding sound and raised his hand to his arm's limit.

Coop laughed again. "What did your recruiter tell you?"

Reyes shrugged. "He said he'd keep me from going to jail."

The Stryker parked at an intersection. The ramp dropped at a speed the boys considered painfully slow. Coop, Reyes, and the truck commander behind the mounted fifty provided overwatch while the rest of the squad dismounted and fanned out in a security perimeter.

Horvath raced out last and took a knee.

"Never get out of the boat," he said, quoting *Apocalypse Now*.

The squad secured the area and set up a traffic control point, which proved fairly simple today with no warning shots and close calls. Word about the IED had spread; the locals were steering clear of the area.

Then *BOOM*. So loud it jolted the nearby buildings.

EOD had detonated the IED in the road. Heads jerked toward the sound, hoping to see the cloud.

"Eyes on sectors," Ramos growled and tilted his head again to continue his dialogue with the lieutenant over his shoulder-mounted radio. "Roger that, Six." Straightening his neck, he yelled, "Mount up! We got another tasking."

As the ramp again raised, he explained over the headsets: "The FOB took some hits from mortars, we've got place of origin, and we're closest."

Reyes grinned at Coop. He'd always dreamed of catching an insurgent mortar cell in the act of lobbing shells at him while he was trying to sleep.

The Stryker roared to life and started rolling. All the Golf Victors rallied on Bab Sinjar and headed back the way they came before veering south onto Ibn al-Athir. Instantly, the buildings seemed to crowd in closer.

"Aw, shit," Reyes muttered. "*This* place."

"Hm-hm," Coop agreed.

They were in Old Mosul now, which carried a higher pucker factor. The population was denser here, the people poorer and angrier, the air ranker with the stench of shit and diesel, the streets narrower and chaotic as a maze.

He found himself coiling again like a steel spring.

The column weaved south into the Wadi Hajar district, which was within light mortar range of FOB Marez. The urban terrain shifted to become less threatening, though being urban, it still sucked.

At last, the platoon leader called a halt.

Reyes looked around. "Do you see any mortars? Because I do not."

Coop grunted. No, he did not either. Another bust.

The street was busy with people walking about on their daily errands. The ramp dropped again, and the soldiers fanned out into another security perimeter. Coop and Reyes stayed on point at their air guard positions.

The lieutenant whistled for Hip Hop, the platoon interpreter, an Iraqi college dropout whose knowledge of English was sketchy at best. At Marez, he was always singing or quoting hip hop lyrics and begging anyone who would listen to help him emigrate to America, where he intended to marry Britney Spears and sire strong sons.

Outside the wire, he wore a mask so no one would identify him. The insurgents considered the terps to be collaborators and marked them for death.

Howen, Coop caught him saying as he helped Stuckey question the locals. The Iraqi word for *mortar*.

Naturally, no one knew or had seen or heard anything.

"Big waste of time," Reyes said.

Coop agreed. In fact, it was beginning to feel a little hairy. More locals had started to gather. As always, the kids laughed and asked for sweets, but some of the adults were angrily gesturing and shouting.

"Hey, Doc," he called down.

Doc turned, his eyebrows lifting to disappear under his Kevlar brim.

"You speak some of the lingo," Coop said. "What are they saying? They're all reporting the location of the mortarmen so we can keep the peace, right?"

"They're mad that Americans have freedom," Doc called back.

"No, seriously. What the hell are they shouting about?"

The medic sighed. "They want electricity and working sanitation and clean water like they had under Saddam. They want jobs. They want law and order. They want us to stop raiding their houses and shooting them at checkpoints. They want us to leave their country and go home. Now you know. Happy?"

Coop waved him off. "Sorry I asked."

He remembered the heady days when he'd first arrived in Mosul, when many of the people here had been grateful Saddam had been overthrown. Proudly hospitable, they'd come out to share fruit and serve them tea on trays.

Those days felt like another lifetime now. Back then, he'd talk to the locals and try to get one smiling, tickled at the open, warm hospitality of Iraqi culture and the novelty of talking to foreigners. He'd try to learn faces.

After five grueling months, they now all looked alike to him and he didn't give a crap about a single one. As far as he was concerned, they were all the enemy. Just another thing he had to deal with on his long journey home.

Reyes shrugged. "I like the sound of going home, though. Interesting concept. You know what? I say we do it."

An Iraqi man in the crowd cried out for a doctor in Arabic. He elbowed through the crowd supporting his wife, who hobbled on an injured foot.

Doc hurried forward, but the lieutenant yelled for the platoon to mount up.

"Let me do this, sir," Doc said. "Just one good thing today."

"Sorry, that's a no-go, Doc," said Stuckey. "We're not getting shot at so you can renew your faith in the Coalition's mission."

Seeing the Americans pack it up, the children surged around them.

"Mistah, mistah!"

"I'll bet they were the ones just shooting mortars at us," Reyes said dryly.

He was joking, except he also wasn't. The insurgents paid poor kids like these two hundred dollars to plant IEDs, with the alternative being a bullet in the head.

One mimed drinking. "Pepsi? Pepsi?"

"Water," a girl said. "Please, mistah."

The Strykers revved. The first Victor rolled forward in a puff of engine exhaust. Then Coop's vehicle started moving while the children clamored close behind. He reached into a pouch, took out a handful of Charms he'd been saving up from his MREs, and tossed them into the little throng, which let up a cheer.

Then a loud bang made him flinch. A second bang.

"Ow, goddamnit!" the truck commander swore. "That one hit me!"

Some kids had come out of a side alley to throw rocks at the departing Americans. Another thumped against the Stryker.

"Fuck you, America!" a little boy called out as he ran, flipping Coop the bird with both fists.

"And this is why I hate Iraq," Reyes said.

Another day in paradise. As they exited the area, Coop spotted a man who smiled and gave him a hearty thumbs up.

Unwinding

Coop awoke from dreamless slumber to discover a hangover. He greeted it as one did an annoying, long-lost uncle coming to visit. He remembered how when he came home from Iraq he'd drink himself to sleep every night, but the alcohol never eliminated the bad dreams so much as postponed them.

Shifting his body into a savasana yoga pose, he took stock of how he was feeling. Not surprisingly, his brain felt dry and set in an irritated, throbbing complaint. His wobbling stomach craved but might buck at the sight of food.

Overall, though, he felt good. Calm and centered. Whatever toxins he'd taken into his body last night, he'd purged far more shit talking with his old comrades.

He padded to the bathroom on bare feet and emptied his bladder in a mad rush. The house felt hot and stuffy and smelled like stale smoke from Horvath's cigarettes. Doc's room was quiet. Horvath snored like a bear.

Dressing in sweatpants and a hoodie from his ruck, Coop put on ratty tennis shoes and went into the living room, where he found Horvath sprawled on the couch like something dropped from a great height. The room smelled of sour booze sweat and soupy sleep breath.

Outside the guest house, crisp white daylight and a refreshing if biting wind struck him. The air rustled through the branches of the maples and alders that grew thick around the lieutenant's property.

The last leaves had fallen over a week ago, transitioning the landscape from vibrant warmth to a barren coldness. The house stood some distance away along with a shed and a swing swaying from the branch of a stout backyard oak.

Stuckey had made a nice life for himself here.

Coop pushed back at the creeping envy, reminding himself that the more you had, the more you could lose. He'd chosen a different path for himself, despite what it could never give him. What it did give him was enough for his needs.

Choosing a bright patch of ground, he sat in the lotus position and meditated until he'd emptied his restless mind and the sun saturated his skin. Unraveling into a standing position, he greeted the dawn with a sun salutation.

This transitioned into another yoga pose and another, wherever his body felt like going. From downward dog to plank to mountain to warrior, ending as it always did in extended child's pose, subservient to the great everything and the even greater nothing.

When he stood again, Coop spotted a feminine face staring back at him from a window in the house. The lieutenant's wife, Carol. He waved, and she offered a shy wave back. Even from here, he could tell she was curious about her husband's past and his war buddies, even as she most likely wanted them all to pack up and go.

Limber now, Coop broke into a brisk jog that took him past the house and back onto the road, where his truck sat parked on the shoulder. Colorful leaves crunched under his shoes. He allowed the wind to sweep him along the asphalt as if he were a leaf himself, happy to go wherever the cool air brought him. There was a liberating joy in wandering, in grabbing trails just to see where they went.

He'd run until he flushed out all the booze and he was smoked, which he suspected wouldn't take long this morning. Another way of self-medicating, though at least it was good for him. Paying down the same credit card as other men like him, only when he'd preferred booze and coffee and cigs, he'd been doing it with steadily growing interest.

Along the way, he allowed his memories to march again across his mental battlespace. He thought about Ramos, which even now roused complex emotions.

Back in Iraq, Coop had feared, respected, sucked up to, and on more than one occasion even hated the man. To call Ramos loveless would be wrong, but it was the Army kind of love. Built like everything else in the big green machine for function and not comfort.

With the maturity gained from his years, Coop now understood that Ramos had protected his squad from themselves to keep them alive. Everything he did was to keep his boys bitching, on point, and breathing. Every action he took in the field was to model how to keep your shit squared away and fight.

The man didn't care about anything else. He didn't have a kumbaya bone in his body. Maybe in his private life, Coop supposed. He pictured the sergeant standing on a little stage in Tacoma, singing his heart out and sounding like Marvin Gaye.

Then he remembered Ramos throwing himself at the grenade at OP Applejack, the day Coop realized what real love was.

Yes, Ramos, in his way, had loved him.

Returning to the guest house sweaty and renewed, he found Doc sweeping bottles into a garbage bag and Horvath mixing Bloody Marys at the bar. His old squad mate turned to bleakly appraise him with a once-over.

"Christ, you're like a warrior monk," Horvath said. "What's it all for?"

"Why does it have to be for anything?" Coop made his reply as glib as possible, though the question had surprisingly needled him. "I do it to unwind. It's a discipline. What do you do to unwind?"

Horvath jerked his tall Bloody Mary aloft in a quick toast. "I'm unwinding right now." As if for good measure, he popped a cigarette in his lips and lit it with a theatrical flair.

"A little PT would do you good." Army acronym for physical training.

The man waved him off. "Been there, done that, for too long."

"I suggested a little hair of the dog," Doc said. "A Bloody Mary gets you Vitamin C, electrolytes, sodium and potassium, some antioxidants, and lycopene, which fights off toxins in the liver."

"Yeah, Doc," Horvath said, blowing a stream of smoke. "That's why I'm drinking it. You hit the nail on the head right there." He took a swig and smacked his lips, which shaped into a sneer. "And how about you?"

Doc regarded him warily. "How about me, what?"

"What do you liberals do to unwind? Get on Twitter and like your girlfriend's posts calling us baby killers?"

Doc's soft face darkened. If this was old barracks banter, it was the pointed kind. He shook it off with a little headshake.

"It's like a form of Tourette's," he said in wonder. "Do people like you actually mean any of the shit that comes out your mouth, or is it all about getting a rise?"

"That's for me to know and you to ponder, Doc."

"Watch me pondering, Ghost." Doc returned to cleaning up.

Horvath scowled at hearing his own old nickname.

In the barracks or when allowed in the field, the guys constantly tried to one-up each other with rough humor, playing the old game of male dominance. There was an unspoken line, however, and each man had just tested it.

"I like to shoot," Stuckey said in the doorway. "To unwind. I'll take you guys out to pop off a few rounds." He held up two paper bags. "But first, breakfast."

"Jesus Christ, LT," Horvath swore, reaching for one. "It's about time."

The men returned to the couches and chairs to pry the lids off tall coffee cups and unwrap bacon and fried egg sandwiches. Famished, Coop devoured his meal, washing it down with sips of the still steaming coffee.

Thinking Doc was onto something with the whole electrolytes business, he chased it with a glass of tomato juice. The food hit the spot, coaxing his hangover headache into a dull, sleepy murmur.

"What's the word, Hud?" Doc asked.

"There is no word," Stuckey said. "Fox and MSNBC picked up CNN's story of Ramos's capture but had nothing new to add to it. I checked out the ISIS propaganda site first thing this morning, and they claimed they had him, but from what I can tell, they haven't executed him."

"No news is good news," Coop said.

The others grunted in agreement.

"Probably saving him for some *Allah akbar* moment," Horvath said. "Celebrate some big win in Mosul or distract the faithful from a big loss."

Coop couldn't refute him. It fit the way the Islamic State did business.

In 2004, Abu Musab al-Zarqawi founded Al-Qaeda in Iraq, a splinter group of Al-Qaeda, the group responsible for the World Trade Center and Pentagon attacks three years earlier. In 2005, he declared war on all Shia Muslims in Iraq, accelerating sectarian violence into civil war.

In 2006, a pair of five-hundred-pound guided bombs dropped by an American F-16 pilot put an end to Zarqawi. This was back when the government boasted of killing the *number one leader* of various terrorist organizations, only for a new leader to emerge as supervillain. Zarqawi's successor rebranded Al-Qaeda in Iraq as the Islamic State, only to die himself in a counter-terrorism raid in 2010.

After the surge and Sunni Awakening in 2007, the organization dwindled. Then it staged a comeback in 2011 following the American withdrawal, largely due to Iraqi Prime Minister Nouri al-Maliki's vindictive rule that marginalized and oppressed the country's minority Sunni Muslim population.

With instability and anti-government sentiment growing, the Islamic State captured territory stretching from civil war-torn eastern Syria to western Iraq. Abu Bakr al-Baghdadi, the Islamic State's emir since 2010, declared the organization to now be the Islamic State of Iraq and Syria, or ISIS.

Festooned with black flags, columns of vehicles triumphantly rolled into the Iraqi cities of Ramadi and Fallujah, which was only forty miles from the capital of Baghdad. In June 2014, a single battalion of fighters took on thirty thousand Iraqi Army troops in Mosul, Iraq's second-largest city.

After a week of fighting, the Iraqi Army crumbled and fled. At the Great Mosque, Baghdadi declared a new caliphate that at its height would rule over some ten million people. For two years, this caliphate terrorized its citizens with a brutal brand of Islamic law while exporting terrorism around the world. In Mosul, the population declined from some two and a half million people to around a million.

An international coalition formed to destroy ISIS. The newly revitalized Iraqi Army recaptured Ramadi and Fallujah in a grinding campaign that brought three army divisions, working with Shia and Kurdish militias, to Mosul's doorstep.

Until October 2016, they cleared ISIS fighters out of the approaches to the city and began shelling it with artillery. In early

November, Iraqi soldiers fought their way in, their generals calling what awaited them the "mother of all battles."

They weren't wrong.

Between ten and twenty thousand ISIS militants, reinforced by a thousand foreign fighters, had entrenched in Mosul. They'd had years to prepare its defenses, and they planned to fight until granted a glorious death.

As expected, the combat was savage, horrific, and merciless. A twenty-first-century Stalingrad in the making. The last major battle of the second Iraqi civil war. If ISIS lost Mosul, it would lose everything.

If the coalition lost, well, the consequences were too horrific to contemplate.

Now the bastards had Sergeant Ramos, a propaganda prize.

Horvath was right. No, they wouldn't squander his execution. They'd wait for the right moment, which might arrive at any time depending on the battle.

"So, we wait," Doc said.

The men fell into a glum silence. There was nothing else they could do.

"I received a lot of texts from the Gamblers," Stuckey said. "We inspired a couple other meetups. Nobody else is coming to join us here, but everybody's talking about it. If we're waiting, we're all doing it together."

Coop found this news heartening, even if it wouldn't affect the inevitable outcome of Ramos's capture. Around the country, veterans from the old platoon had formed vigils. He hoped Ramos knew that he was in his comrades' thoughts and prayers. That he didn't feel alone as a result.

"Yeah, yeah, kumbaya," Horvath growled. "We got a very limited window for a course of action. We should be doing something."

"What can we do?" Doc said.

"I don't know. Get on Fox and scream all the way to the top. *Something.*"

The room became silent again. They all wanted to do something. Stuckey sipped his coffee and cast a cunning glance at the man. For a moment, Coop expected him to say, *Okay, gentlemen, load your nuts*, but he said nothing.

Policing his trash, he took a quick shower, brushed his teeth, and dressed in his usual blue jeans and black T-shirt. Stuckey caught him in the hall outside his room and gestured for him to follow.

"I need a hand," the lieutenant said.

He led Coop into a small room he'd converted into a study. Books about the Middle East and the Iraq War crammed a small bookshelf. Mostly nonfiction: *House to House, Generation Kill, Fiasco, My War, No True Glory, The Forever War, The Last True Story I'll Ever Tell,* and others. A few fiction titles like *Redeployment* and *Billy Lynn's Long Halftime Walk.* Pens, papers, and half-filled notebooks littered the desk around a laptop and a framed photo of the lieutenant and Sergeant Dixon grinning in full battle rattle in front of their Stryker.

The lieutenant ignored all that and went to a tall safe, which he dialed open to expose a small arsenal of rifles, holstered pistols, pouches, and boxed ammunition.

Coop gestured at the desk. "Are you working on a project here, LT?"

He still wanted to call Stuckey *sir* as an old reflex. The lieutenant didn't want that, but it still didn't feel right calling him by his first name. So, like Horvath, he'd decided to simply call the man *LT*, the same as he'd once done in the field.

Stuckey bleakly inspected the mess. "My magnum opus. I'm working on a book about the war."

"How's it going?"

"I started it in 2006, so you tell me."

Coop let out a low whistle. "Harder than it looks, I guess."

"Not really," Stuckey said. "Getting the words down is easy enough. I'm having more trouble with the thoughts."

"Thoughts?"

"You can tell people easily enough what you did day to day over there. You probably have a few funny, scary, or sad war stories on file when you need them. But can you really explain it to a civilian? What it was like?"

Coop thought about it, shook his head. "I guess not."

"I can't even explain it to my wife." Stuckey frowned with frustration and maybe even self-loathing. "Christ, Coop, sometimes I can't explain it to myself. Mostly, I just sit at the desk staring out the window, thinking about it."

"Permission to speak freely—?" Coop caught himself with a little sigh.

"Say what's on your mind."

"I don't think war has a single simple truth. All I know is being a soldier is a boring, dirty, dangerous job. War is what it is. What it all means is up to the soldier, whatever gets him through the shit. Anybody else can think whatever they want, but they can't tell that soldier any different, bad or good. He earned it."

To Coop, one of the only things a soldier truly owned was his perspective, and he was allowed what he believed even if it flew in the face of harsher facts existing outside his situational awareness.

"Well put," Stuckey told him.

"I don't know." Coop flushed a little at putting himself in a position to teach the lieutenant anything. "I'm probably not the best guy to ask."

"It's just—I see so much good in what we did over there, you know? A whole lot of good. Only I see what's going on now, and I wonder if all we did was open Pandora's Box. It's hard to reconcile meaning with reality."

"I believe the last thing that came out of that box was hope, LT."

As if awaiting just this cue, Stuckey removed a Colt AR15 carbine from the safe and handed it over along with its smell of gun oil and the memories it produced.

The AR15 was basically a semi-auto civilian version of the Army's M4. Coop felt its familiar shape, bringing on other conflicting emotions. He hadn't held a weapon since he got out. He'd sworn never to shoot in anger again.

At the same time, it fit him like a missing jigsaw piece.

"Come on, let's go shoot something," Stuckey said. "Hope always goes best with action."

Shoot

The veterans tramped through the woods. Doc and Stuckey led the way, Coop and Horvath behind. Their boots crunched and rustled the dead leaves carpeting the trail. Bare trees crowded their view.

Each man was equipped with a weapon and pouches containing eye protection, accessories, earplugs, and ammunition. Doc carried a Remington bolt-action hunting rifle, Stuckey an old Army M1 carbine, Coop an equally ancient Soviet-made AK47, Horvath the AR15.

"Are these guns actually legal to own in New York?" Doc asked Stuckey.

"All the rifles except that Remington are more than fifty years old and therefore qualify as antiques," Stuckey said. "And they're registered."

"Too bad Clinton lost, Doc," Horvath said. "Now she can't take *all* the guns."

Doc sighed without turning around. "You voted for Trump, did you?"

"That's right."

"The guy who said invading Iraq was a mistake?"

"Let's enjoy this fine day," Stuckey said like a warning.

Coop nudged Horvath. "Doc's not the enemy."

The man shrugged and grinned. Coop suspected he trolled to blow off steam. Stuckey liked to shoot antique rifles, Horvath his mouth. Horvath hadn't been trying to make a point so much as get a rise out of Doc. Mission accomplished.

During the war, he hadn't been much different. He'd antagonized Coop every chance he got. But there'd been a hilarity to it, as if they were acting out some Laurel and Hardy routine where Coop was forever doomed to play the straight man. This felt different. Mean-spirited. Based on anger instead of boredom.

The trees broke at a long, grassy field where the lieutenant had set up a shooting range. A barebones plywood table marked the firing point. Downrange, pairs of wood stands awaiting paper targets stood at pistol and rifle practice range. At the far end, in front of the backstop consisting of sandbags heaped up the slope of a tall berm, a steel target with a vaguely human shape dared them to hit it.

Stuckey and Doc marched ahead to haul target stands until the four formed a line around ten yards in front of the steel one. They began to affix simple human silhouette bullseye targets to the wood with clamps.

Heading south for the winter, birds chirped from their rest stop perches in the high branches of the trees. Coop breathed in the fresh, clean country air and smiled. This was a good place. A man could live here. Really live.

"You got out too soon, Coop," Horvath said. "You missed a hell of a show."

"You got out later than I'd thought. *Staff Sergeant* Horvath. I never thought I'd see the day. You moved up in the world."

He wasn't listening. "What was Ramos doing over there, anyway?"

Coop had wondered the same thing. "He changed after OP Applejack."

"He went soft, you mean."

"He left something there. Some part of him. Maybe he went back to find it."

Horvath snorted. "Okay, Oprah."

"You asked." Coop shrugged.

"Me, I see a man who couldn't handle the Army anymore but couldn't leave the shit, so he told himself some story to make it work."

"Both could be true."

Maybe even more than both. Maybe Ramos had gone back because he wanted to rewrite his war's meaning. Maybe he'd simply had a need to do something righteous, and the Knightingale Commandos offered him a chance to do the most good. Maybe he was simply addicted to combat.

Or maybe, just maybe, none of the above.

The only man who knew the truth was Ramos himself, and Coop suspected even he would be hard pressed to explain what the hell he was doing over there.

There was only one thing about which he was dead certain, which was Ramos had suffered a moral injury at OP Applejack. This was when a soldier did or saw something that went so strongly against his moral beliefs that he couldn't make peace with it. Some guys with a moral injury, they didn't know what was right anymore. They became angry, bitter.

When the grenade didn't go off, he believed, Ramos had directly confronted his mortality—in a sense, he'd died that night in the reeds by the Tigris—and by extension, exactly what he was dying for. He'd been willing to die for his boys, but in natural tandem he'd made a decision to die for his war.

Coop had pondered and studied that night for eleven years. He remembered the battle cross Ramos fashioned out of his own gear and contemplated, how puzzling and disturbing the scene had looked. At the time, he had wondered what the sergeant had been trying to tell him. Only later he started to think maybe Ramos had been trying to explain something to no one but himself.

Horvath eyed him. "You changed."

"So did you."

"You used to be this high-strung, needy kid. Hassling you to keep myself laughing was as simple as picking what string to pluck to make you sing."

Coop thought of the way he hassled Doc. "You used to only play at being an asshole. You didn't armor yourself in it."

Horvath laughed at the tough love. "Not Oprah. I'm gonna call you Dr. Phil."

"I'll bet you still like Olivia Newton John, though."

"I *don't* like her," Horvath grumbled. "I *love* her."

With the targets all set up, Stuckey returned with Doc.

"Let's get battle ready," he said.

The men geared up for shooting and fingered rounds into their magazines.

Horvath went first, trying out the AR15 on iron sights. The rifle popped and spat hot shell casings into the grass. Coop caught a pungent whiff of the nitroglycerine used in the gunpowder, a scent he associated with Iraq.

Stuckey peered through a scope to inspect the result. "On target. Good shooting."

Showing off, Horvath shifted aim and popped off three shots in succession, rewarded with the satisfying metallic pings of two rounds striking the steel target.

Its magazine went dry. He inspected its firing chamber, set it to safe, and put it down.

"Child's play," he bragged.

"If it wasn't, I would have given you shit, Sergeant," Stuckey said.

Horvath grinned. The man thrived on tough love, coming and going.

"I'd love to try out that old carbine."

"You'll get the chance. Coop, let's see what you got."

Coop picked up the AK47 and inserted the magazine into the magazine well, where it clicked with a snug fit. He planted the fixed wood stock against his shoulder and pulled the charging handle to place his first round in the chamber.

Locked and loaded. While he aimed, his thoughts clamored for attention.

During most of the war, he'd shot off indirect fire, shooting at positions more than people, a frustrating thing but probably a small mercy. At Yarmouk Traffic Circle, he'd killed two insurgents close enough to watch them die.

The jihadists had aimed rifles at him just like the one in his hands. Coop still carried a 7.62 round from one of the magazines in his pocket. Sergeant Ramos had told him it was the one that was going to kill him, and as long as he had it, it could never do its job. An old soldier superstition.

Even years later, he refused to part with it, because you never knew. Some rounds traveled around the world, over and over, waiting for their time.

Controlling his breathing, Coop allowed the stormy waves of these thoughts to pass through him. Shooting using the rifle's iron sights, he shifted his focus from the target onto the front sight and allowed it to naturally align with the rear.

He squeezed the trigger. Seven foot-pounds of recoil hummed against his shoulder. The shell casing flickered in his peripheral vision.

Even with the earplugs, the boom was a little louder and had a deeper pitch compared to the sharp metallic crack of his old M4, familiar in a way that electrified his nerves with alarm.

"A little high," Stuckey said behind his scope.

Coop fired again, this time hitting the silhouette where a man's arm would be. Responding to the lieutenant's corrections, he eventually walked his shots within the kill circle. He then shifted stance, brought the more distant steel target within his sight picture, and fired five rounds, pinging it on the last.

The rifle clicked empty. Despite his alarm—his body asking repeatedly, *Are we really doing this, is there a threat?*—he set it down feeling a deep if fuzzy calm. At last, he'd scratched one particular psychic itch.

Stuckey smirked at him. "Blow off some steam?"

"I guess I did," Coop confirmed.

"Not bad shooting, after so long."

It was Doc's turn next. He sat on a stump and propped the heavy scoped hunting rifle on a little bipod shooting rest Stuckey had set up on the table.

He blinked, as if unsure what to do. Overall, he looked shaky. Horvath threw a gloating smile at Coop, who responded with a brief warning headshake.

"Back in the saddle, Doc," Coop said. "Then you own it."

Nodding, Doc embraced the gun in a sitting shooting stance, eye kept back from the scope to avoid the harsh jerk of recoil.

The gun roared with a flash. Aided by the magnification optics, the round sailed true to pop against the steel target's head. Wearing a sour grimace, Doc worked the bolt, positioned, and fired again.

"Nice shooting," Stuckey said when he was done.

Doc set the rifle down, regarding it not with fear now but anger. The lieutenant stared off at some distant point that interested him. Horvath eyed the man's M1 carbine hungrily, itchy to shoot again. Coop looked around at all the natural beauty, marveling again at the life Stuckey had here and this time wishing he'd settled down somewhere and built something more permanent for himself.

Doc noticed Stuckey's eyes. "You all right, Hud?"

The lieutenant seemed to snap out of it.

"I'm going to Iraq," he said.

"I'm sorry, what?"

Horvath guffawed. "Goddamn, LT. That is some Bravo Zulu shit right here."

Bravo Zulu, military slang for, *You did good.*

Stuckey said, "I've given it a lot of thought. One of my men is going to die, and I can do something about it. If do nothing except wait and watch it happen, what kind of man am I?"

"A husband and father to two kids who need you," Doc said. "That's who you are either way."

"We got a man down," Horvath said. "Leave no man—"

"Dead bodies attract more dead—"

"I'm going," Stuckey cut them off. "And I have a proposition for you men."

Doc and Horvath started talking again, but Coop raised his hand and whistled. "Listen up, guys. Let's hear him out."

Though he knew what Stuckey was going to say, and he didn't want to hear it.

"Thanks, Coop," the lieutenant said. "Tonight, I'm going to book the first available flight to Erbil. Any man who wants to come with me is welcome."

Before the men all started shouting again, Coop said, "What exactly is the mission, LT? How are you planning to get in and out?"

"We fly into Erbil in Kurdish territory and drive until we find friendlies around Mosul. We start with Knightingale and work our way up the chain—Iraqi Army and any American Special Forces we come across. We put pressure anywhere we can on local forces to locate and rescue Sergeant Ramos. I see us being over there a few days, maybe a week, tops. That's it."

Doc fumed. "You'll be flying into a war zone without weapons or gear, and with no big green machine watching out for you. No dustoff, no fire or air support, nothing. You don't even speak the language."

"We'll buy what we need when we get there. Hire a terp. As for support, the Iraqi Army will be providing security. If anybody needs casevac, we've got Knightingale, but I don't see that happening. The plan is to talk, not fight."

"I'm with you, LT," Horvath said. "Or I would be if I weren't broke."

"As you can see, I'm a man of means," Stuckey said. "I'm willing to cover the entire cost of our trip."

The man's homely face broke into an excited grin. "Then I am definitely in."

"My travel agent is holding seats and waiting for my call. Think of it as me hiring you all as security contractors for room, board, and travel expenses."

"Just like old times," Doc muttered.

"You and Coop can sit this one out," Horvath said. "Me and the LT got it."

"They're welcome to come," Stuckey said. "What do you think, Coop?"

Coop was thinking this part didn't feel like coming home. It felt like signing up. He was thinking the lieutenant's plan sounded reasonable and possibly even safe. Only as they all well knew, plans rarely survived first contact with the enemy. He was thinking Doc and Stuckey were out of shape and might not be able to handle it. He was thinking Mosul was a living hell right now and that he might need to fight to defend himself, only before today he hadn't held a weapon in eleven years and all his old experience and know-how had gone to rust.

He was thinking about what he owed Ramos, a man he hadn't even really known or even particularly liked.

"I guess I'm still thinking," he answered.

"You've got a few hours to decide." Stuckey looked at his watch. "Almost lunchtime. Let's head back. Leave the brass on the ground, I'll pick it up later. I have to make arrangements and spend some time with my family. You're welcome to hang out, order pizza, drink my booze, whatever. After supper, I'll drop in and see where everybody stands. Understood?"

"Hooah," Horvath said, all interest in shooting the antique carbine forgotten.

They double-checked to make sure the weapons were cleared and then packed them and the gear into bags. Hoisting them onto their shoulders, Horvath and Stuckey strode off toward the guest house, fleshing out their plans.

Doc watched them go. "They're going to get themselves killed."

"You hate it."

"Typical Army mission. Sending the gullible to do the suicidal."

Coop let out an amused snort. "Are you definitely out?"

"I was there too, you know. I saw what Ramos did."

OP Applejack.

"I do know," Coop said.

"So you should know I don't know what I'm going to do."

"Yeah. Okay."

Doc shook it off and started walking toward the trees into which Stuckey and Horvath had disappeared. Coop kept pace, thinking his own thoughts.

"Hell," Doc said after a while. "Maybe tomorrow he'll sober up and forget all about it."

"He sounded pretty sober to me."

"If he isn't drunk, then he's nuts to show his face anywhere near ISIS."

Or to leave this place to risk his neck, Coop thought.

Then again, he did seem lonely. Stuckey appeared to somehow need this.

One last adventure, perhaps. A way to get off the hamster wheel and finish his story. Maybe having it all wasn't enough for a man who'd seen war up close.

No one knew for sure but Stuckey, who might be lying to himself.

"You'd think after Iraq, we'd at least have a healthy respect for our mortality," Doc added.

The light dimmed a little as they walked deeper into the forest. The birds had stopped singing. The little bubble of serenity Coop had imagined here seemed to pop. He'd have to keep driving until he found it again, his eye of the storm.

In his mind's eye, half of him did just that, while the other half flew back to Iraq.

Doc jarred him from this reverie. "You're in, aren't you?"

Coop said, "I don't know what I'm going to do, either."

"Roger that."

"I guess we have a lot to think about."

"Whatever happens," said Doc, "it's been damned good to see you, man. You changed, and for the better. You grew up." He thrust out his hand.

Coop shook it, thinking Doc hadn't changed much at all. "You, too. Try not to let Horvath get on your nerves. He grew a chip on his shoulder over the years."

"You know, the best thing about getting out of the service was not having to be hard all the time. It took meeting Marjorie to teach me how to be weak again in the right ways so I could be strong in the right ones."

"That's good to hear, but I'm not sure—"

"I feel *sorry* for Joe."

"Ah," said Coop. "Just don't tell him that."

They returned to the guest house. Mixing another Bloody Mary, Horvath winked at them. Doc disappeared into the room he'd claimed. Coop found Stuckey in his little office, carefully placing his rifle collection back in the safe.

"You need a hand, LT?"

"No, I've got it, thanks. Unless you want to talk to Carol for me." He cast Coop a quick, rueful smile. "I am gonna be in so much shit for this."

"Well. It's a crazy idea."

"Too crazy?"

"No," Coop said. "I guess it's not."

"Go do your deep thinking. I'll need your answer by 1900."

Withdrawing to his room, Coop lay on the bed, took out his phone, and plugged into Stuckey's Wi-Fi. Then he pulled up everything he could find being reported about the battle raging in Mosul for the past month.

The operation to clear the sprawling city involved a hundred thousand men, four divisions of the Iraqi Army including the Golden Division, the American-trained special forces who did most of the fighting.

Supporting them: Shia militias, Saddam's old Baathists, the Kurdish Peshmerga, and a coalition of nations that included the United States and Iran. ISIS had united the country and the Middle East at a level America had never been able to impose. Everyone hated ISIS and wanted them destroyed.

Facing the Iraqi Army and its partners were around ten to twenty thousand ISIS fighters. Only half of whom probably had real training, the other half being poorly trained fanatics, teenaged boys, and even child soldiers.

The Iraqi Army had the manpower, equipment, and plenty of air and artillery support. ISIS enjoyed advantages of terrain, civilians used as human shields, IEDs and even more dreaded vehicle-borne IEDs, weaponized drones, and an outright eagerness to die for Allah.

A general called it the largest urban battle since the Second World War.

In terms of manpower, the good guys outnumbered the bad by ten to one at best and five to one at worst. Typical military doctrine called for at least a three-to-one advantage for an attack to succeed. One would therefore think the Iraqi Army would mop the floor with ISIS, but he'd be wrong.

Infantrymen feared urban operations for good reason. The Iraqi Army was advancing, but it was painfully slow in the nightmarish terrain and with all the civilians still there, and it involved virtually destroying the neighborhoods they liberated. If ever a village had to be destroyed to save it, it was Mosul. The Iraqi soldiers and the civilians they'd come to save were dying like flies.

Ramos was somewhere in that seventy square miles of living hell, if he was even in the city anymore. A needle in a haystack made not of hay but burning buildings, broken bodies, and hot flying metal.

Stuckey and Horvath had cooked up a loony plan to visit the most dangerous place on Earth. Coop pictured tagging along with them, useless after so long out of arms, playing war tourist in a pointless attempt to do the impossible.

They'd be going for honor or to scratch some other deep itch, not to accomplish anything real. Which made the whole idea to fly over there feel like dangerous cosplay to him. Like something not entirely honorable.

He returned to the living room and passed Horvath, who sat on the couch eating a massive submarine sandwich with both hands.

"I got a hoagie for you too if you want it," the man called after him through a mouthful of bread and lunchmeat.

Coop grunted and went outside. Let Horvath go back to the devil he knew, Stuckey back to the devil who'd tricked him into thinking he'd once been his best self in war. He started walking to his truck. If he stuck around, he'd up and do something stupid like reenlist.

If he was going to escape this horrible idea, the only way out was to just go.

Passing the main house, he heard shouting from inside, most of it coming from Carol. In the ranks, the boys called soldiers' wives the Household Six for a reason, recognizing their ultimate command authority.

Coop wished her success. If anyone could talk sense into Stuckey, it would be her. He suspected she wouldn't have her way this time, however.

The lieutenant had his itch, and it wasn't going to let him go until he'd given it a good scratch. Honor and duty were a soldier's catnip. These lofty notions gave all the inanity and suffering meaning.

They didn't end after one left war and service.

Two boys sat on the back porch, elbows on their knees, glum faces cupped in their hands. Their eyes warily followed Coop's path across the backyard.

"You must be Jeremy." The kid the spitting image of his dad. Coop next winked at the younger boy. "And you look like a Doug. Is your name Doug?"

The boy replied with a smile and shy nod.

"Did you fight in the war with my dad?" Jeremy said.

"I did. He was a good officer. He did right by us."

"He never says anything about it."

"That's because war is bad, even if it's done by good men trying to do right."

Doug finally spoke up. "Did you kill anybody?"

"I was proud to serve with your dad," Coop said. "That being said, I can't think of much I did over there I'm particularly proud of. But I did my job and my duty."

No longer talking to the boys but to his comrades, his unit, the Army, the country he'd served, the universe.

The kids scowled back at him. His answer was far too grownup to be satisfying. They wanted a juicy story, not an essay on the duality of war.

He shrugged and kept walking until he'd returned to the comforting confines of his old Dakota. Even the clunky slam of the broke-dick door sounded right to him.

All he had to do now was slide the key into the ignition, and he could burn rubber for new destinations unknown. Follow the open road to the next place it and his restless spirit took him. Maybe quit his familiar Yankee territory this time and follow the birds in search of warmer climes for the winter.

"Yeah," Coop said. "Fuck all this."

He didn't move. He sat frozen in a different, far more agonizing kind of meditation. The picturesque, leaf-strewn road called to him as it always did, but this time it had competition.

The siren call of duty to the skull tattoo that permanently branded his shoulder, the sweet smell of warrior catnip. The man he owed a deep and lasting psychic debt. And something far, far more seductive.

The promise of a strong purpose, lost all these years since he got out.

His instinctive drive to help those who needed it.

The idea he could make a difference to do something good.

This was the only desire he still encouraged in his fairly monastic life. Coop had given up believing that God kept score and gave a crap about him enough to intercede in worldly affairs, but one of the aspects of Buddhism he'd adopted was karma. The basic principle was the more good intent and deeds you put out in the universe, the more the universe rewarded you. Simple cause and effect. Coop's sense of it was a little different, visualizing a massive scale balancing the good and harm he'd done and simply wanting the good to win.

Maybe if he went over there, they *could* get Ramos out.

What if?

No way, Coop thought. This was different than his usual temptation to do the right thing. And he wasn't putting his neck on the line for an idea again.

Been there, done that, got the T-shirt and a few scars to boot.

Back in Iraq, he wouldn't have given it a second thought. One of his people was in trouble? He'd set his rifle to kill and charge in, compartmentalizing his searing terror to save it for a long, hard think later. Shoot first, then ask questions.

The only thing was he wasn't in Iraq anymore. A lot of years separated Coop from the man he was on Mosul's mean streets and the men he'd served with there.

Still, he didn't move, however, held in place by an old and powerful gravity. The hours rolled past. The afternoon bled away.

The sky dimmed toward twilight. Soon, night would fall like a curtain on his planned escape.

It's harder to fight with yourself than the world. An old Iraqi proverb.

"Damn it," Coop growled.

He left the truck in a state of self disgust and trudged back to the guest house, for once not mindful or even hypervigilant but utterly oblivious to his surroundings. There should have been some comfort in letting go and surrendering to something bigger than himself. He felt only trepidation.

He'd gone as far as the guest house when he realized no one was shouting anymore. Aside from wind gently whistling through the trees, silence blanketed the property. The main house glowed in isolation.

He went inside the guest house. Horvath now sat on the couch talking into his phone, ordering pizzas for delivery. Empty glasses cluttered the coffee table by an overflowing ashtray. The cigarette smoke hung in drifting layers. The man seemed to be making up for lost time by consuming everything in sight.

Horvath hung up. "I hope you like pepperoni."

Coop sank into the couch next to him with a sigh. "Give me a cig."

If he was giving up to desire, he might as well go all the way.

Horvath quickly torched the tips of two Marlboros and passed one over. Addicts loved company, but more than that, he sensed Coop had made the right call. Sharing a cigarette would welcome his old comrade to the team.

The chemical rush made Coop blink, but it didn't take his body long to welcome it. Resuming habits was like getting back on a bike. He wondered if it would adjust so easily to banging around a war zone.

"Where's Doc?" he said.

Horvath jerked his thumb toward Doc's bedroom. "Talking to his old lady."

As if awaiting his cue, Doc entered the room scowling and flopped into one of the easy chairs. He looked like Coop felt, like a man awaiting his execution.

"Did she give you hell?" Horvath asked him.

Doc grimaced. "She understands."

"Well. Good." His voice gentle, knowing this was a time to go easy, not hard.

The door opened, and Stuckey, looking worse for wear himself, entered in a gust of brisk fresh air.

"Is this the doghouse?" he said. "Because I am in the doghouse."

"You're in the right place," Coop confirmed.

"Who's out?" Stuckey read the answer on their faces and nodded with an expression of absolute pride he switched off before it turned saccharine. "Good. The game is on, but I'd like to show you something, in case you still had any lingering doubts. Brace yourself. It's a tough watch."

The lieutenant held up his smartphone and pressed a button on the screen. A video began to play.

Dressed in an orange jumpsuit, Dante Ramos knelt on a concrete floor. A very tall and thin man wearing black stood behind him, only his torso visible along with the machete glinting in his tight grip. An off camera voice rattled in Arabic.

"Jesus Christ," Doc breathed.

Ramos's worn, battered face wore an expression of utter despair. This was a man no longer afraid but sadly accepting his death. A man without hope.

On his forehead, visible against dark skin glistening with sweat, his captors had written a message in English in white paint: NO GOD BUT GOD.

Horvath snarled. "Goddamn animals."

When the video ended, Coop realized he'd been holding his breath. He sucked in air but still felt choked, like he was being slowly strangled.

By some miracle, the show hadn't ended in Ramos's beheading.

"They're bragging they have him," Doc said.

Stuckey nodded. "He's alive."

Coop's face hardened. Right then, he knew he'd made the right choice.

Forget the Army. Forget brotherhood born under fire. Forget his debt.

If he could help Ramos, he had to try. It was that simple.

"Load your nuts," said Stuckey.

Then he withdrew to his office, where he bought tickets to Iraq.

Insurgent

May 2004.

Two months after a Sunni Muslim insurgent group attacked Shia holy sites in multiple cities and broadcast the burned remains of four American security contractors hung on a bridge. This group would soon become Al-Qaeda in Iraq and evolve over the years into the Islamic State of Iraq and Syria, or ISIS—

One month after torture of detainees held at Abu Ghraib prison became known to the world, which fueled the anti-American insurgency and marked America's surrender of the moral high ground—

Mere days after the same insurgent group beheaded American businessman Nicholas Berg in direct response to Abu Ghraib. The man who murdered him was Abu Musab al-Zarqawi, Al-Qaeda in Iraq's founding father—

Seven months into Coop's deployment—

In the tactical operations center, he manned up for action.

Tonight, the Gamblers hunted.

After chow the day before, Lieutenant Stuckey had passed down the operations order. A night raid on two houses occupied by suspected insurgents. Two line squads would be riding, along with an HQ element.

He'd pointed at locations on a map depicting the area of operations. He'd laid out the times of movement, line of march, who was on overwatch and who was going in, and the rules of engagement, or ROE, which defined the conditions under which his shooters could use lethal force.

For the first raid, 1st Squad would be on overwatch. For the second, Ramos's boys were going in.

These raids were part and parcel of occupation, and they'd significantly stepped up in the last month after insurgents attacked local police stations and tried to overrun some other government buildings. The Americans were fighting an enemy indistinguishable from the locals, an enemy both invisible and hiding in plain sight, an enemy that was everywhere and nowhere and was growing bolder.

As a result, they relied on intel, largely produced by informants, that told them where these insurgents lived. Tonight, they'd storm these houses, search for weapons and documents, and bag and tag some bad guys for interrogation.

For Coop, sometimes Iraq felt like he was a diplomat doing humanitarian aid work, other times that he had a pivotal role in the reality TV show *Cops*.

More bullshit, but then Lieutenant Stuckey reminded him it wasn't.

"Intel says these are the guys who have been shooting mortars at you," the platoon leader had said. "Taking pot shots at you. Planting IEDs. Running guns and bombs into the city. Keeping Iraq in the shit. Tomorrow night, they're ours."

The Gamblers heartily hooahed this prediction.

A day later, Coop popped fresh batteries into his night vision goggles, or NVGs. The room smelled like bolt oil and pre-op jitters. Around him, hands roamed to check weapons, pouches, and radios. ROEs and crib sheets protruded from breast pockets. A few final rounds were fingered into magazines, the magazines sliding snug into weapons or chest ammo racks. Weapon bolts slid into place with a satisfying clack. Doing a shakedown test, Murray bounced on his heels a few times to make sure all his equipment was securely fastened.

Standing with Sergeant Dixon, Stuckey checked his watch. He looked up from his map board and said, "Gentlemen, load your nuts."

In full battle rattle, the squads filed out the door to the motor pool, where their Strykers warmed and waited with ramps lowered. Sergeant Ramos performed a quick pre-combat inspection on Coop to make sure he was squared away and patted his shoulder.

Good to go, Coop tramped aboard and parked his ass on the hard bench next to Horvath. Reyes filed in behind and sat on his other side.

"I was talking to Basam," Horvath said. "Just to get a rise, I asked him why Iraqis hate freedom so much."

Basam had been the Gamblers' interpreter for the past two months, ever since Hip Hop one day had stopped showing up at the base to work. His English was fluent, but unlike Hip Hop, who was practically starry eyed about Americans, it was obvious Basam thought they were all idiots.

Before the country collapsed, he'd been an English literature professor at Mosul University and seemed to hate every minute he suffered this job of relaying unwelcome news to his countrymen. He didn't seem to mind the risk of being murdered as a collaborator so much as he was simply too old for this shit.

"How did he answer?" Coop said.

In a spot-on imitation of the terp, Horvath pinched his nose in painful frustration. "'They do not hate American freedoms. They hate *you*.'"

All aboard and eavesdropping on the exchange, the squad burst out laughing. In his own way, Basam talked a fearless brand of shit as well as any grunt in the barracks, which made him a bit of a badass in their book, an Iraqi worthy of respect. Even the usually cool Ramos, who stayed out of the barracks banter unless one of the boys was feeling his oats enough to test him, let out a chuckle.

"He's starting to sound like Doc," Murray said.

"After the meeting yesterday, I heard Doc bitching about the raid," Coop said. "He was saying the intel is often wrong, and there was a good chance the guys we're nabbing tonight are people the informant doesn't like or owes money to."

It was Horvath's turn to play. "What did you say?"

"I said, 'Doc, as far as I'm concerned, they're all insurgents.'"

Another round of laughs. Despite the tough talk, Coop had tried to soften his take on the locals he felt like he was trying to save from themselves. He'd asked Basam to help him brush up on the Arabic he'd forgotten from his orientation course. On ops, he used it to set Iraqis at ease while gleaning little bits of what they were saying around him that they thought he couldn't understand.

Practically speaking, it didn't change anything. After seeing five men from his platoon killed or wounded by IEDs, Coop's motto was *better safe than sorry*. Maybe all Iraqis weren't terrorists, but they weren't his friends. If being nice and using the right words helped ensure his survival, though, he was all for it.

The first target lived in a small family home in Mosul's northwest. Another ride up MSR Tampa, another swing through the Yarmouk Traffic Circle, that major hub used by American soldiers and Iraqi insurgents alike.

The compartment went dark.

"NVGs on," said Ramos. "We're coming up on the target."

Coop reached up to the NVG attachment on his helmet and pulled it into place over one eye. The optical lens sucked any available photons in the compartment's gloom and passed them through a vacuum tube that converted them into electrons producing an amplified image a thousand times more visible than the naked eye delivered. The resulting monocular view appeared rendered in a multitude of greens—green added to the gray image because it was the easiest color to look at for extended periods of time in darkness. Night vision.

The view offered lousy peripheral vision and no depth perception. One didn't use optical attachments on weaponry while the NVG was in use. Blobs of light like headlights and exploding ordnance could flood them out and be blinding. Using them for extended periods of time was tiring.

Nonetheless, they gave the Americans yet another dominating advantage.

The ramp ground down until it touched earth. The squad hustled out the way they'd rehearsed, the same as they'd done many times before, and established security in its overwatch position for 2nd Squad, which raced up to the house and assembled into assault and follow-on assault teams.

Coop took a knee and eyeballed the houses across the street rendered in shades of green. The other squad banged the door open and charged inside, setting off a flurry of barks from dogs around the neighborhood.

A loud sigh sounded behind him. He glance over his shoulder to see Doc looking at the target's house.

"Doc, get over it," he said. "It's happening."

"Everything we do, we end up making more terrorists."

"What's that supposed to mean?" Murray asked him from Coop's left.

"If he isn't a jihadist tonight, there's an even chance he will be by the time the detention center gets through with him."

On Coop's right, Horvath chuckled. "Doc, why did you even sign up?"

"Do you really want to know?"

"Hey, if you don't—"

"GI Bill," Doc answered. "I can't afford college otherwise. But a big part of it was Saddam was a monster. I wanted to help these people."

"Is that what your recruiter told you?" Reyes said. "We help people?"

"You sold your principles, Doc," Coop chimed in to ride him even harder.

They all laughed at that until Ramos growled to bring them back on point.

Behind them, 2nd Squad emerged from the house on stomping feet. Coop glanced over his shoulder again to see two of the soldiers pose on either side of the detainee, who stood cuffed with a sandbag hood over his head.

Another soldier snapped a quick picture of the trio.

"The banality of evil," Doc muttered.

"Shut up, Doc," Murray said.

"Fo'real, dog," Horvath put in. "Save it for the chaplain."

The prisoner stowed and the house searched top to bottom, Lieutenant Stuckey ordered the platoon to mount up. Ramos hustled his squad back into the Stryker's dim compartment. The engine's steady whir enveloped them along with the vehicle's familiar smells.

Coop raised his NVGs. "That went well."

"Our turn next," Murray said. "Do it like we trained it."

"Hooah," his fireteam said.

The Stryker powered down to its next stop. Overwatched by its sister squad, 1st Squad exited down the ramp. Ramos flashed hand signals, and Coop and the others hustled toward the narrow shoebox house with weapons at the low ready.

One by one, his fireteam stacked nut to butt next to the door. They would be the assault team, Bravo team the follow-on.

Reyes appeared behind him and tapped his shoulder, indicating he was in position. Coop gulped, thinking about who was in the house, what kind of weapons they might have, what might happen when he went charging in.

Horvath was in front of him. Coop was second in line.

With a running start, Horvath stomped the door with his boot. The door burst wide with a crash. Coop surged forward on Horvath's heels, sweeping through the foyer and into a long, spacious *majli* or traditional sitting area, what Americans would call a living room.

This being night, it had been converted into a sleeping space. On the green circle his NVGs offered, people sat up on thin mattresses placed against the walls. Their eyes gleamed with surprise and fear. An old woman was already screaming while children whimpered and cried.

In moments, the room had been secured. Coop stayed to cover the Iraqis while Horvath, Murray, and Reyes surged across the patterned carpet to another living area beyond.

He loved this part, the rehearsed and choreographed ballet of clearing a house. He also hated this part, the screams and terror, the lack of control, the madness of the violence of action, where men panicked and did stupid things.

In Arabic, he yelled at them to stay put and remain calm, hoping he wasn't mangling it.

The old woman shrilled at him, but they otherwise did as they were told.

"Door, left!" Horvath called out and kept going forward into what appeared to be a kitchen. Murray, meanwhile, shifted left and emerged moments later escorting a man and a woman back into the sitting room.

Bravo had entered the house, but it was essentially over. Coop raised his NVGs as someone found a light switch. The room flooded with a weak overhead light, its incandescence revealing ornate if sparse furnishings. Cushions, shelves, a table lamp on a little dresser, the women hastily covering their heads with scarves.

Ramos and Basam talked to the couple, who sat on the floor with their children. The man wore a plain white tee and pajama bottoms. The old woman continued her berating until Ramos turned to fix her with his immovable stare.

After a few more words—*la'a, la'a*—and a flinging gesture, she pointedly looked away as if he didn't exist and fell silent.

Ramos started his questioning in a tone of calm authority, Basam murmuring his translations. Murray called Coop into the bedroom. Together, they ransacked it. They searched under the floor mattress, spilled boxes from shelves, rummaged through clothes neatly folded in a dresser.

They found nothing and left a mess.

Back in the sitting area, the man had been zip-cuffed behind the small of his back. The entire family wailed now, and for the first time, Coop saw them as human beings. As terrified and desperate people.

The mother hugged her three wide-eyed, weeping children, a boy of maybe twelve or thirteen, a girl no older than nine, a little boy who looked around five.

The sight of them filled Coop with a fury too big to comprehend. He wanted to smash his rifle stock into this man's face for putting his family through this trauma. For forcing his country through so much suffering. For killing and maiming men Coop knew. For keeping him here in Iraq when he could be home already or at the very least not having to do this shit to people.

We're here to help you, he fumed. *And you'd rather kill us.*

The man now ignored Basam's questions and focused on his oldest son, who gaped back at him with dark eyes watery with anguish.

"Looks like we're done here," Ramos said.

The man spoke in rapid Arabic, and then the hood went over his head.

Murray and Sergeant Franks, Bravo team's leader, reported to Ramos that they hadn't found anything. Ramos passed it up to Stuckey outside and then twirled his finger next to his face.

"Let's go," he said. "We're Oscar Mike."

On the move again.

Coop shifted his gaze to catch the boy staring at him. The boy was no longer weeping for his father. Wasn't weeping at all.

He sat dead still, just staring.

Glaring pure hatred and murder directly into Coop's eyes.

Murray frogmarched the suspected insurgent toward the door. The squad fell in and tramped out after them. Behind, the women let up a low, almost animal keening.

Outside, Coop caught Basam's shoulder.

"What did he say?"

The terp replied with a puzzled frown behind his balaclava. "Did you think he would confess? He said he is innocent, of course."

"No, I mean what he said to his kid."

"Ah," Basam said. "He said, 'Kaseem, now is your time to be a man.'"

Welcome to Iraq

Six and half miles above the Atlantic Ocean, Qatar Airways Flight QR750 flew toward Doha on the Arabian peninsula. From there, after a brief layover, Coop would board the next plane that would take him to Erbil, Iraq.

Nearly eight thousand miles. The trip would take close to a full day.

Due to his height and frame, he'd won the window seat, from which he'd watched America shrink and disappear. Now the view only offered thin air and a bright world of cottony clouds, what medievalists thought Heaven looked like.

"So we're doing this," Doc said.

"It's something, huh?" Coop said.

The man looked dazed. "Oh yeah, it's something."

"You're not happy."

"I think this is stupid even for Gamblers."

"Why'd you come?"

Doc glanced across Horvath and the aisle at Stuckey's satisfied profile. "You could say my recruiter is a hell of a salesman."

Coop laughed. "I'm starting to I wish I'd hung out with you more back in the day."

"I was too full of myself telling you the war was stupid."

"You still do believe that, though, don't you?"

"There's a time and a place to be right," Doc said.

The pretty flight attendant returned in her red, vaguely military uniform to deliver their drink orders from her trolley. Though Qatar was a Muslim country, QR750 was an international flight and so alcohol was served. Doc accepted a vodka on the rocks, Horvath whiskey poured neat, Stuckey his gin and tonic.

Coop received a bottle of water. He twisted off the cap and took a swig.

After she'd moved on, Stuckey raised his little plastic cup toward his comrades. "Drive on."

"All for one," said Horvath.

The men drank. Stuckey leaned closer, raising his voice a little to be heard over the plane's muted roar.

"Joe and I were talking about how we're going to work together," he said. "We agreed that I'll run the big picture. Everybody's used to that, and, well, not to be crass or anything, but I *am* paying for the trip."

Coop didn't object. This wasn't a vacation but a mission, and missions worked best under command. He'd already assumed this was how it would work.

Stuckey went on, "I intend to go home to my kids at the end of this, which you can take as ironclad assurance we are *not* going there looking for trouble. We'll be behind the lines, so I don't see it happening. But if trouble does manage to find us, Joe here will take tactical command. Any objections to that?"

"You mean besides the fact Joe's an ignoramus?" Coop asked.

Horvath guffawed at the old barracks humor.

Stuckey smirked. "Yes, let's take that drawback off the table for a minute."

"Then none from me, LT."

Doc answered with a wag of his head but couldn't suppress a wince. Aside from the fact Horvath could be grating, this part probably felt too much like the real Army for him. Even the idea they might see combat, however remote, was worrying.

"Good," said Stuckey. "Joe has the most squad experience, so we'll be in good hands if we get into a jam. Plus we've got the best medic in our old battalion."

No one had any questions. They settled again for the flight. Still looking sour, Doc went back to the ad hoc tourist guide to Kurdistan and Erbil he'd thrown together from the internet and printed in the lieutenant's office.

Coop plugged buds into his ears to listen to music.

"Hey." Horvath reached across Doc's shuffling papers to give Coop's leg a little poke.

He removed his earbuds. "What's up?"

"I know this was a tough sell for you. But we're going to do some good."

"You know what I think?"

"Tell me."

"I think Doc might be right, and we're looking for hajji tanks."

Horvath blinked as he remembered, and then he guffawed again.

"Which we did end up finding," he said. "Go, Wolverines."

With a wry smile, Coop returned the buds, which emitted a plaintive musical interpretation of the Hindu mantra *Om Namah Shivaya*.

He realized how exhausted he was, waking up at oh-dark-thirty to hustle down to New York City to scour its all-night pharmacies for medical supplies and then rush to JFK Airport for their flight. The music, along with the plane's soft roar and the air pressure, quickly lulled him into sleep.

He dreamed of Iraq.

In a rocky stretch of desert, Sergeant Ramos trudged through oven heat in full battle rattle. Topping a rise, he looked down into a dry basin.

A tractor trailer idled down there, its refrigerated conex filled with Iraqi dead.

"I'm in mourning," Ramos said.

He thrust his rifle barrel-first into the dirt and stuck his Kevlar over the upraised stock. He removed his dog tags and draped them over the grip. Sitting in the dust, he next stripped off his boots and placed them facing him.

Coop approached as Ramos knelt barefoot in front of his battle cross.

"Who died, Sarnt?"

He woke with tight shoulders and stiff joints. Night had fallen. The Airbus cabin was dark and quiet. His window was black.

Under a reading light, Doc sat next to him still taking notes from his mass of papers but bleary-eyed and nodding off. Across the aisle, Stuckey snored, head lolling and mouth open. Horvath's seat was empty.

Coop recalled his dream. The details had been all wrong. Ramos had built his battle cross behind the chapel at FOB Marez, not in the desert. He did it the morning the platoon returned from OP Applejack.

By then, it had been months since they'd seen the refrigerated truck they'd once guarded in the desert. The truck had meant little to Coop at the time. It was just another bullshit tasking. He hadn't thought about it since.

And no one had asked Ramos who died. The squad found him without knowing how long he'd been kneeling there. They noticed the battle cross had been made with his own gear and tags.

Already unsettled by what happened at the lonely observation post on the banks of the Tigris, no one had spoken at all. *This is some kind of soldier juju at work*, they thought. *Some arcane magic known only to the hardcore lifers.*

The heavy dread Coop felt in the dream was spot-on accurate.

In his Airbus seat, Coop shivered. He hoped his dream wasn't a premonition.

Thinking this, he realized he was starting to hope.

Starting to think this might not be a fool's errand and might actually help.

What if was a whole different kind of soldier magic, and it could be white or black magic, good or bad.

Horvath walked down the aisle fuming and plunked back into his seat bitching about the line for the lavatory.

"You're gonna get a fine," Coop said.

Horvath snorted. "They haven't caught me yet."

"What's going on?" Doc asked.

Coop mimed taking a drag on a cigarette.

"Oh, great. They'll force a landing in Istanbul and ditch us there."

Swaddled in a blanket across the aisle, Stuckey awoke with a puzzled frown, as if surprised to find himself on at airplane. He looked over with a sleepy smile.

"Where the hell are we?"

Coop glanced at the little screen on the back of the seat in front of him. "Somewhere over Germany."

"Berlin, then," said Doc.

They'd continue down the Balkans, cross over Turkey, and then actually pass Iraq before landing in Doha and catching a flight back north.

Stuckey turned on his light to read a magazine. Horvath sweated with desire to light up. Doc's head slowly tilted to the side, and he started snoring.

Coop set his watch seven hours ahead to Iraq time and studied his comrades with puzzled affection.

He didn't really know them. At the same time, he felt like he knew them as well as he knew himself.

Meeting again, they'd dropped anchor in the past and tested each other in the old way. Ahead lay the harder work of building something new.

"Why'd you stay in?" he asked Joe, starting there.

Horvath scowled. Somehow, this was a deeply personal question.

"You could say I made a promise to Ramos," he finally answered.

Horvath didn't explain. Instead, he told a story about Ramadi, which had been like the Battle of Mosul only even harder and stretched out over months instead of a week. He bitched about the rules of engagement that denied him air support, the rear-echelon career generals running the Sandbox wars on PowerPoint slides, and Obama bringing the troops home so all their labor and sacrifice could go down the drain.

"Afghanistan," he said with a rueful and incredulous shake of the head. "Now, the 'Stan was even more screwed than Iraq, if you can believe it."

Again, the kid-glove ROE to avoid civilian casualties, which always happened anyway in a hot war zone. The nicer the Americans played it, the more ruthless the Taliban got, and guess who was winning the battle of hearts and minds?

Alexander the Great had it right when he took over, Horvath pontificated. Everywhere he went, he yanked one out of ten men and killed him on the spot. A message the Afghans understood. They ended up revering him as a god.

Again, Coop found himself wanting to agree with everything Horvath said. If *what if* motivated men to act, *if only* acted as a balm after they did. Oversimplifications carried a natural moral weight; they certainly made being a soldier easier even if these statements were dangerous. He would have hated to have done his time in Iraq carrying Doc's tortured soul on his shoulders.

Coop was older now, however, and far wiser than his dumbass twenty-year-old self the government had trusted with a rifle and a qualified license to kill. If there was one thing he'd learned about his war, if not all wars, it was how much it had enjoyed curb-stomping easy narratives.

He kept all this to himself and just listened. When Horvath finally spent himself on his rant and sagged against his armrests, Coop spoke again.

"So what promise did you make to Sergeant Ramos?"

"Enough about the Sandbox," Horvath said. "Christ, I just got out. Tell me about that club you worked at and all the hot girls who danced there."

For hours, they laughed, listened, and shared, establishing themselves in each other's mind as the men they were now, not a list of memories from back in the day. At the same time, this was all familiar, using words to kill time the way they had in Iraq, when they'd shoot the shit at some boring, mosquito-ridden observation post or while kicking back on crates in a camouflage netting-draped smoke pit on base.

Horvath marveled at how easy Coop's life appeared on the outside. Coop missed Horvath's purpose and admired both Doc's fresh start with med school and the seemingly idyllic family life the lieutenant had built.

Again, it felt good to talk. In a way, it felt like home.

Dawn paled the sky as their Airbus touched down at Hamad International Airport in Doha.

"Look alive," Stuckey told them. "We've got about two hours to kill."

The men stirred in their seats and waited their turn to deboard. After spending half a day breathing recycled, pressurized air while strapped into a chair, they looked far more like something hung out to dry.

"How do you do it?" Doc groaned at Coop, who appeared utterly alert.

"Chair yoga," Coop explained. Periodic stretching to relax and get his blood moving. Overall, he felt a little wrung out but good to go.

"Maybe there is something to all this Buddhism business."

"Oh, yeah," Horvath enthused. "Don't have any fun, and you'll live longer."

They exited the plane into the new grand, posh airport filled with hustling Qataris and other travelers dressed in a mix of traditional and Western fashions. A glittering airport shopping mall awaited them. Marveling at the wealth on display, Coop saw an image of the prosperous Iraq the war planners once envisioned.

The last time he'd flown to this part of the world, he'd been wearing fresh desert cammies, ruck and weapon stowed and seat in the upright position, packed in with other excited and fresh-faced American youth. All of them feeling earnest and gung ho and trying hard not to let it show, each warned by his mother not to try to be a hero but determined to be one anyway once he got in the shit.

Arriving in Kuwait, Coop boarded a bus that hauled him to a camp that processed him and punted him to another camp, a veritable city made out of tents. There, he did his PT, trained to react to ambushes, and shot live ordnance at targets. The battalion commander raised the unit tomahawk and delivered a rousing speech about killing while Coop and the boys screamed *Aieyah!* back at him, thinking, *Can we get this over with and go already?* Soon enough, they mounted their Strykers and drove north through the Sunni Triangle all the way up to Mosul.

Years later, Coop was now returning to the Sandbox, though this time he had far fewer illusions.

Gathering his little troop in the gleaming airport, Stuckey doled out orders.

"'All respect, I'm gonna stop you right there, LT," Horvath said. "I'm going to the smoking lounge. See you later, suckers."

"See you later, Ghost," Doc said.

Horvath threw him a dark look and then chuckled.

Coop watched him go. "You nailed it, Doc. He's still a shammer."

The men drove on without the sergeant's cheerful presence. Stuckey confirmed their connection to Erbil. Doc ran off for some duty-free shopping of cigarettes they'd use to buy favors in Iraq. Coop checked ISIS's snuff channel and confirmed Ramos hadn't been executed while they were in the air.

After breakfast—or late night snack, as Coop's brain was still catching up from New York's time zone—they boarded the connection to their final destination of Erbil, home to nearly nine hundred thousand people.

Around two hours later, Kurdistan sprawled in the haze outside his window.

As the plane descended into this northern region of Iraq, patches of farmland appeared in the large steppe stretched between the surrounding Zagros Mountains. Then the city hove into view, a handful of high-rises at the center of housing tracts and other buildings radiating into the surrounding empty landscape. Its ring roads gave it the appearance of being constructed of interconnected spoked wheels.

Erbil was one of the oldest cities in the world, the site of the decisive battle between Alexander the Great and King Darius III that spelled the end of the Persian Empire. Now much of it appeared modern and new, the result of the economic boom in this region that followed Saddam's fall and it being spared much of the violence that had plagued the rest of the country.

For Coop, this was to be his new forward operating base.

Doc leaned to have a look for himself and paled.

"Stupid even for Gamblers," he repeated to himself.

Coop took a deep cleansing breath and let it go.

The plane's wheels whumped against the tarmac. Touchdown. The men waited for the door to open and tramped off the plane in surly silence, raw and singular after the endless travel. They collected their bags from the spinning baggage carousel and anxiously hustled to Passport Control, their final hurdle.

Kurdistan was the only region in the war-torn Republic of Iraq currently welcoming tourists. Stuckey had figured the best way to play it was to tell the border agent they were there to distribute aid in Mosul with Knightingale, which would explain all the medical supplies they'd bought and boarded as luggage.

If Knightingale had gotten in, they could too.

The only trick was Mosul was outside Kurdistan's current regional borders, and there was no quick and uncomplicated way to gain travel authorization from Iraq's shaky federal government.

Wearing a gray uniform with gold stars on his black epaulettes, the officious mustached border agent examined their passports and listened to Stuckey's explanation. Looking at the man's bland expression, Coop wondered if the man even understood what was being said.

"Mosul," the man prompted. "You are medical?"

Stuckey thrust his hand into his pocket in case the situation called for some palm greasing. "Yes, we're medics. We're here to help the people of Mosul."

The agent promptly stamped their passports, granting them permission to stay in Kurdistan Region for thirty days. Longer than they intended to stay.

"Welcome to Kurdistan," he said. "Welcome to Iraq. And thank you."

Erbil

The gun shop owner wore a fierce mustache and struck Coop as a cross between a Hell's Angel biker and Rambo.

"Rojbash," the man welcomed them in his loud, harsh voice.

"Salaam alaikum," Doc said, hand over his heart. *Peace be upon you*, a standard polite greeting in the Muslim world. He squinted at his notebook and started banging his way through an elaborate Kurdish phrase.

The lieutenant took charge. "Do you speak English?"

The man's stoic deadpan shifted to accommodate a brief, shy smile.

"A little bit," he said.

His name was Zoran.

In serviceable if pidgin English, he told them he'd once served in the Kurdish militias called the Peshmerga, "those who face death." He'd built a trade repairing weaponry for them, over time accumulating enough arms to open the shop.

"Everything for sale." Zoran gestured around the room.

"What about ammo, accessories, tactical vests?" Stuckey asked, miming the outline of a chest rig over his torso.

"Balé, balé." The man jerked his thumb toward the back rooms.

Taking that as a yes, the lieutenant's eyes lit up. "Excellent. Gentlemen, we've come to the right place."

He was right; they'd found the local Walmart of refurbished weaponry. Coop checked out the wares. Weapons of all makes and vintages covered every inch of the walls. Others lined the concrete floor near the base of the walls.

He spotted WWI-era Ottoman rifles, Bulgarian machine guns smuggled into the region long ago by the CIA, an Africa Korps MP40, a stand of peeling rocket launchers, and a pair of American thirty-cals shipped to Israel after the Second World War.

"What a bunch of junk," Horvath said.

"Hm-hm," agreed Coop, whose hands practically itched for his old M4.

In the corner, a giant young Kurd with a buzzcut and jowly, stubbled face sat behind a worktable cluttered with pliers, screwdrivers, machined parts, and spray oil cans. He looked up from repairing a pistol to deliver an annoyed glare.

"Pearls before swine," said Stuckey, who was a collector.

Horvath snorted. "If you say so."

The lieutenant crouched to run his hand along a battered drum-fed machine gun with an attached bipod. "Do you know what this is?"

"That would be a machine gun, LT," Horvath deadpanned.

"Not just any MG. This little beauty is an Egyptian-made RPD. Soviet design, damned hard to find. One of the SAW's granddaddies. The RPK replaced it."

The sergeant gazed bleakly at an AR15 on the wall that appeared to be there purely for show, as it was no longer serviceable. "If we end up in combat, would you trust it with your life?"

"Well, I…" Stuckey frowned, remembering his mission. "Maybe not."

"We're heading to Mosul with Third World weapons."

The far wall offered a wide selection of Kalashnikovs, arguably the most popular combat rifle in the world. Cheap, simple, and durable, it also had a range and compact size well suited to close-quarters urban fighting. The weapon could be put through just about anything and shoot at the end of it, with jams being rare.

Coop picked out a fairly new RK62, a modern Finnish take on the original Soviet AK47 design by way of Poland. In addition to the standard three-pronged flash suppressor, this particular model included a folding tubular metal buttstock, which still carried its cleaning kit inside, and a top rail for mounting optics. Otherwise, it fired the same 7.62 ammunition used everywhere in Iraq.

The rifle was scratched up and had seen action in its day, but it appeared to be in working condition, and it wasn't corroded or pitted anywhere he could see.

She wasn't his old M4, but she'd do.

While giving the rifle a closer inspection, he caught Zoran staring at him.

"You know guns," the Kurd said.

"Yeah," Coop sighed. "I guess I do."

Horvath appeared toting a Super 90 semi-auto combat shotgun.

"Hey, Doc," he said. "Ask Kurdish Chuck Norris here how many twelve-gauge shells he can give me with this."

Coop eyed the weapon. "Good choice."

"Where we're going, goddamn right, I'll take the stopping power."

Zoran waved his arms in front of his face. *"Na! Na, na."*

Doc appeared helpless. "I asked him about the ammo, and he's telling me no, but I think he just doesn't understand me."

"After all that studying of the lingo you did on the plane? I am disappointed."

Doc gave him a sour look.

Horvath shrugged. "He'll figure it out. If he wants to sell me this boom stick, he'll need to cough up something to make it go boom."

Coop stepped aside for the lieutenant. Stuckey selected a Russian-made AKM, an updated version of the AK47. Doc took a step forward to scoop a rifle seemingly at random, which turned out to be a Yugoslav Zastava semiautomatic rifle with a hardwood stock. Not a terrible choice. It was a workhorse, and it used the same ammunition as what Coop and Stuckey would be carrying.

Zoran grinned as the Americans laid their weapons on his sales counter.

"Sidearms too," said Stuckey. "Go pick out a pistol."

"Thanks, but no," Doc said.

"I'm sorry, Doc, but it isn't optional. I can't lead you into that city unless I know I did everything possible to make sure you can defend yourself."

"Yes, sidearms," Horvath agreed. "I'm going with all the weapons and ammo I can carry. Hell, I'm hitting a goddamn knife store on the way back."

Tokarev and Makarov pistols slapped the table next.

After that, Zoran brought out Rhodesian recon chest rigs, canteens, holsters, and pouches, all of it looking like it had been dragged through multiple bush wars, one rig having a bullet hole to prove it. Cleaning kits and an assortment of magnification and red dot optics of varying quality arrived next. Spare magazines and boxes of ammo stacked the counter, including Horvath's shotgun shells.

Lastly, the Kurd set out a flak jacket and heavy civilian body armor plates that looked like they'd gotten banged enough times to make their future effectiveness at stopping rounds a dice roll. Regardless, Coop would take what he could get. As a man who'd once been hosed at close range, he was a firm believer in it.

The Americans picked out what they needed.

Horvath blinked as it all added up. "You sure about all this, LT?"

Stuckey nodded. "I want us being able to handle anything."

"Hey, I'm not arguing. Semper Paratus, right?"

Coop looked at the piled hardware and gear and wondered if Stuckey was fronting all this just so they could feel safe. Where they were going, the things that would kill them likely weren't the kind they could outmaneuver or suppress with gunfire: mortars, drones, car bombs, IEDs.

At the same time, if it was an illusion, it was a comforting one. The illusion he'd possessed even a modicum of control over whether he got his ticket punched had gotten him through his war in Iraq. In an active battlespace, being able to shoot back topped the hierarchy of needs.

No, Coop wouldn't refuse guns, a little body armor, and a knife as a backup.

Grabbing a box of ammo, Zoran beckoned them to pick up their weapons and follow him through a bead curtain into the back of the shop. They walked past several rooms filled with metal junk and a kitchen space where a woman prepared a steaming meal that wafted the rich smells of cumin and cardamom.

At last, they emerged into a shooting range set up in an open-air courtyard surrounded by taller structures. From the looks of things, the Kurds were pretty relaxed on noise ordinances.

Coop fired five test shots at twenty-five yards and shredded a spread of holes a good ten inches to the right of the bullseye. Smooth action, but inaccurate.

Zoran picked up an empty shell casing and pinched it with pliers. Then he took the rifle from Coop. Fitting the shell casing over the front sight, he gave it a few savage twists to manhandle the sight alignment and then handed the rifle back.

Coop planted the RK62 against his shoulder, aimed, and smoothly pulled the trigger. The rifle banged angrily in his hands.

The rounds mashed the center of the target in a solid grouping. The rifle was now zeroed.

"Ah," Zoran let out as a positive exclamation.

Coop nodded, impressed. "I think I'll take it."

Once all the weapons had been test driven and calibrated, the Kurd led them back into the shop and commenced his haggling with the lieutenant.

Coop walked away to give his mind a chance to clear. Back in Poughkeepsie, agreeing to Stuckey's loony plan had given him the peace of relief. For the first time since then, he was now starting to feel as anxious as Doc looked.

Because the plan was beginning to feel very real.

He wasn't afraid of dying. Life was temporal itself and therefore just another illusion. When his time came, it came. He couldn't control it. At the same time, he didn't want to die, and he found he didn't want any of these men to get hurt.

Too late to back out now, Coop thought and told himself to let go.

For better or worse, he was in it. They were doing this.

Money changed hands at the counter. A colossal amount of Iraqi dinar handed over in literal bricks tied up with thick rubber bands, though with an exchange rate of fifteen hundred to one, the total in American dollars wasn't bad at all for the guns and gear, which went into two duffel bags.

Stuckey asked where he could hire a guide and interpreter, receiving only a quizzical expression as an answer. Doc jumped in to help.

Finally, the shop owner said, "Okay, okay."

The man whistled at his beefy worker, who stood behind his cluttered worktable to glower at the Americans.

Zoran swept his arm in introduction. "Eylo." He turned back to the Americans with a frown, realizing he didn't know any of their names. He shrugged. *"Ameriki."*

With that, he jabbered at length. Eylo nodded.

"He will help you," Zoran said.

Stuckey stepped forward and thrust out his hand.

"Nice to meet you, Eylo. We're—"

The big Kurd stabbed his finger in the air in the universal gesture for *wait one* while he took out a cell phone and placed a call.

"Sazan, chawa ye?" The giant chortled into the phone.

Horvath's face darkened with impatience. "Whiskey Tango Foxtrot, guys." Army slang for, *What the fuck?*

"I am at a loss as well, Joe," Coop answered, more curious than anything.

"Balé." The man hung up and walked out the door.

Stuckey shot Zoran an annoyed stare, but the gun seller appeared nonplussed.

"He will help you," the man said with a shooing gesture. "Good luck, bye."

Coop shrugged, hoisted one of the heavy rucks over his shoulder, and followed. Horvath grabbed the other and tramped after him.

"Spas," Doc blurted in parting, showing off that he'd learned enough of the lingo to at least say thank you properly.

Out on the busy street, Eylo shot into the crowd on tall strides. Coop and his comrades set out after him. They walked past shops whose rolled-up carpets, percussion instruments and flutes, handbags, and other wares spilled in stacks onto the sidewalk. Men baked naan in large ovens, throwing the bread onto piles. A neighboring eatery's shawarma and kebabs added to the exotic mix of smells.

The ancient citadel loomed on its mound in the distance, partially under renovation. The fortress had once withstood the Mongols and was a top candidate for oldest site of continuous human habitation in the world. Today, it remained as a symbol of Kurdish resilience and self-determination.

Stuckey led the way, happy they were still making progress to their objective. Doc had picked up prayer beads from somewhere and thumbed them as a fidget relief. Horvath glowered, visibly warning no one to mess with him, his Russian pistol already loaded and tucked into the waistband of his jeans.

As for Coop, he marveled at the people and scenery, the old and new, the familiar and utterly alien, and was again tickled by the feeling that being in a foreign country had once inspired in him. Otherwise, his eyes continued their exhausting, never-ending chore of checking windows and doors and what people had in their hands.

When they passed a liquor store, Horvath's glower softened a little. "Finally, progress in Iraq." The rest of the Muslim country didn't permit the sale of alcohol. "We'll have to hit that on the way back."

Coop knew what he was thinking. The warm and friendly hospitality, the beautiful women in Western clothes, the modernity fueled by economic progress, and with liquor stores to boot: *Why couldn't we have invaded here?*

Eylo turned into a narrow alley that cut across to another street.

"And this is where we get robbed and murdered," Horvath now grumbled.

"They probably should have done that before selling us a lot of guns," Coop told him. Nonetheless, his eyes roamed ambush points.

The big Kurd led them out onto another busy street, never looking back to see if the Americans were following. After a few turns, he entered a café.

It was a tea house, small but somehow grand with its arched and ornately painted ceiling. Lanterns and a few recessed lights illuminated tables and stools and the decorative cushions that lined benches zigging around the perimeter. A series of framed photos celebrated historical heroes of the Kurdish resistance.

Eylo turned to Stuckey and fixed him with an incredulous frown, as if surprised the Americans had actually followed him. He gestured for them to sit at one of the little tables and stomped away toward another table where a man and woman in paramilitary-style garb lounged over tea and cigarettes.

The man packed up his gear and left. Eylo and the woman talked for a while, ending their conversation with a laugh. The big Kurd whistled for the Americans, who moved to join her. Then he left too without even a wave.

"Welcome to Hawler," the woman said, using the local name for Erbil. "My name is Sazan. My brother tells me you need an interpreter."

As Coop settled in, he had time for a good look at the young Kurdish woman. While bright, her eyes communicated the kind of weariness that came with constant struggle toward an elusive goal. Her olive-green jumpsuit, unzipped in the front to reveal a white halter top, clad a stout but shapely body. She'd bound her long black hair in a practical ponytail, but her head was otherwise uncovered.

"And a guide," Stuckey said as he picked his own stool to perch on. "We're going to Mosul to make contact with the Knightingale Commandos."

Sazan nodded. "I know Mosul, and I know Colonel Reynolds."

John Reynolds, the fierce warrior monk who'd founded Knightingale.

"Anyway, I'm Hud. This is Kyle—we call him Doc—and Coop and Joe."

At the mention of Horvath's name, Coop glanced over at him, expecting him to scowl as he always used to at the idea of women going anywhere near a war zone. Instead, Horvath gazed at her striking if severe face with open lust.

No, not just that, Coop mused. The man looked like he was actually smitten. When his tea arrived in a tall, steaming glass, he didn't even look at it.

"Are you Peshmerga?" Stuckey asked her.

Sazan lit a slim Turkish cigarette. "Yes. KDP."

As a people of some twenty to forty million, the Kurds were the world's largest stateless nation, spread across northern Iraq, eastern Turkey, western Iran, and parts of Syria and Armenia. After the fall of the Ottoman Empire following the First World War, the treaty that would have established an independent Kurdistan was never ratified and ended up superseded by a separate treaty—yet another case of poorly drawn post-colonial borders sowing the seeds of future conflicts.

The Kurds had never stopped wanting their own homeland, however, and Sazan had that earnest look of nationalist hunger about her. Multiple revolts only ended up crushed. During the Iran-Iraq War of the 1980s, they rose up again, which resulted in mass executions and the Iraqi Air Force killing five thousand civilians by dropping chemical weapons onto a town captured by Kurdish guerillas. Coop and his squad mates had once spent one very hot month thirty clicks north of Mosul guarding a Kurdish team engaged in exhuming the dead for proper burial.

After the American invasion deposed Saddam, the Kurds gained an officially recognized level of autonomy. While a part of Federal Iraq, they had their own functioning government and something of a military—two militaries really, each predominantly controlled by one of the two major political parties. Sazan served in the Peshmerga affiliated with the Kurdistan Democratic Party, or KDP.

During Coop's war, the Kurds were the good guys, allied with the Americans. He'd found them committed if disorganized, the bulk of the Peshmerga fighting more as an ad-hoc militia than an army. They traveled to the front on anything with wheels, fought for a month with scavenged, hand-me-down weaponry, and then rotated home. Nonetheless, Coop had been glad to have them on his side.

During the Battle of Mosul in '04, the Kurds had helped pacify the convulsing city, even if the insurgency had taken root there because the Americans had gotten too friendly with them, which threatened the Sunnis. Again, it was a complicated war. Now the Kurds were an active part of the coalition against ISIS, marking the first time the Peshmerga fought alongside the Iraqi Army instead of against them.

The Peshmerga recruited women, though the KDP didn't allow them combat roles. Nonetheless, Sazan had received military training, and her open and fearless body language spoke of time spent around soldiers. Currently on leave, she was available. She could speak English and Arabic. At university, she'd learned English, which she spoke with a clipped, military precision, and she'd spent enough time in Mosul that she could find her way around.

"She's perfect," Horvath interjected while Stuckey was explaining their mission. Perfect for what, Coop could only guess. "Hire the lady, LT."

Sazan blew a stream of smoke and gave him a knowing look. "I have not said I am to be hired. What are you paying?"

"Twenty-five U.S. dollars a day," Stuckey said. "We'll be here a week, tops."

She regarded him coolly. "Your Army paid fifty."

"We aren't the Army."

"You look like soldiers. And fifty is the standard rate."

"We can do fifty," the lieutenant conceded.

Sazan laughed. "My point is you are a rich American who can afford more than the Army paid. I am charging you one hundred."

"Oh, my God," Horvath grinned. The man appeared to be in love.

Coop suppressed a laugh. The walk over here from the gun shop had imparted a clandestine feel, and finding the tough, sexy Kurdish fighter at the end of it made the whole thing seem like a trope in an espionage movie. The shitty and improbable sequel to his Iraq War, which had been like watching *Freddy Got Fingered* on repeat.

But here she was, negotiating her pay while the lieutenant, who'd dropped a small fortune on flights and gear, was haggling purely because he didn't want to feel ripped off. It was all so mundane that it made their mission here real again.

Sazan added, "I can translate, defend myself, and get you through the Peshmerga checkpoints we'll run into on the way to Mosul."

Scowling, Stuckey kept at it until they settled on eight-five.

"When do we go?" she said.

"Tomorrow morning at 0800." He told her the hotel.

"I know it."

"I guess that's it," Doc said, dazed again.

The Gamblers had almost everything they needed to return to the field.

Tomorrow, they were going to the most dangerous place in the world.

Ambiguous Loss

July 2004.

One month after the U.S.-led Coalition Provisional Authority handed the reins of government back to the Iraqi people, recognizing a new interim government. The ceremony took place in the "green zone," a heavily guarded area in downtown Baghdad where the coalition and Iraqi leadership lived and worked—

Nine into Coop's deployment in the "red zone," which was pretty much most of the rest of Iraq—

Only three more until he was scheduled for redeployment stateside, marking him as a short timer—

At the edge of the Nineveh Plains bleached to desert brown by the dry season's angry sun, near a town whose name he already forgot, the Iraqis dug up their dead.

Coop eyed the refrigerated truck, where they stored the bodies.

He wanted to get inside it. Just for a minute.

Feel that beautiful and glorious cold.

His squad had been detached from its rifle platoon and tasked to provide security for the exhumations. Every morning, they rolled outside of Mosul past wheatfields, olive groves, and lonely shepherds tending their flocks to this desolate patch of *Mad Max* country.

Their mission: ID and pat down the Iraqi workers and then stand around stupefied in roasting heat that shimmered off the ground in convection waves.

The armored Stryker rested on its eight big wheels on a patch of dirt, its commander munching a protein bar in the turret behind the swivel-mounted heavy machine gun. Sergeant Ramos leaned with his back against the vehicle, rock still in the blinding sunlight, eyes inscrutable behind ballistic sunglasses.

A soldier had many enemies from bullets to the chlorinated water that still gave Coop the painful shits, but on this particular op, the worst had to be the climate. The climate was Biblical in its temper, flinging wind and choking dust and swampy mud and burning heat.

Hell, everything in Iraq felt Biblical. The geography, all brooding mountains and vast deserts and life-giving rivers, the kind of land where a prophet could go mad. The camels loping across the sands. Even the bugs, from the biting fleas to the monstrous camel spiders and scary scorpions. And of course the people, many dressed in fashions that struck Coop as being popular when Jesus was a corporal.

But back to the climate, which dominated his current thoughts.

Like his squad, today Coop wore Kevlar and armor, cammies, five-quart Camelbak, and M4 carbine clipped to his harness puffed with ammo magazines. Sixty-five pounds in all and getting heavier by the minute.

The temperature, meanwhile, hovered around a hellish one hundred ten. For a man born and raised in wintry Michigan, this was murder weather, blackout weather, riots and murder spree weather.

Since he'd deployed to Iraq, he'd been shot at and almost blown up. Now even the sun wanted to end him.

"I didn't sign up for this," he muttered.

Horvath laughed. "Yeah, you did, ya dumb-dumb."

The heat wrung the sweat out of Coop faster than he could replace it, body temp elevated to a constant hundred and three.

Sunburned, raw, bored, dried out, and pissed off.

He bit the business end of his Camelbak tube and sucked a sip, tasting rubber, his teeth crunching on grains of sand. The water was almost too hot to drink now.

The cloying smell of the dead filled the air, no escaping it.

"Maybe somebody will take a shot at us," he said.

Over his deployment, his craving to shoot had only intensified. Right now, he was hoping for *anything* to alleviate the boredom and take his mind off his deep exhaustion, the sand that got into everything, his face melting.

Horvath's homely face grinned behind Ray-Bans. "Nothing's gonna happen, dog."

Coop sighed, said nothing, resisted looking again at his wristwatch.

Horvath: "Tick, tock, tick, tock—"

"Just shut up. For five goddamn minutes."

A short distance away, a mechanized backhoe had scraped the arid topsoil into ragged piles, exposing human remains dried and hardened to leather. The machine itself so old it barely had paint left on it. Signs next to the pits showed arrows pointing north toward the Zagros Mountains purpling the horizon.

Men and women crouched among the corpses, snapping pictures and beginning the painstaking process of removing them into body bags.

A dozen mummified bodies already lay on tables in a nearby tent, where they were examined along with artifacts such as clothing and identification cards. Pelvic girdle and skull to identify sex, teeth and bones to estimate age.

Bullet holes in the base of their skulls to determine cause of death.

During the Iraqi dictator's twenty-five years of rule, Saddam Hussein "disappeared" more than a quarter of a million people, many of them Kurds. Mass executions. From '87 to '89 alone, the Iraqi Army wiped two thousand villages from this region off the map.

At least a hundred of Saddam's victims were buried at this site. Probably more. Possibly a lot more. Past the laborers hacking with pickaxes and shovels, a man swept the ground with a metal detector looking for buried shell casings.

Coop's gaze shifted to an Iraqi fixing a spare tire and finally rested on the refrigerated truck.

He wondered how cold it was in there.

Much colder than the Stryker, now heated to broil. Where the impotent air conditioning barely moved the air around. Where the driver had yanked the plastic hose from his nuclear, biological, and chemical attack mask—which attached to an air purifier with a fan in the vehicle—and stuck it down his shirt for hillbilly AC.

"You could always pitch in on the digging," Horvath said.

Coop growled. "At least they have something to do."

Ramos called out from the Stryker, "You need a tasking, troop?"

"No, Sergeant." He wisely clammed up. As bored as he was, one never volunteered in the Army, where the volunteering always found you.

"Mm-hm," Ramos said doubtfully, as if the jury were still out on whether Coop indeed appeared occupied enough to pull his weight today.

By this point in the deployment, Coop thoroughly doubted the man was human. The worst things got, the more his squad leader seemed to enjoy it. Infernal heat, bugs, getting wrung out with the spasming shits, no sleep, IEDs jolting Strykers on the road, mortar shells randomly falling on their base at night.

Sergeant Murray walked over with Specialist Reyes.

"God, it really stinks today," said Reyes, eyeing the mummified bodies.

He wore what appeared to be some Special Forces gadget taped onto his helmet, and then Coop realized it was the man's little camcorder he'd gotten in the mail. Ready to record action, if any action were to happen.

"Yeah, dog," said Horvath, adding thoughtfully, "I'd still do her, though."

Coop shook his head while the other men let out a disgusted guffaw at the graveyard humor. Over by the pits, a middle-aged Frenchwoman paused in her work to glare at them. A forensic anthropologist with a humanitarian organization working with the Iraqi International Commission on the Missing.

"You're a sick man, Horvath," Murray said, chuckling.

"A soldier in the field will screw anything," Reyes noted.

Normally, they'd squeeze every second and chortle out of an odd topic or flash of comedy, however lame or brutal. Yesterday, they'd spent an hour redesigning the Camelbak with dry ice insulation and a solar panel powering little AC fans that would clip onto their shoulders and hose cool air under the chafing body armor. That done, they'd proceeded to ride each other mercilessly for laughs.

When they weren't laughing, they were thinking about the heat, how their feet hurt, how their ass hurt, how far they were from home, how badly this all sucked and how they were doing it for a measly fifteen, sixteen hundred bucks a month.

So, yeah, they laughed every chance they got.

Only their hearts weren't much in it now. It was too hot, the morbid smell was something best ignored than talked about, they had sand literally crawling up their ass, and the dead bodies dug out of the earth struck them as too damned sad.

Murray and Reyes kept on walking, going nowhere and killing time. Coop looked again at the cold truck. His brain felt like it was boiling under his helmet.

If he walked over, he could make up an excuse to get inside it. A grisly idea, with the dead stacked in there, like sitting in a crypt. But it was *cold*, and that's what he wanted more than anything right now.

Five minutes. Just five measly minutes of not suffering.

Ramos wouldn't buy his excuses. *But I had symptoms of heat exhaustion, Sarnt. I needed to restore combat effectiveness. My mind wasn't thinking straight.* Too bad. Suffering was part of the service. They even gave it a name, *the Suck.* You embraced the Suck. You made the Suck your friend and mentor. The Suck set you apart, made you better than other people, defined you ironclad as *not a pussy*.

The Army thrived on paradoxes and Catch-22s. Spotting them in the wild passed as sport for grunts. Ramos had embraced the one that said if you didn't completely love the Suck, then the Suck made you its bitch and owned you. As for Coop, he'd done his best to imitate the veterans and try to make pain his friend, but in the end, pain was pain. It hated his guts, and he hated it back.

No, the sergeant loved the Army and in particular his squad, but it was a tough love, so tough one could easily mistake it for something else entirely. Sneaking into the truck would likely earn Coop an Article 15.

A misdemeanor, though, not a felony. After the usual sneering and ritual humiliation to set an example, Ramos would end up slapping him with a week or two of gate guard duty, maybe some time burning waste from the shitter barrels, running laps around the FOB until he was good and smoked. None of it a fun time.

Coop smiled as he measured it all out, what he'd be gaining and losing.

Yes, as scared as he was of Ramos, it'd be worth it.

"Hey." Horvath raised his rifle and aimed it at the wastes to the south.

Coop stiffened at his battle buddy's tone. He wheeled and raised his M4 to take a look through his scope. "What have you got?"

"Three hundred meters. At your one o'clock."

He scanned the brown landscape pulsing in rising heat waves. "What is it?"

"You see it?"

"No. What am I looking for?"

"Oh, I found a rock."

He lowered his rifle with a pressure cooker hiss. "I hate my life."

"I think it's hostile," Horvath said. "Should I shoot? Should I *shoot*?"

Coop stomped off toward the mass graves.

"Where are you going?"

"Taking a dump." He waved at Murray, who gave him the go-ahead.

As he neared the pits, he slowed his pace. The little camp's port-a-shitters stood like white tombstones in a cloud of moondust raised by a passing four by four. Their insides were ovens swarming with black flies that seemed to materialize out of nowhere in this country.

The refrigerated truck stood near these portable toilets. A group of Iraqi gravediggers smoked their lousy Miami cigarettes by the cab. The cloying stench of death was even stronger here.

Coop ran some mental calculations. He wanted to glance over his shoulder to confirm sightlines and see if anyone was paying attention, but he knew, just knew, that he'd find Ramos eyeballing him from behind his Oakleys.

His mission suddenly felt hopeless, but he'd try anyway.

"Hello, soldier," a female voice said.

He turned in surprise to see the Frenchwoman frowning at him. She wore olive-green cargo pants, dirty T-shirt, and blue plastic gloves. She'd pulled her graying hair back into a practical pony tail. Her face was caked with dust.

"Can I help you, ma'am?"

Instinctively, he postured himself to display zero weakness and otherwise control the encounter. Nonetheless, it'd be cool if this woman liked him, despite the perpetual look of disgust she directed everywhere except at the bodies she studied. He was a twenty-year-old male stuck in a forward operating base dominated by men, which automatically placed this older, somewhat attractive female somewhere near a "ten" in his book.

"Do you know what we're doing here?" she asked.

"You're identifying the dead so they can be returned to their families," Coop said, repeating what he'd been told.

"It is so much more than that."

He glanced at the refrigerated truck, now tantalizingly close. "Sure."

"Your guns will not fix Iraq." She gestured toward the mass graves with her gloved hand. "*This* will fix Iraq."

"I'm afraid I don't follow that logic, ma'am."

"Imagine your lover or perhaps your mother worked at the World Trade Center when it was hit. The towers collapsed. Her body was never found. You never knew for sure if she was alive or dead."

"Wow," Coop said, uncomfortable with talking about 9/11. He'd signed up with Uncle Sam in part because of the attack. It was still a sensitive subject, though, especially in the direct way she'd made it personal to him, even hypothetically.

"It is called ambiguous loss. I imagine it is exhausting, draining, maddening. Not *knowing*, not being able to say goodbye. That is why we are doing this, so these people can heal and move on. These graves are also a crime scene. With these forensics, we can hopefully bring the men who did this to justice and make sure anyone who would do this in the future knows they can be held accountable."

"It's good," Coop admitted.

He envied her, in fact. She had a simple, morally clear mission.

"As you can see, most of the people working here are Iraqi Kurds," she went on. "Doctors, archaeologists, manual laborers. Some have a relative they hope to find. All are considered collaborators with the Americans and therefore risking their lives to do it."

He wondered why she was telling him all this.

Then—

"I get it," Coop said.

Every day, the soldiers cracked jokes and grab-assed to pass the hours within earshot of the forensics team. She was asking him to show a little more respect. If not to the dead, then to the survivors here who labored to take them home.

He flushed with a little shame. She had a point.

On the other hand, his squad had been tasked to stand in more than sixty pounds of battle rattle day after day going rock happy in baking heat. This after facing bombs and bullets and mortars for nine months.

For soldiers in the field, it was either bitch or mope. Crack jokes, or let all this shit get inside your head.

Keep it all bottled up until later, or make mistakes that got men killed.

Coop's mouth set in a hard line.

"Do you know what *we're* doing here, ma'am?" he asked her right back.

Before she could answer, Coop squared his shoulders and marched back to his post, all thoughts about sneaking into the refrigerated truck forgotten.

To Mosul

Outside Erbil, the Nissan Pathfinder hummed along Federal Iraq Highway 2 past oil tankers and palm trees and farmers selling figs on the roadside. Despite a transmission issue, the vehicle was four-wheel drive, powered by a V8 engine, and just roomy enough for five passengers and all their weapons and gear. The truck would get them to Mosul. The only real downside was it wasn't bulletproof.

Getting the vehicle loaded had taken some time, a puzzle Stuckey tackled with gusto. Organization and logistics were his province. Sazan showed up wearing a fully loaded chest rig and webbed belt with a revolver strapped to her thigh. Standing next to her wearing his fresh fleece pullover, chest rig, and blue checked keffiyeh around his neck, clean-shaven and fresh from a hotel shower, Coop felt like some rich American on safari. A war tourist.

The lieutenant took the wheel with Sazan riding shotgun and Coop wedged into the back with Doc and Horvath. Starting the engine, he navigated them outside the city limits.

They drove west across the steppe, which sprawled largely empty except for distant electric transmission towers. Wormwood and spiky scrub dotted the thirsty land, which awaited renewal in the season's nourishing rains. The radio played Kurdish dance music, traditional warbling tenor sung to modern beats.

"So," said Sazan, all business. "Where do you want to go first?"

"I figure we start with Knightingale," Stuckey said. "See what they can do to help us. After that, we'll try to make contact with any American forces and work our way up the Iraqi command structure."

"That is all?" She seemed to expect more from Americans.

Stuckey shrugged. "I'm afraid it's the best we can do. We're hoping something will come up once we're on the ground. We're honestly kind of winging it."

"Winging," Sazan said in wonder.

"Making things up as we go," Doc deadpanned, his tone betraying exactly what he thought of that.

"Ah. The last I saw Knightingale, they were with 9th Armored in Intisar." A district on the southern edge of Mosul.

Stuckey said, "I didn't know the Peshmerga were operating that far south."

"My duties require me to talk to the Iraqi Army."

Sazan said the Peshmerga were primarily in the north, clearing out villages outside the city. She was a military liaison with the Iraqi Army, however, which often brought her south into their areas of operations.

"What exactly is your rank?" Coop asked.

"Sergeant," said Sazan. "I drive the liaison staff officer."

"I was just wondering if I'm supposed to salute you."

She laughed. Horvath leaned forward in his seat to say something, but Stuckey cut in.

"The first step is to get there in one piece." He patted the wheel as if for luck. "Your side controls the whole road between here and Mosul, right?"

Sazan shrugged. "The last time I drove it."

"That's not completely reassuring." Stuckey shot a look into the rearview. "If we run into a checkpoint, we'll need to get frosty, gentlemen."

"Roger that, LT," Coop said, sounding more confident than he felt. He imagined running a roadblock in this flying bullet magnet while shooting out the window with an old Russian pistol, and he did not like what he saw.

"Frosty," Sazan echoed the word, as if savoring its taste. "Cold, yes?"

"It also means be ready for anything," Doc explained. "More slang."

"Ah." Seeing this as sensible regardless, she said nothing more.

All along, Horvath sighed through his nose with impatience. Sensing a break, he jumped in. "So tell us, what do you like to do for fun, Sazan?"

She gave a little clap of delight as a favorite song came on the radio, a man belting out a stirring cry over a bouncy dance rhythm. She cranked the volume.

Coop smiled at the back of her head, which swayed side to side with the music. He remembered life as a soldier on deployment, how the little things carried him through a difficult day and how he'd snatch fun wherever he could find it.

Then he turned to Horvath and raised his eyebrows in a teasing lilt. In response, his comrade scratched a spot on his cheek with his middle finger.

Men roared a martial chant as the chorus.

"What are they saying?" Coop shouted over the music.

"'We are coming, Nineveh!' It is the name of the operation against ISIS." She smiled. "Soon, we will have Mosul surrounded and shoot them down like dogs."

"Hooah," said Horvath.

The song ended, and she turned the volume back down.

"So you like to dance and you like to kill ISIS," he added.

She turned in her seat to throw him a brief, sly look.

"Among other things," she said.

Coop and Doc grinned as Horvath flopped back gripping his chest.

As they approached the Great Zab River, the landscape steadily shifted to lusher shades of green. Through the air conditioning, Coop caught a whiff of the poultry farm they passed among the brownish hills on their left. In the distance, he spied the fencing and blue Quonset huts of a refugee camp.

Skirting the town of Kalak, the highway humped a reservoir and then carried them across the Great Zab. A flatbed truck flashed past going the other way, packed with terrified Moslawis likely headed to the camp, followed by a military ambulance carrying wounded from the front.

Reminders of the civil war that awaited the Americans at the end of the road.

They were in Iraq proper now, at least as the borders of Kurdistan Region were ratified back in '05, and it quickly morphed into the country Coop remembered. Cultivation and desert and towns and endless dust, bits of trash carried everywhere by the wind, the buildings all utilitarian and shabby as if made on the cheap and then neglected for several decades.

"I do not wish to give you sorrow," Sazan said, "but convincing the Iraqi Army to rescue your man will be difficult."

She told them that after weeks of fierce fighting, 9th Armor had barely taken Intisar at the edge of the city. Even if its generals knew where Ramos was being held, they had far bigger concerns than staging an impossible rescue.

Stuckey frowned. "What about the Peshmerga? Are they going in?"

"Iraq claims Mosul is theirs, so their blood will pay for it."

Back in Poughkeepsie, Stuckey's plan had appeared crazy, yes, but generally simple and sound. Establish a base with Ramos's organization, weasel intel from American forces about his location, and then convince the local nations to stage a rescue.

Now that they were here, it fell apart like sand.

Coop envisioned their course of action narrowing to waiting until the Iraqi Army had finally reconquered the city, which might take months beyond too late. Even if they stuck around, in the end, they'd be searching for a corpse in rubble.

Stuckey, God bless him, wouldn't give up.

"Is there any unit in the Iraqi military that knows what it's doing?" he asked.

"The Golden Division is doing most of the fighting," the woman said, referring to the Counter-Terrorism Service, an elite unit trained by American Special Forces. "If your people will not help, the CTS may go where you will find your friend."

"Okay." It was something, and he'd take it.

"Drive on, LT," Horvath encouraged.

"The war rains luck," Sazan said. "You may catch the right drop."

She stared out the window at the fleeting scenery.

"Just remember," she added, "that every bad has its worse."

Mosul appeared as a gray smudge that slowly spilled across the horizon like some desert mirage. Black smoke plumes reached into the haze. Packed with cowering refugees, another olive-green flatbed truck flashed by.

"Checkpoint up ahead," Stuckey said.

"Frosty," said Sazan, as if she'd been awaiting the chance to use the novel word.

Coop slid his Tokarev pistol from its old holster against his thigh, did a press check, and dropped his hand to rest by the door, ready to shoot if needed.

If refugees were traveling along this road, the checkpoint was almost certainly manned by friendlies. Nonetheless, he was nervous. Their visas gave them permission to visit Kurdistan Region, but this was Federal Iraq.

In short, they were here illegally, and a local with an axe to grind against America—which Coop guessed at this point might include a whole lot of Iraqi citizenry—might arrest them.

But he doubted it. They'd come to help in the Iraqi struggle against ISIS. If there was one thing Coop had learned about this country's sectarian warfare, it was the *enemy of my enemy is my friend.*

At first, this principle had played in ISIS's favor. A staple goal of insurgency was to provoke a brutal government response that turned the population against it, and Prime Minister Maliki had happily obliged in Mosul. When ISIS arrived under their black flags, the Iraqi Army fled with barely a shot fired; some said Maliki had inexplicably ordered them out just as he'd earlier abandoned Anbar Province. In any case, Moslawis celebrated in the streets at what they saw as their city's liberation while jihadists paraded in captured American Humvees and tanks.

Ruling benevolently until they'd achieved complete control, the Islamic State soon unmasked itself as a police state founded on terror and destruction. New laws outlawed smoking, alcohol, condoms, wearing perfume in public, homosexuality, the sale of underwear. Men had to grow beards; women had to cover themselves in burqas and abayas. Most of the university was shut down, all media suppressed.

Christians were told to leave the city, convert, or be executed. Shia properties were confiscated. The Yazidis were outright massacred, their women taken and trafficked as sex slaves. Every day came new religious laws, more brutal punishments.

The Hesba, or religious police, raided homes to round up alcohol, satellite dishes, and cell phones. They lashed men for smoking, stoned women to death, cut off hands and heads, burned people alive, crushed them under the tracks of tanks, pushed them off buildings. They razed churches and ancient sites. They posted almost daily executions to the internet, attracting religious radicals from all over the Middle East and even Europe, Russia, and America to join the Islamic State.

In a sense, history had repeated itself. Mosul started as a fortress some six thousand years ago, facing Nineveh—known only through the Bible until its ruins were finally discovered—across the Tigris. Sennacherib, king of the Assyrians, made Nineveh his capital and dedicated it to Ishtar, the goddess of sex and death. Everywhere they went, the Assyrians raped and massacred to satisfy her.

ISIS was the Assyrians' modern expression, a violent mass cult that had taken religion's obsession with sex and death to a whole new level. They sought to appease God with violence to fulfill the divine mission to purify the world. To ISIS, never-ending state murder was simple culling, a matter of societal hygiene.

The Pathfinder rolled to a stop at the checkpoint. Cradling automatic rifles, the squad of Iraqi soldiers crowded smiling around the vehicle. Coop had done enough guard duty in his life to sense how happy they were for something interesting to come along and break the monotony.

Their squad leader didn't look as pleased. Glowering under bushy eyebrows, he leaned into the open window. Coop appreciated this too. Regardless of what this man might be feeling, he had a job to do and would do it.

"*Salaam alaikum,*" Stuckey said.

He had the passports in his lap and a thick wad of dinar wedged under his leg just in case. Sazan barked a short exchange with the soldier, however, and the soldier stepped back and motioned them forward.

"*Shookran, Ameriki,*" the soldier said. *Thank you, American.*

Stuckey didn't ask, didn't argue. He shifted back into drive and pressured the gas pedal until they'd left the checkpoint in the dust.

"It's like the war we never had," he said in wonder.

"How's that, LT?" Coop asked.

"Iraqis doing the fighting and dying for their country against the vilest terrorists in the world, while we help them and get thanked for it."

Horvath laughed. "Thank you for your service."

Coop chuckled with him, though his anxiety continued to nag him about danger. The little helpful genie who'd fought at his side during his war had flared back to life during the tense stop and insisting on sticking around.

This genie had turned malevolent when he got home. It remade America into his own personal war zone. It warned him of ambushes in big box stores and screamed at him to be wary of high schoolers lugging suspicious backpacks.

Thanks to his Buddhist practice, Coop had starved and chained it until its voice no longer jolted him. He'd almost forgotten it was there, doing its silent duty in his constant yellow threat awareness level. Now that it was back, he wasn't so sure he wanted to return it to its lamp, given he was driving straight back into the shit.

This was the devil he knew.

Next to him, Doc appeared to be thinking and feeling along the same electric lines. The man was visibly shaking, his face slick with flop sweat. He seemed to be clamped to near suffocation by his flak jacket.

Coop placed his hand over Doc's shoulder and squeezed.

"You're okay, brother," he said.

Doc nodded but didn't speak, as if he was holding back vomit.

"Don't fight it," Coop added in a calming voice. "Use it until we get home."

During the Battle of Mosul back in '04, he'd watched in a state of incredulous amazement that was almost disdainful as Doc made one suicidal run after another through enemy fire to save lives. Coop knew Doc had the genie in him just as he had it in himself. The man only had to put it to work.

"We're here to help, Doc. Keep your mind on that."

Telling himself as well as Doc.

Doc's head jerked in a nod. "We're here to help."

Saying it aloud made it real.

At last, the man's breathing calmed even as the scenery outside the window steadily became more terrifying.

During the Battle of Mosul in '04, hundreds of insurgents had overrun, looted, and burned police stations across the city. They razed the governor's house to the ground. At one point, they controlled most of the city, hunting down Iraqi police and leaving them dead in the street. This was the insurgency that would eventually evolve toward humanity's bottom until it became ISIS.

For the first time, the jihadists fought American forces in pitched battles. Jets roared overhead, guiding missiles to targets. Coop killed two men so close he later found their blood spray on him. Even average Moslawis got in on the act, taking advantage of the lawlessness to engage in wholesale looting. By the time the Americans retook the city with the help of the CTS and Peshmerga, many buildings had been burned and riddled with ordnance, and the soldiers shot the wild dogs they found eating the headless corpses sprawling everywhere.

All that had been nothing compared to the devastation and horrors that greeted Coop and his comrades as they tentatively drove past Mosul's outlying Gogjali district. Iraqi special forces had blasted through it and left it a ruin for 9th Armored to mop up. The horizon was heaped with the shattered skeletons of buildings, charred and twisted vehicles, splayed hands thrusting from piled rubble.

Horvath reacted with typical soldier's humor.

"It looks like they redecorated since we were last here," he said. "I really love what they've done with the place."

No one laughed. The radio off, the vehicle was silent except for the men's labored breathing and the distant muffled booms of civil war.

Long before he became the Buddha, Siddhartha had served in the Sakya army as a warrior knight. Coop wondered how he'd handled it.

He wondered if Siddhartha had made the same grisly jokes to laugh at death. Wondered what he had to do to survive and whether he'd compartmentalized while doing it. Wondered if his future philosophy was an ultimate reaction to all the things he'd seen and felt that he had never found a proper place for.

Knightingale

The SUV skirted Gogjali's ruined edge toward a long column of Iraqi vehicles lumbering into Mosul proper. Through the dusty windshield, Coop spotted armored personnel carriers, Humvees, trucks, bulldozers, and massive battle tanks. Cheering children pursued the vehicles, falling out one by one as they caught khubz loaves tossed down by grinning tankers flashing victory signs.

Under an overcast sky, the column marched toward a smoking urban landscape bursting with the ominous flashes and grinding thunder of falling ordnance. The tons of steel churned the trodden dirt into a dusty haze that wafted up from the landscape like the aftermath of an airstrike. Far beyond the column, an M1A1 Abrams tank stopped and fired with a flash that raised a line of dust devils.

While this dreamlike vision of armored power growling to the front inspired awe, the swarms of refugees forming an endless river flowing in the other direction was nothing short of heartbreaking both in scope and detail.

This harlequin horde staggered in shemagh headscarves, tattered suit jackets worn over dishdasha robes, black abayas, leather jackets, even tuxedoes and formal dresses as this was one way to take their best clothes with them. They hauled what was left of their lives in anything that moved or with their hands. Entire families dragged bulging luggage, a husband heaved a wheelbarrow carrying his maimed wife who clutched photo albums, a large man carried an old granny on his back.

The military-age men had hastily shorn off their beards to avoid being detained and disappeared. Some carried white flags, though this did not stop ISIS from sporadically shelling the

Moslawis for betraying the caliphate by abandoning their duty as human shields. They hustled as one when a random mortar shell burst nearby and then stubbornly slowed again, too goddamned tired to try any harder. Or maybe by this point they were too fatalistic to make more than the expected effort, embracing the Iraqi motto of *inshallah*, as in *we'll survive the journey out of Mosul, inshallah* or *our house will still be there when get back, inshallah.*

From his Iraq days, Coop knew the word all too well: *If God wills it.*

Taking it all in, he absorbed the atmosphere of sledgehammer violence that permeated the Iraqi civil war. It all felt more like World War Two than his own, a comparatively intimate affair intricate in its precision and care. Focusing on the refugees stumbling dazed against a backdrop of smoke and ruin, he quickly revised the associations the apocalyptic scene inspired. He no longer regarded it as being like any one war but more like a modern portrayal of God's smiting of Sodom.

"Holy shit," Doc summed it all up.

They joined the column and passed a T-72 tank slumped on the side of the road awaiting a tow, one of its tracks broken by a mine and lying unspooled behind it. Soldiers emerged from a half-standing structure to gaze curiously at the Pathfinder, expecting it to stop and deposit a bigwig who would tell them what was going on.

Sazan leaned out her open window to call to them. A machine gunner shouted back, and then she rolled the window back up.

"He said to keep going and we will find them," she said.

Gritting his teeth, Stuckey said nothing. He gripped the wheel so tightly his knuckles glowed. He could barely see through the choking dust filling the air from the Soviet-era BMP infantry fighting vehicle tracking ahead. Somewhere behind, fifty tons of M1A1 heavy tank drove similarly half blind. Coop squirmed with the sensation of being a bug caught in a vast geared machine, a sudden shift in which might squash him into paste without even noticing he was there.

"I got something," Horvath called out. "Hajji triage station on our ten." He glanced at Sazan. "Iraqi triage station, I mean." Saying it the American way, *eye-racky*, but at least he was being polite to their guest.

Stuckey cut through a gas station, still taking it slow, tires mounting scattered pieces of concrete and crunching broken glass. Crossing an empty lot strewn with trash and a handful of rusting oil drums, he drove into what was recently a school playground and was now used for a triage station for the wounded of 9th Division's 36th Brigade.

The lieutenant parked the car and blinked out the window, looking like a man wondering just what the hell he did last night after his tenth drink.

Horvath reached to pat his shoulder. "Not bad driving, for an officer."

"Right." He killed the engine.

No one moved. The Pathfinder had gotten them here, and therefore it was safe. Sazan looked over at Stuckey's clenched profile. The lieutenant glared out at the Iraqi soldiers writhing on the ground like a man at war with himself.

"We made it," he added.

Duty had brought him here, and no doubt his duty to his family was screaming at him to go the hell home. This psychic scream so loud it was almost audible in Coop's ears.

Gripping his rifle, Coop got out. The weapon was his Pathfinder now; as long as he held it, he would be safe. The superstitious logic of war zones proved to be yet another old habit that came back so easily.

And boy, did this place scream *war zone*.

The warm, humid air felt electric with impending rain, smoky and acrid with an almost tangy burning chemical smell. His boots crunched shell casings and cinderblock chunks blown across the yard from the nearby school, which now flew the tricolor flag of the Republic of Iraq. A squad of soldiers in various shades of uniform stood around near its doors, their idea of maintaining a security posture somewhere between lax and not giving a shit.

The ground trembled as another steel tracked monster lumbered past. A jet roared overhead in the murk.

Coop absorbed these details in fragments, his brain hustling to fit them together as the local normal and not some postwar fever dream.

Then he looked down to discover a medium-sized white dog with a wedge-shaped head growling up at him.

"Good boy," Coop said.

The dog bared its teeth.

"Iman!" a voice called out. "*No.* They're good guys."

The dog gave Coop a final warning glare and retreated.

A paunchy, middle-aged man in dusty wire-rim glasses approached him. "Sorry, she's pretty protective of the camp. Who the hell are you guys?"

He was American, dressed in civilian clothes. Stuckey got out and walked over with his hand extended for a friendly shake. The man gestured helplessly with his own, covered in bloody latex gloves.

"Is this the Knightingale Commandos?" Stuckey asked.

Stripping off the gloves, the man gestured across the wounded soldiers groaning on blankets. The gurneys, bloody tables, boxes overflowing with iodine bottles and IV bags and miles of gauze. The exhausted Iraqi orderlies smoking on desert camo lawn chairs.

"This is 36th Brigade's triage station," he said. "But yeah, the colonel has us set up here to do what we can to help."

Coop looked around and wondered how much help they were actually doing. Their effort struck him as a Band-Aid slapped on a sucking chest wound, pluckily heroic but ultimately futile.

Still, they were doing *something*. Looking at it from the perspective that every Iraqi life mattered, they were probably doing a lot. Like him and his mission to save Ramos, at least they were trying.

The man added he was a doctor and his name was Peterson. "So who are you? You don't look like press."

Stuckey introduced himself and his team. "We're here about Dante Ramos."

"Wait." The man blinked behind his wire frames. "You know Dante?"

"We served with him."

"Jesus. Wow. Well, I don't know what to tell you guys. Daesh took him."

Daesh was basically the acronym of ISIS as it was written in Arabic and said aloud. ISIS hated it because it sounded similar to a verb meaning to stomp, trample, or crush something. Also to a noun describing a bigot.

Its enemies used it all the time, as the shoe fit. ISIS responded by threatening to cut out the tongue of anyone who did.

"We're trying to learn everything we can," Stuckey said.

"Of course. But why?"

"So we can maybe convince a unit to get him back."

Now that they were here, it sounded even more feeble in Coop's ears.

Peterson flushed red. "The colonel loves his people like family. You think if there was any chance to save Dante, he wouldn't already be doing it?" He bowed his head with a wince. "Sorry, guys, it's been a long—"

A Humvee roared onto the yard and ground to a halt in a puff of dust. Iman dashed off to circle it bounding and barking. Moments later, a rickety, bullet-scarred ambulance retrofitted with a Frankenstein layer of hillbilly armor arrived, rocking on the rough earth until coming to a stop.

Men spilled out of the vehicles and rushed three wounded men on stretchers over to the tables. The Iraqi orderlies snatched frantic final drags on their cigs and then jogged over to help. Peterson was already there, pulling on fresh gloves.

Doc lurched forward like a man who wanted to run the other way but whose inner compass had other ideas. Packed into a satchel looped around his neck, his med kit flapped at his hip as he hustled over to help. Snapping on his own gloves, he quickly sized up a patient and packed QuikClot gauze into an entry wound while Peterson wrapped a screaming burn victim in paraffin gauze.

The Humvee door opened with a protesting creak, and a man got out wearing rugged paramilitary clothes strapped with a chest rig, body armor, and secondary weapons. Its frayed brim worn low over the eyes, his baseball cap bore the Knightingale seal of a red cross inside a circle of stars. In contrast with his camo browns and grays, a bright American flag bandana was tied around his throat.

Holding a Kalashnikov loosely at his side in one hand, he stooped to scratch Iman around the ears. Then he straightened to slap his heart in an Arab welcome.

"Volunteers?" he said, flashing bright teeth.

This was Lt. Colonel Reynolds, who'd founded Knightingale after four Sandbox tours. He'd once tried to help Iraq as a Marine Corps officer, now he was doing it his way as a praise-the-Lord-and-pass-the-ammunition-style Christian.

Coop had expected him to be a physical giant like the former Special Forces, Rangers, and Navy SEALs he'd collected for his group and who now stomped around the triage station. Reynolds, however, was medium height and wiry, seemingly made of rope, gristle, and leather, his eyes hard and penetrating as bullets, his smile disarming. While hardly imposing in stature, he had the kind of presence that swept everyone and everything into its orbit.

"It's a pleasure to meet you, sir," Stuckey said. "We're here about Ramos."

"We are praying every day for his release. How do you know Dante?"

The men walked off a ways to talk. Coop looked at Horvath, who smiled back through a cloud of cigarette smoke.

"I feel like I'm in *Saving Private Ryan*," his friend said.

"Things seem pretty calm right now."

"Methinks the jihadis are praying."

He was right. It was around the time for midday salat. Out in the city, the mullahs called the faithful to prayer from the minarets of the mosques. Muslims prayed five times a day, and ISIS was observant even if it was diabolical.

Coop eyed the former Special Forces and SEALs guys cleaning out the ambulance and inventorying their supplies. At one time, he'd have earned major bragging rights being anywhere within five miles of their units doing an op.

"It's a weird outfit," he said. "You have to admire it, though."

"'Are my methods unsound?'" Horvath said, setting aside *Saving Private Ryan* to quote *Apocalypse Now*. He turned his head and answered himself in full Martin Sheen: "'I don't see any method at all. Sir.'"

With that, he deviously twirled the pointy tip of the mustache he didn't have and sauntered over to the Pathfinder to offer Sazan one of his Marlboros.

Coop found himself alone again with the dog, who gave him the stink-eye.

"Hi, girl," he said. "Iman, right?"

The dog showed him its teeth again and snarled.

So much for that. Backing off, he walked over to where Stuckey and the colonel conferred over a map laid out on a stack of ration boxes.

"The sniper pinned the entire platoon we were joined with down on this street, between the mobile phone repair shop here and the mosque." Reynolds glanced up to acknowledge Coop with a nod. "I was just telling Hud here a rule of Mosul: Stay low. Daesh snipers are damn good."

"Good to know," Coop said.

"That day was a serious cluster. Anyway, the sons of bitches grabbed Dante in one of the buildings on that street. Apparently, they forced a little girl to call out for help, and when he ran in, they nabbed him. Right now, he could be pretty much anywhere. I seriously doubt he's even alive."

"He is." Stuckey took out his phone and showed the video to Reynolds, whose face darkened. "We haven't seen anything since this was posted."

"If you find him, you be sure to let me and my boys know."

"Will do, Colonel. I was wondering if you wanted to team up."

"You mean work together to drum up intel on his posit?"

Posit, military shorthand slang for *position*.

"That's right," said Stuckey. "Anything, really—"

"No can do," Reynolds cut him off. "Our mission is to help civilians. Every hour we're not on mission, innocent people die."

"Colonel, they have one of *your* people."

"Understood, son. Trust that I do. But Dante knows the score and accepted it when he signed up with us. If I was the one got captured, I'd expect all my people to do the same."

"Damn," Coop said. This was cold.

"Look, if God sees fit to show you the door, me and the boys will come to personally kick it down and go to guns to get him back. You can count on it. Until then, our Christian mission puts the people of Iraq first."

Sagging, Stuckey started to fold up the map. "Roger that."

"Wait, one." The colonel ran his hand over Mosul's neighborhoods and tapped it. "If you want to get straight in it, CTS is north of us. They're pushing harder than anybody else, and their commanders have real fire in their balls."

The lieutenant squinted at the map. "Aden?" A little neighborhood on the east side of Mosul.

"Yep. They're all around that area." Reynolds grinned. "If in doubt, follow the sound of the guns." The grin just as quickly faded. "If you do somehow find Dante on your own, tell him that the commander-in-chief needs him back on line and the Iraqis miss him."

"C-in-C?" Stuckey said.

"They miss Sergeant Ramos?" asked Coop, equally puzzled.

"I'm talking about the Lord, son," the colonel answered Stuckey and then took aim at Coop. "Dante sings to the Iraqis. The man can sing the heck out of an Al Green tune. Now give me your hands so we can pray for his safety and your success."

Stuckey's eyes narrowed to impatient slits, but Coop shrugged and reached to accept the man's warm, leathery grip. What could it hurt? The lieutenant grudgingly did the same.

"Dear Lord," Reynolds prayed, "we—get down. *INCOMING!*"

The earth shook with a deafening roar.

Salat was over. The jihadists were back in the fight.

Reeling in the blast of heat and light, Coop curled into an armadillo ball. Shouts and an agonized scream rang from the billowing dust cloud.

"What the hell are you doing?" Stuckey said.

Coop peeled his eyes back open to see the colonel stomping across the ground while another mortar shell blew a geyser of dirt into the air around him.

The man turned. "The Lord is watching over me!"

"You're going to get yourself killed!"

Reynolds laughed. *"Inshallah!"*

Then he walked off to help the screaming man, raising his hand to signal to Iman that she should stay in the little cement pipe where she'd taken shelter.

"He's a goddamn nut," Stuckey growled.

Coop was shaking. "I don't know, I think he might be onto something."

A shrill kettle whistle, followed by another gut-clenching boom so loud it blanked out his mind. The earth bucked again. Clods of dirt rained around him.

Staying as flat as possible, his head jerked to locate his comrades. Stuckey lay nearby, unhurt but pissed off. Horvath and Sazan spooned on the ground near the Pathfinder. Kneeling next to the screaming Iraqi orderly who'd been hit, Doc flinched as Reynolds laid his hand on his head to pray for him, and then he returned to applying a seal over a sucking chest wound.

Striding off into the flashes and steel rain, the colonel raised a defiant fist to the west and roared an Old Testament verse, "'And if you fail to learn the lesson and continue your hostility toward me, then I myself will be hostile toward you! I will personally strike you with calamity seven times over for your sins!'"

As if summoned by Reynolds, the wrath of God manifested in the clouded sky. An eerie crashing sound filled the air like a vast ghost train rushing overhead. The sound alone punched Coop in the chest and left it tingling with primitive awe.

The booms followed moments later, equally beautiful and terrifying. Artillery shells falling on Mosul and turning a stretch of it into blazing rubble.

"Shot out," Stuckey gasped. "Those are ours. Paladins."

Massive self-propelled howitzers delivering salvos of 155-millimeter shells from a nearby firebase, dropping anvils on flies. Not God but a U.S. Marine Corps artillery battery, which, when it came to wholesale destruction, was close to the same thing.

The mortars stopped falling, which felt like a divine miracle in itself. Coop slowly uncoiled to sit up as the outgoing fire mission's final salvo rippled and flared along the horizon, the flashes barely visible through a heavy veil of dust.

He looked at Reynolds with emotion caught between incredulousness and envy, wishing he had the kind of fierce faith that would make war's murderous randomness fall into place and armor him against both terror and shrapnel.

A rock-solid faith there was a God and that he was watching, he was angry, and he was on Coop's side.

Oasis

Coop swam.

In swift, deft breaststrokes, he reached the far side of the hotel's swimming pool, kicked off, and lapped back.

Over and over, the physical effort its own form of meditation.

They'd returned to Erbil in a silent stupor, suffering a collective combat hangover shared by all except Horvath, who joked around until he read the room and zipped it. Back in the hotel's luxuriant safety, the group parted ways with an agreement to rally up at 1700 for dinner.

Acting on some deep officer intuition, Stuckey had invited Sazan to join them, which proved to be a good call. They perked up to avoid bumming her out. The Peshmerga woman, meanwhile, had been around soldiers long enough to read them, and she set herself on some basic mothering.

At dinner, she did the ordering. The servers brought sharing plates loaded with olives, meat dishes, vegetables, and yogurt along with plenty of beer. Then the raki arrived, a clear brandy with an anise ouzo taste that turned a milky white when mixed with water and ice, giving it the nickname "lion's milk."

By the end, they were laughing again, back on point.

After he'd digested it all, Coop went out to the pool for a nighttime swim.

They'd shown up in Mosul and received an education. This wasn't the old wack-a-mole with insurgents but an all-out war involving tanks and planes and infantry. More a replay of 1942's Battle of Stalingrad than 2004's Battle of Mosul, which had been bad enough. They'd learned just how daunting it would be to figure out where Ramos was being held and then motivate a force to act.

In short, it had been a sad day with no real breakthroughs.

On the other hand, the game wasn't over. They still had cards to play. Tomorrow, they'd make contact with the Golden Division, Stuckey said. Reynolds had told him about a little base they ran where they might find out something useful. No light yet, the lieutenant added, but at least they were in the tunnel.

American grit on fully display. That or the usual sunk cost fallacy; they'd come this far, so they might as well keep going as long as there was a way forward.

Another lap across the pool and then another.

Reaching a point where his body was smoked and his mind a gentle blank, Coop hauled himself out of the heated water. Steaming in the brisk night air, he waited until his breathing found its own sweet spot and then reached for a towel.

Sitting in beach chairs with drinks in their hands, Horvath and Doc regarded him with baleful stares. Sazan lounged at the far side of the pool, seemingly contemplating the sky. Stuckey wasn't around, having disappeared after dinner to call his wife.

Horvath plucked the earbuds from his phone, on which he'd been listening to some playlist of favorite tunes.

"A great thing about being out is you don't have to do PT anymore," he said.

Coop finished rubbing his short hair dry and pulled on a bathrobe. "You'd be surprised how quickly you go soft without it."

"Yup." The sergeant slurped his drink. "I earned it."

"You never told me why you re-upped. The promise you made."

"Nope. I didn't."

"I think you did it for the PT. Usually, I meditate right about now. I'd invite you to do it with me, but I'll bet you've already got Olivia's greatest hits on deck." Olivia Newton John being Horvath's path to serenity.

"You know me too well." The man frowned a little. "Seriously, it's unnerving." He shifted his gaze to Sazan and sighed. "Thirteen years…"

Huddled in a blanket, Doc tilted his head. "Thirteen years, what?"

"Following orders. Now what? I go to college and argue with kids too young to learn anything real? Get a job and take orders again from even bigger shitheads?"

Doc shrugged. "That's life after the Army. It's not all bad."

"Coop here has the right idea. Live free with nothing tying you down. He calls his own shots. Army of One."

Coop thought again of Stuckey's life of commitments with its righteous purpose and solid borders. "It's not as terrific as it sounds."

"Maybe I'll sell out and sign up with the mercs," Horvath said. "Keep on doing what I do best. Make the mad money and then coast on it until I figure it all out."

The security contractors had been ubiquitous in Iraq, working lucrative contracts in a highly privatized war. The Gamblers hated them for their *Soldier of Fortune* gear and Special Forces beards and the fact they earned comparatively enormous salaries to basically kill anyone they wanted and make the Army's job that much harder.

Coop followed Horvath's stare until his sightline reached Sazan, who gazed up at the moon. "You could always settle down with a great woman."

"Hell, yeah. I should marry a girl like Sazan and live here. This place is the Wild West. There's barely a government. Can you picture it? Me, carving out a goat farm on some rocky hill, raising a crop of kids? Then every once in a while, me and the wife will clean our AKs and go to war to punish the deserving."

"Oddly enough, I can picture it," Coop said.

He'd noticed that Horvath had lightened up a great deal since they'd arrived in Erbil. The niceties and complexities of civilian life appeared to thwart him. For him, flying back to Iraq to survive a mortar barrage was pure adventure.

"She's right over there," Doc teased.

Horvath sagged. "I should go to my room and clean my rifle."

"Dear God, I sincerely hope that's not a euphemism."

"What the problem?" Coop asked. "Straight talk."

"I don't know how to talk to women," Horvath growled. "I'm not good at it anymore. There. Happy? It's been years since I've had a real conversation with a lady who either wasn't wearing a hijab or asking if I wanted a lap dance."

Coop exchanged a glance with Doc and with it the telepathic thought: *Jesus, he's actually smitten.*

He said, "I'm not sure you were ever good at it, Joe. Anyway, one thing I've learned, all the sweet talk is overrated. You should take a page from Sergeant Ramos and go over there and sing her a song."

"A little Al Green, and she'll melt like butter," Doc confirmed, though his eyes bore the playful glint of a kid mixing chemicals in a chemistry set just to see what happened.

Horvath's own eyes flashed under his heavy brows. "You know what, for once in your lives, I think you guys are talking sense."

Before Coop and Doc could save him from himself, the sergeant heaved himself to his feet and stomped to the far side of the pool, where he pulled over a chair and parked next to the Peshmerga fighter.

"Holy crap, he's actually doing it," Doc said.

They watched him with sharp if reluctant anticipation, as if they were being forced to witness either a horrific vehicle accident or the climax of a rom-com.

Sazan nodded, and Horvath handed her one of his earbuds while he kept the other. He pressed play on his music app, and moments later they were both bobbing their heads to Olivia Newton John.

Coop wheeled to blink at Doc, who was grinning.

"Thatta boy," said Doc. "There's hope for him yet. To be likeable, I mean."

"What is it about the Army? It makes you grow up in about a week, but then in a lot of ways you don't really mature until you get out."

Doc chuckled. "Even then, it can take a long time. Some of us don't pull it off until we meet the right lady."

"Speaking of ladies, don't you want to call Marjorie?"

"Seven-hour time difference. I'll call her later tonight when she's off work. When are you gonna get somebody you can call?"

Coop thought about all the relationships he'd had. Too many to recall all at once, which a guy like Horvath would likely find enviable. The confident detachment that made him interesting to some women also kept him from sticking around. When it came to romance, he was a jack of all trades but master of none.

"When I finally grow up, I guess," he said.

Doc took a pull from his raki glass. "That's what you'd call a Catch-22."

Coop sighed and considered turning in. He was worn out and cold and getting colder by the minute. A long day awaited him tomorrow.

Hope took a lot out of you, as much as worry did.

Perched on the edge of his chair, he didn't move. This moment, this pool, felt like an oasis in both time and place, its own meditation. Once he moved, reality would return and tomorrow would come.

"You know, you were a real superhero today," Coop said. "I just sort of stood there trying not to get bit by the dog until we got mortared."

Doc squirmed. "I did what I had to do."

It summed up their whole mission. Coop's return to desire wasn't without rewards. The truth was they were no superheroes. They were just ordinary guys. But what they were doing felt superheroic.

After a long pause, he said, "You know even better than me that getting Ramos back is pretty much going to be impossible. Why did you say yes to it?"

"Are we doing straight talk?"

Coop nodded.

"I thought maybe I could do it right this time," said Doc. "Fly over here, do something good, go home, and everything would finally feel complete. I don't know. It sounded better in my head when I decided. What about you?"

Coop shrugged. "I figured if I'd signed up to fight over a year here for my country, I could put in some effort a week or two for my squad leader."

"That's—"

"I owed the sergeant something," he said, correcting his lie. "A piece of me. And paying him back was bigger than my bullshit. That's it."

There was the reason he told himself, and then the real reason.

Paying his debt. Bringing his karma back into balance. He owed Ramos a piece of himself, and by giving it, he'd get a missing piece of himself back.

"I remember what he did," Doc said quietly. "I guess a part of me thinks he deserves this. Men caring enough to try. If there was one thing Ramos taught me, it was how to love humanity. You do it with real courage, even if it's just trying."

"Okay," said Coop.

"Okay?"

"If you're going to stick your neck out for an idea, it's a damned good one."

"Right." Doc shivered again. "I hated it today. Civil war. We were only in it for a few hours, and my nerves are already shot."

"It's bad." Actually, *bad* didn't come close to covering what it was like to cower through the mortar barrage, but it was the best he could produce.

"So much for staying behind the lines where it's safe." He sighed. "This is a freaking horror show. I hate being here at all. It pisses me off. We did this, Coop. I don't mean you and me but America. We broke Humpty Dumpty real good."

Since the invasion, at least two hundred thousand Iraqis died in the violence, even more were wounded, and nine million ended up refugees in their own country or abroad. The brutality of Saddam lived on in Maliki, whose authoritarian regime made a mockery of the freedom America had tried to export. The war only seemed to create more terrorists that had to be fought *over there* so they didn't have to be fought *over here*. Al-Qaeda took root, flourished, and eventually morphed into the grotesque Islamic State. In Ramadi in '06, the group started using chemical weapons in the form of chlorine bombs and was now using them in Mosul.

In short, the war directly led to the creation of the very problems on which it had been justified, the biggest paradox of all. Meanwhile, America had paid for an act of sheer hubris with its treasure and blood. Trillions of dollars that could have been more productively spent on almost anything else. More than four thousand dead soldiers, more than thirty thousand wounded. Another paradox: America won every battle, and the more it did, the less it achieved its overall mission.

A cluster, to borrow a term from Colonel Reynolds's colorful repertoire.

Coop shifted in his chair. He didn't need all that on his karma, a debt he'd never pay back. He'd taken part in the occupation, but he wasn't responsible for its outcome, and he'd never done anything for which he had any heavy moral regret.

"We did our duty," he said. "It wasn't up to us. We followed legal orders and acted with a hell of a lot of restraint. And it wasn't all bad. We did a lot of good. The rest was on the Iraqis, who shot at each other and at us for trying to help and then screwed up their country far worse than we ever could."

"Like I said, I didn't mean you and me. We were used. Anyway, what I'm trying to say is I'm doing my duty now. My duty as a human being. I want to do something good this time and make things right. Now is the time and place."

With that, he tossed back the remains of his drink, returned his glass to the little table next to his chair, and stood with his blanket still wrapped around his shoulders.

"Speaking of which," Doc added, "I have medical supplies I should get sorted for tomorrow. It was good talking to you. Good night, brother."

Coop nodded vacantly while the man departed, his good vibe replaced by an unsettling sensation of karmic ripples. Iraq was bleeding, but didn't he bleed as well for it? During the Battle of Mosul, only a few inches had separated him from eternity. He'd watched good men get shot and explode and get burned alive.

What did he owe Iraq?

And just as valid, what did Iraq owe him?

In the end, he'd happily call it even, but it still nagged at him a little. As always, it was hard to wrap his head around, as Iraq was and remained far more Pandora's Box than Gordian Knot.

On the outside, it looked like any other Third World basket case that with all its oil should have been rich but had squandered it on war and internal strife. Then you took a hard look at its artificial borders imposed by colonial powers, its virtually landlocked geography at the mercy of its neighbors, and its sectarian and ethnic fault lines dividing haves and have-nots. And you realized how truly screwed it all was, which made the American mission here seem even more steeped in hubris and fanciful thinking.

Standing in the chilly night, Coop looked over at Horvath and Sazan on separate chairs under a common blanket, heads touching as they shared a love song under a waning moon.

They've got the right idea, he thought.

Then he went to his room to await tomorrow, which always came.

QRF

November 2004.

    Seven months after the first battle of Fallujah—

    Three after the battle of Najaf—

    Two after the battle of Samarra—

    Thirteen into Coop's deployment, which had been extended along with his active duty service due to the overstretched Army's "stop loss" policy, which the boys called the *backdoor draft*—

    The Strykers rolled up MSR Tampa at full throttle.

    Mosul had become a full-on war zone.

    Rifle between his knees, Coop sat in the Stryker's rider compartment. Directly across from him, Ramos inspected his combat knife's edge.

    The 350 HP engine whirred around them. The axles hummed across a pot hole. Sandbags covered the floor as up-armor against IEDs. The *Maxim* pinup girls plastered along the ceiling appeared to shimmy in the vehicle's vibrations. Exploding ordnance boomed outside.

    Ramos caught him looking at the knife. "Semper Paratus."

    Then he winked and sheathed it.

    Coop gulped but nodded. *Always prepared.* Ramos had prepared him well for this. In his squad, every man had to know how to do everything with proficiency. After endless drilling, each man could shoot, man the radios, run the weapons, give life-saving first aid. For this ride, they'd brought as much ammo as they could carry.

    He was as prepared as he was ever going to be.

    A little video screen behind the commander's hatch showed the tactical situation on a graphical map of Mosul. Little blue dot icons marked friendly forces, including 3rd Platoon getting shot up at Yarmouk Traffic Circle.

Red triangles tagged enemy positions.

Another popped onto the screen accompanied by an automated voice: *"Warning! Enemy in area."* Then another. *"Warning! Enemy in area."*

Judging by the force tracker, 3rd Platoon was virtually surrounded.

In the past seven months, the insurgency had leveled up, engaging American and Iraqi Army troops in several cities and trying to capture territory. Wack-a-mole with ordnance. This morning, the violence had finally come to Mosul.

Heavy booms had sounded in the city, producing distant plumes of smoke that reached into the haze. Hundreds of insurgents were out there taking on Iraqi security forces for real, a replay of the April violence that shook the city but this time on a far bigger scale. Units across FOB Marez were alerted. Some kind of Tet Offensive was happening, and Coop's entire battalion was Oscar Mike.

One by one, they'd marshaled out of the motor pool and rolled past Marez's razor-topped Hescos to support the Iraqi security forces and secure vital infrastructure, including the bridges of the Tigris that split the city in two.

But not Coop, who chafed at the order the Gamblers were staying behind on quick reaction force status, ready to move in a hot minute. After more than a year in Iraq, his crucible had finally arrived, and he appeared destined to sit it out.

Then the frantic calls had come into the TOC. Mayday, mayday. Troops in contact at Yarmouk Traffic Circle. Then: two Whiskeys and multiple possible Kilos, Army phonetic for wounded and killed in action.

A Nine-Line request for emergency casevac. Multiple requests for close air support. The platoon sergeant was calling the shots, not a good sign.

It was real war out there. All-out contact. This was *Blackhawk Down* shit.

And the QRF was ordered into swift action.

Mount up, mount up. Shouting soldiers hustling everywhere in the motor pool, Strykers growling exhaust in the hot air, an atmosphere of martial drama lending a heavy significance to every action. Rolling out past the wire, Coop had been surprised to hear the enraged bangs of ordnance, alarmingly close.

"Holy shit," said the truck commander. "They're attacking Marez."

Again, Coop had that heady zeitgeist feeling, the same as he'd felt the morning of the World Trade Center attacks. A sense of history at the crossroads.

His hands sweated in their gloves. His gloves kept a tight a grip on his rifle. His mind raced as it pictured the traffic circle and what awaited him.

In his mounting stress, he no longer trusted his thoughts. He'd have to rely on his training. He'd trained like he'd fight, and now he'd fight like he'd trained.

Coop gaped at the force tracker screen. The platoon was getting close.

"Two minutes out," the truck commander said.

Careful what you wish for, troop. He'd wanted real action, and he was going to get it. *You're in for it now, boy!*

He shouldn't even be here. Stop loss. The backdoor draft. He should be home pounding beers and working on getting a girlfriend, a woman who was warm and impossibly soft and who wouldn't try to hurt him if he was ever weak.

Another bang outside. The Stryker didn't break stride. The boys grimaced under Kevlar brims. Only Ramos appeared calm, as if this were a mundane op, just another day at the office.

"The mission: engage to kill and get 3rd Herd out of the shit and back on objective," the sergeant said, repeating what they already knew.

He paused to allow his steady tone to seep into their pre-combat nerves as ballast. No hooah speech from the sarge. If he'd done that, they would have mentally updated their wills. Instead, he displayed the usual cool leadership, reminding them that he'd see them through this.

"The ROE: cleared hot," he added. "You see a weapon, you shoot."

Kevlar bobbed as the boys nodded. The Stryker rode toward the thunder.

"You're the best fucking infantry on the planet. Let's get it done."

"Hooah, Sergeant," Coop said with the others.

Shouting it like a war cry, meaning it this time.

Best fucking infantry on the planet. President Bush could have flown over to give them a rousing pep talk about democracy, the War on Terror, and mom and apple pie all rolled into one, and it wouldn't come even close to the motivating power of Ramos's simple pronouncement.

The muted thunder outside grew louder. *Holy shit*, pale faces mouthed before returning to a look of stony professionalism. Someone was getting lit up out there, possibly everyone.

One of the mounted FM radios was set to 3rd Platoon's frequency. Punctuated by pops of radio static, a cacophony of strident voices competed for attention.

The breakdown in radio discipline got into Coop's head even more than the noise. *This is bad.* Then an authoritative voice came on and growled at everyone to *clear the fucking net.*

The Stryker veered to the left. Something thumped against its armored hide, reminding Coop of Iraqi kids throwing rocks only a million times harder. More impacts thumped and whammed, as if a group of enraged people outside were going to town on the Stryker with sledgehammers.

The truck commander flinched low in his turret. The vehicle steered even harder to the left as an explosion crashed outside and shrapnel splashed the Stryker. RPG! A moment later, Coop's head cracked against the bulkhead as the vehicle scraped and plowed against something solid, tearing crashing chunks as it straightened out.

"Jesus Christ," Horvath swore. They weren't even in the fight yet.

"We're having fun now!" said Murray, hugging the Suck for all he was worth.

Cursing, the truck commander stood tall again behind the fifty-cal and started shooting. The machine gun was a beast, hurling six-inch slugs at three thousand feet per second that punched through concrete and tore humans in half. In the distance, a Mark 19 grenade launcher joined the fifty's drumbeat with its distinctive *whump*, answered by the cascading crashes of impacts.

The Stryker commanders were getting some.

Horvath: "Can we *please* get the hell out of this vehicle?"

Coop seconded that thought. The insurgents were shooting RPGs out there, and he was sitting in a giant rocket magnet.

If I'm going to get hit today, give me a chance to do something first, he prayed.

Outside the vehicle might not be much safer than in here, but he could at least face his fears head on rather than sitting here inflating them with his imagination.

Ramos had grabbed the handset for another mounted radio, which was set to his own platoon's freq. Exchanging words with the platoon leader, he rogered and hung up as the ramp dropped to blinding sunshine.

Then he addressed his squad.

"Dismount and form a perimeter. Our Victor is up against a wall here. Another Victor is moving on our right. We'll use it for cover and lay suppressing fire to buy some breathing room and unwind this clusterfuck."

"Hooah," the squad shouted at it exited.

Coop charged down the ramp into oven heat tinged with tangy gun smoke. Rounds snapped past his head as he dashed to the shadow of the nearby Stryker. From the buildings all around the highway, muzzle flashes burst in windows with the distinctive *crack* of Kalashnikovs and the menacing rattle of a Russian-made belt-fed PKM machine gun.

Out of the frying pan, he thought.

A section of façade dissolved in boiling concrete clouds under the withering blast of the fifty-cal hosing an apartment building directly across the highway in a Z-shaped pattern. The clouds drifted to be sucked into the thick black smoke billowing out of a burning Stryker down the road close to the traffic circle. The top half of a palm tree ejected in a burst of splinters to tumble to the ground.

Horvath stood to let off a few rounds. "It's a goddamn kill zone!"

Gulping terror, Coop looked around to puzzle the tactical situation. In the distance, a Stryker slumped, disabled by an IED. One of 3rd Platoon's. Near it, another burned energetically, its ammo cooking and popping off in flashes and streaming sparks. Pieces of it sizzled on the road.

Accurate rocket fire had taken it out.

The surviving 3rd Platoon vehicles straddled the highway, their big guns rocking, the dismounted troops stuck between them fully engaged and giving everything they had in a savage, balls-out contest for fire superiority. On both sides of the roadway, it was literally raining building as glass and brick and dust fell in a continuous tumble onto MSR Tampa.

All by the book. React to ambush, return fire, get behind cover, call out enemy positions, use the Strykers in support, maneuver, call for close air support.

Coop's old fears about the traffic circle being ripe for a complex ambush, it seemed, had come true on steroids. Judging by the volume of fire, at least a hundred insurgents were here, and they weren't shooting and scooting this time.

His own platoon deployed in support. Some of the squads were already blasting two buildings across the way from which they received fire.

Murray paused in his aiming. "What the hell is *he* doing?"

It was Doc, doing the hundred-meter dash down the highway and going for the record, bullet impacts dusting the ground in his wake.

"Covering fire," Ramos called out. "Make it hot!"

Coop fingered his selector from safe to kill and stood to peer through his rifle's optic with its little red dot. He swept the buildings and spotted a muzzle flash coming from a parking garage. He shifted aim to zero on where it had come from and squeezed the trigger to produce an angry metallic report.

In his peripheral vision, he saw Doc run the final gauntlet stretch to reach the burning Stryker. The medic opened the back hatch and jumped back as flaming bodies spilled out and tumbled onto the ground in a burst of black smoke.

Command vehicle, Coop thought. *Their platoon leader is dead.*

Holy shit, holy shit.

Then Doc granulated and dissolved as Coop's brain amped to tunnel hyperfocus on what was directly in front of him. The Stryker he used for cover growled into reverse, turret swinging as the mounted M240 machine gun searched for a new target, found one, and returned to hammering.

Christ, all the big guns are going full cyclic.

He paced the vehicle's slow progress along with his fireteam, though every step took him farther from his own and its promise of quick egress. A smoke grenade popped in front of the Stryker, spewing a cottony white screen. A Kiowa helo roared overhead, pounding down the road and stirring the cloud. A Stryker let off a TOW missile into the parking garage, a beautiful sight in training but truly awe-inspiring as the real thing. Someone's car flew out into the street in the ground-shaking blast. Murray paused to stress-vomit onto the road and then resumed shooting as Ramos called out an enemy position at their two o'clock.

With all the shouting, smoke, gunfire, and snarling vehicles, this was pure chaos, but all the Strykers' jockeying appeared to have a purpose. The lieutenant was trying to organize the platoon for best effect, which would later give Coop a new respect for officers, who had to think at chess level while a ton of shit was flying straight into the fan.

As for his own brain, it had already gone into autopilot, working past the paralyzing terror running an express train between his brain and balls.

Frying pan, he thought again. Coop couldn't get that phrase out of his head. It kept looping like some kind of self-protection spell.

The insurgents still couldn't shoot for shit, but there was a whole lot of them out there spraying and praying, and they seemed to be in it to win this time.

Reyes whooped as the machine gun position he'd been hosing finally fell silent. "You want some fries with that, you hajji fuck?"

The SAW gunner had reached the sweet spot of controlled battle madness. His exclamation pushed Coop over the edge into an endorphin-rich state of joyous rage himself. He couldn't get hit. Okay, he'd definitely get hit, so why worry. Either way, he was in this to the hilt now. He felt fully alive as the stock hummed against his shoulder and his M4 clacked and spat brass and he pounded hot metal into distant windows in the hopes of killing a motherfucker trying to kill him.

Otherwise, he was out of his mind with terror, acting on his training.

"Frying fuck pan!"

Horvath chuckled at his outburst. "We're finally earning our combat infantry badges today, huh, dog?"

Wearing his war face, Coop ignored him, focusing on the battle.

Shoot until his M4 went black.

Drop the mag, jack in a full mag, release the bolt, and shoot again.

Pause to drink some water.

Compartmentalize all these emotions.

The fight falling off and ramping up, ebbing and flowing.

Check the time. *Holy shit.*

The firefight had been raging for over two hours.

Helos crossed overhead, shadows flickering across the street, guns rattling.

Murray ducked. "RPG!"

Coop hesitated long enough to see the rocket stream down before falling into a crouch as it splashed into the asphalt near the lieutenant's Stryker. Gripping the side of his neck, the truck commander wore an odd look of disappointment as he quit the fight and dropped below the hatch.

Raging into a handset attached to his radioman, the LT jabbed a finger at the empty turret. A man from his vehicle's rifle squad scrambled up to take over the turret gun. An AT4 rocket hissed up into the building the RPG had fired from.

Then Doc appeared out of nowhere, running through fire again up the ramp to treat the wounded man in the platoon's commander's vehicle.

"How is Doc still alive?" Reyes marveled.

"Run, Forrest," Horvath called out.

The insurgents had received reinforcements or a strong second wind, and the fight ramped back up again. The bright daylight seemed to modulate from all the tracer rounds. Rounds pinged along the road and cracked against the Stryker's armor that protected Coop from death. A rocket exploded against it with a flash, but the armor held and the truck commander barely paused his shooting. Another banged off the hardtop, and then yet another whooshed overhead into a window, which belched pieces of furniture out around Coop in a dimming cloud, ending in a fluttering, smoldering thing that turned out to be someone's rug.

For the first time, it truly hit him that peopled lived here. They were almost literally fighting in someone's house.

He pushed the thought aside, as it didn't help him survive and changed nothing. *Compartmentalize.*

"Hajji Victor in the road on our nine! White van in the road!"

The call relayed up the line about the possible VBIED. The rear Stryker's fifty was rocking, joined by the rifle squad using it as cover. As the car bomb promised Armageddon, Coop paused in his shooting to watch it come. Horvath, who'd been sitting on the ground taking a smoke break, jumped to his feet and joined him.

The tracers streamed south now, back down the roadway, converging on the windshield of a white van sparking in the sunlight. The glass cratered and disappeared, the grille gaping with sucking chest wounds until the engine bled streams of smoke. Reyes hoisted his SAW, but Ramos swatted the muzzle down to keep him from shooting past friendlies.

Still, the horrible van kept coming. At the rear Stryker, a rifleman skittered away from his squad to aim an AT4 rocket launcher.

"Fire in the hole, fire in the hole!"

Back blast pluming behind it, the shoulder-fired tube whooshed. All the expensive training paid off. A beautiful shot. The missile streamed into the grille, vaporizing the front of the van in a movie fireball that stopped it in its tracks.

While his squad cheered, the rifleman grabbed his nuts and jigged, flipping the van the bird. "Who's your daddy now? *Who's your daddy?*"

With a cathartic shudder, Coop returned to the firing line. Ramos had long gained a feel for the fight and continued to direct his shooters for maximum effect instead of just lighting up buildings. He now had Reyes adjust his fire with a mild scolding about fire discipline, as he was burning ammo.

Firing off a few more rounds at a silhouette flashing along the distant rooftop, Coop checked his own loadout. Empty mags and brass lay around his boots. He'd spent a lot of rounds in the on again, off again battle and would have to start conserving himself, as even now the insurgents had fight in them.

Three hours had passed. Four by the time the Iraqi National Guard showed up. They arrived in a column of pickup trucks bristling with rifles.

Ramos whistled for his squad's attention. They gathered around. Their leader's face was caked with dust streaked with fresh rivulets of sweat. His hard eyes inspected his boys, and judging from their proud glint, they liked what they saw.

"New plan," he said. "LT says these ING guys are going to clear the buildings, and then we can break contact with these lunatics."

Coop and the others nodded. He'd yearned for the crucible of battle. He'd fantasized about being tested under fire. He'd lusted for a real fight where the enemy finally stood his ground and went at him punch for punch.

Mission accomplished, and now all he wanted was to get the hell out of here.

"Weapons Squad will continue fire support while 3rd Herd sets to RTB," Ramos told them.

RTB, return to base. That sounded great.

"What about us?" asked Franks, Bravo's team leader.

"LT thinks the ING guys won't do their jobs unless they have Americans going in with them. I think he's right."

The boys groaned. His uniform saturated with sweat and dust, Coop gazed up the pockmarked length of the smoking building looming four stories, currently infested with jihadists.

"Get ready to gamble." Ramos gestured to the building. "Our squad has this beauty. All we got to do is clear the stairwell, and the ING will take it from there for the room clearing. Everybody got that?"

"Hooah," Coop said, as there was no other response to give, though his squad mates chimed in with others.

"Lima Charlie," said Franks. *Loud and clear.*

"Solid copy," said Murray, his face blackened by gunpowder.

"We're with you," Thompson said in pure PFC mode.

"Sounds just fucking great, Sarnt," said Horvath, pure deadpanned sarcasm.

"Then let's get it done," Ramos told them.

It took a while for the ING company to get itself organized. By the time they were ready, they'd already taken casualties. Ramos whistled again at his squad and flashed hand signals.

Go.

"Bounding!" Murray called out.

Alpha team rushed across to the building's door and stacked. In the distance, another squad bounded to lead the ING into another building. The platoon had shifted to offense. It was time to end this fight.

"Set!"

Bravo followed. Franks blew the door lock with a shotgun. Ramos kicked it open, and they poured in rifles first to clear the small vestibule.

The stairs led up into the gloom.

Coop withdrew a SureFire flashlight from his kit, attached it to his M4, and turned it on. Ramos ordered them forward with more hand signals, but his worn-out squad got confused, and the two fireteams went up in a mix. Coop found himself behind Sergeant Franks in the lead, Thompson behind him.

Around and around they went, up and up, as the battle muted to a gentle roar punctuated now and then by sharp bangs that vibrated through the walls. Below them, ING squads peeled off to clear rooms.

Franks's beam illuminated two anxious faces on the next landing. He froze, Coop pulling up short behind him.

The man in front spread his hands, yelling in Arabic that they were civilians and not to shoot them.

Franks yelled back at them to put their hands in the air.

Okay, okay, the man said.

The second man stepped to the side, raised an AK, and opened fire at the same time Franks squeezed his own trigger.

The sergeant's ceramic armor caught the first slugs, the impacts making his aim wild and ineffective, shotgun roaring to spray buckshot against the ceiling. The next round entered the two-inch gap between his Kevlar and body armor, glanced along his neck protector, and tumbled into his body, twisting him away from the steam of bullets.

The next shots cracked against the plate over Coop's solar plexus, shoving him violently against the wall and punching the air out of his lungs. But he was already firing back, unloading on the jihadists with everything he had.

More through luck than control—the pounding he was taking forced his aim high, and the men were above him—his aim proved true.

The rounds stoved in the armed jihadist's face, the jihadist collapsing like an abandoned puppet. As he fell, his comrade scrambled for the AK while Coop regained control and put aimed rounds into him at almost point blank range.

At each hit, the man jolted but didn't stop trying to kill him, as if he were some kind of zombie in a horror movie. At last, he grabbed his rifle and raised it with the usual Arabic cry, handy for either victory or death, that God is the greatest.

Weeping with pain and frustration, Coop emptied his magazine into him. The rounds splashed across the twitching man's face and throat.

Die, he thought. *Just die.*

At last, the jihadist staggered away choking while Coop reloaded his last magazine and raised his rifle to finish it. Only it *was* finished. The man had fallen to his knees, hanging briefly onto the safety rail before collapsing.

Then Coop crumpled to his knees gasping for air. His chest was on fire, his armor seeming to crush it while also keeping it from falling apart. He wanted to vomit, only if he did, he believed his heart would come out.

Feet stomped past him as shooters moved up to make sure the enemy was down for good.

Ramos suddenly snapped into focus. "I asked if you're hit."

"Sergeant Franks…" His voice rasping and breathless.

"We're taking care of him. Are you hit?"

Coop gently tapped his battered armor plate, producing an alarming stab of pain in his chest. "The armor caught it. I'm good to go, Sergeant."

A familiar voice called out: "Make a hole!"

He looked down at the anxious faces of his squad mates and below them, the curious and shocked faces of the ING waiting to advance.

Doc pushed his way through to drop to his knees next to Franks, who sat slumped and wincing against the wall but breathing. Pulling on fresh latex gloves, Doc checked the disinfected gauze someone had packed into the wound and then rummaged in the man's personal med kit for the IV bag and tubing. He asked if anyone had given Bravo's team leader morphine. Someone said he had.

His job: ensure his patient was breathing, stop the blood flow, cover the wound, treat for shock, encourage him, and if possible, alleviate the pain.

The clock was ticking. The golden hour had started. If Franks could be kept alive long enough to casevac to Marez, he stood a good chance.

Coop touched the man's boot and gave it a gentle squeeze. Franks's dull stare flickered to focus on him.

The man produced a weak smile that morphed into a grimace.

"You sure you're okay?" Ramos asked Coop.

"He wouldn't die," he murmured. "I kept shooting."

"Probably gave himself an adrenaline kick."

They'd all heard how some of the insurgents injected themselves with little vials of adrenaline during combat. The body didn't feel pain and refused to go into shock, allowing it to take incredible damage and continue to fight to the last breath.

He'd just seen what that looked like in combat.

"I'm sending you out on the casevac."

"Yeah," Coop rasped. "Fuck that sideways."

No way he was leaving his unit right now.

"I don't think I heard—"

"I said *no*, Sergeant. I'm good to go."

Ramos gave him an appraising look and nodded. "All right, but you're done here. Get back downstairs. You did good today, troop."

You did good today.

From Ramos, this was praise about as lofty as a soldier could hear. On another day, Coop would have performed any amount of heroics to hear it.

Right now, however, he felt nothing at all.

He tramped down with his rifle, whose weight had suddenly seemed to multiply tenfold. For all his tough talk about staying in the game, he was smoked. His chest was purpling into a massive bruise, and even walking and simple breathing hurt. He was at the loopy edge of heat exhaustion.

His wild-eyed squad parted to let him pass, gently patting him on the shoulder as he went and asking and then telling him he was all right. The ING gaped and whispered. Then he was back outside, where the volume of fire had lessened and was now mostly coming from inside the buildings around him.

He sat on the ground behind the nearest Stryker and focused on his breath, idly picking at a pair of bullet holes he discovered in his pants. Franks came out of the building a minute later on a stretcher and was hustled off to casevac.

Only then did Coop realize how scared he was during the firefight but especially in the stairwell's fatal funnel, half-blinded by the flashes, the agonizing glance of Franks spinning away, the helpless feel of rounds hammering him in the chest like monstrous living things unstoppable in their hate.

Fear, he'd learned, had levels and shades, and right then he'd discovered mortal terror's nirvana in a singular moment that had blasted through his brain like an angel's apocalyptic trumpet. Today, he'd seen men puke and piss themselves and get the shakes so bad that they appeared to be dancing while they reloaded. None of that had happened to him, but now that it was over, his body had reached its own stressed out Whiskey Tango Foxtrot state, which turned out to be utter numbness.

He felt absolutely nothing. His limbs had turned to lead.

Regarding the street from the emotional distance of outer space, Coop managed to light a cigarette and blew a stream of smoke in a heavy sigh. Finally, he had some time to think about what happened, and too much to think about. He'd killed two men close enough to feel the pink mist. Close enough to look into their crazy eyes, eyes that had probably mirrored his own, the intimacy of it a hell of thing he'd like to understand at some point when he had the energy.

What he did think about now was how close he'd come to buying it. A burning pain that filled the world, then lights out, good night, as you find yourself being dragged into dreamless eternity. The rounds had hit his armor. A few inches north, and it would have been a race of dying by bleeding out from a busted jugular or choking on his own blood.

What he was thinking about was what he would have died for. In one sense, it would have been for his brothers in arms, for peace and stability in the Middle East, for the protection of his own country against international terrorism, for the cause of spreading freedom across the globe. In another, he would have died to capture a stairwell in a war he'd grown to have a tough time explaining to himself.

Coop took another drag on his cheap Iraqi cigarette and closed his eyes, feeling drawn deeper into the depressed state that was a severe combat hangover. More than ever, he didn't want to die, but he wouldn't mind at a bit if he fell asleep and never woke up. Just sleep straight through it all and wake up in his old bed at his Mom and Dad's house in Milan, Michigan.

He certainly didn't want to think about killing and dying and what it all meant anymore. If he did, it would mess him up. He'd no longer be combat effective. He had to stay in the game. He didn't want to let anyone down, most of all himself. So he stopped thinking.

He saved it for later, as one must, and focused instead on his breathing, which hurt a tiny bit less now.

Sergeant Ramos emerged from the building. He handed Coop a 7.62 round.

"What's this, Sergeant?"

"That came from the insurgent's mag. It's the bullet that was going to kill you. Hang onto it. As long as you do, it'll never touch you."

Coop pocketed it. "Thanks."

"You all right? You look a little flaky."

"I'm good to go, Sergeant."

The sergeant studied him for a few more moments and grunted.

"Good," he said. "We're Oscar Mike soon."

3rd Platoon rolled out to the south, back to Marez. A half hour later, the Gamblers, dangerously low on ammunition and water, mounted up again and took over its sister platoon's mission, rolling northeast to seize a bridge and hold it.

The battle of Yarmouk Traffic Circle had felt like being in a war movie, and if this was a movie, its runtime would be coming to a touching end. The heroes would go home savoring their victory and reflecting on their sacrifices and the hard lessons about life and death they'd learned. Roll credits.

Only it wasn't a movie. It was just another day at war.

At the third bridge joining an embattled East and West Mosul over the River Tigris, 1st Squad chowed on MREs at their defensive positions, watched smoke plumes sprout from distant airstrikes, and waited.

Each of them having plenty of time to think his own thoughts.

Kill Chain

The Pathfinder groaned and banged on rubble carpeting the road. The road led up an incline to the highest point in East Mosul, where an enormous building dominated the view like a modern Parthenon.

This was the Mosul Exhibition and Trade Center, built with oil and reconstruction money. A place for displaying innovation and showing the world Mosul was ready to do business. A jewel of the new Iraq left derelict during the bleak Islamic State years and shelled in the first days of the siege.

Now the CTS used it as a forward operating base. This was where Colonel Reynolds suggested Stuckey's team start for mining useful intel.

Coop expected some strongarming at checkpoints, but nothing happened. As Stuckey drove up, the only security in sight was a squad of soldiers resting in chairs and who seemed more interested in their phones than the new arrivals.

The lieutenant parked between two Humvees with doors painted in the attacking eagle insignia of the Iraqi Special Forces.

"Bingo," he said.

He pointed at two black joint light tactical vehicles parked near the center's main doors. These boxy, heavy trucks were slowly replacing the American Humvee fleet, promising greater survivability against IEDs.

A pair of bearded, muscled giants in black uniforms and desert-tan chest rigs stood with their backs against one of the vehicles, staring back with professional suspicion. One held an MP5 submachine gun in a relaxed but moment's-notice grip that Coop guessed was second nature for him. The other cradled an

M4-based weapon system bristling with high-tech accessories to the point of science fiction.

"They're Americans," said Coop.

"Operators," Horvath agreed.

Physically, they were cut from the same rock, rope, and iron as Colonel Reynolds's humanitarian army. Otherwise, it was obvious they were part of some elite subset of America's military might.

Green Berets, maybe: the snake eaters. Delta: the Unit, the D-Boys. Navy SEALs: the Frogmen, the Teams.

Lacking any visible unit insignia and wearing uniforms that allowed them to more or less blend in with the CTS, they weren't advertising who they were. *Don't mind us, we're not actually here.*

"They're not going to talk to us," Coop predicted.

Stuckey set his jaw. "We'll see."

"They're going to tell us to piss off back to the States."

"Let's just go start something and see what happens."

Coop shrugged. "You're in charge."

They exited the vehicle with their weapons hanging loose on their straps, their hands visible. The operators absorbed what they needed to know with a single glance, their expressions subtly shifting from suspicion to casual disdain.

The lieutenant marched over to talk to them. Coop followed at a slower pace. Horvath and Sazan stayed behind, passing a cigarette back and forth and giggling. Refusing to look up from his book, Doc stayed in the Pathfinder, as if he'd decided he wasn't moving an inch unless someone actually needed him for something directly useful.

Glancing at Horvath, Coop thought, *It must be love.* At one time, the man would have rushed over to hump the operators' legs in the hopes that some of their cool would rub off.

The operator with the MP5 responded to Stuckey's questions by jerking his head toward the doors. The lieutenant followed him into the building.

Coop arrived just in time to face an awkward moment with the other man.

"The Iraqis are pretty lax with their security posture," he said to fill the air. Soldiers' small talk.

The silence stretched. Coop heard the faint hum of a portable power generator.

"Yup," said the operator.

Suppressing a flash of annoyance, Coop wandered away toward the building. The man's bigger-dick attitude hadn't rankled him so as much as its implied message: *Go home, dude. You're not doing anything and you're in the way.*

Coop had flown nearly eight thousand miles to try to help save Ramos's life, which had sounded noble and all back home but over here probably struck these operators as some kind of Tom Clancy cosplay.

He wasn't sure he could argue with that.

Noble or foolhardy? In his mind, both might be right. He guessed the true answer would come out in the result.

To find out, he had to keep going.

A CTS officer stormed out the main doors yelling at his phone in Arabic.

"You." He glared at Coop.

Coop placed his hand over his heart. *"Salaam—"*

"Yes, yes, *salaam, salaam.* Tell me how to fix this bitch shit with WhatsApp."

The man was tall and gaunt, his scarred and swarthy face taut and severe around piercing green eyes. He wore a dusty black CTS uniform with Iraqi flag and CTS patches, fully loaded chest rig, and patrol cap. His insignia marked him as an officer at the rank of major.

Coop figured he knew about as much about apps as this man did, but he accepted the phone and asked what the problem was.

"The bitch dog will not complete its update," the major growled.

Judging by the clutter on the man's phone, the problem turned out to be easy enough to figure out.

"You may be at the limit of your storage," he said. "You might trying clearing the cache of apps you aren't using or delete apps you don't need anymore."

The Iraqi officer snatched his phone back. *"Min sijak?"*

He'd asked Coop if he was kidding him. Coop shrugged, as it was just a guess.

After some poking and swiping and a restart, a brief smile tugged at the corner of the major's mouth. "Now I can coordinate an airstrike."

The man went back inside the building on long strides. Curious, Coop followed. The Iraqi soldiers regularly texted and called home during lulls in the fighting, and they endlessly posted photos and combat videos to Facebook in what was arguably the first selfie war.

He hadn't heard of messenger apps ever being used to coordinate close air support, however. This he had to see.

The exhibition hall was an enormous, cavernous space. The skylights and clerestories had been blown out by violent shockwaves, and rock pigeons had come to roost and strut on the ledges, emitting their throaty coos.

Boxes of equipment lined one wall, where antennae ran all the way up to poke at the overcast sky. Propped against sandbags stacked along another wall, ladders offered access to hilltop views of the city.

Sitting on boxes while listening to an Iraqi general give a briefing, several Americans turned to give Coop a cursory once-over. He quickly sized them up as journalists, while they dismissed him as just another security contractor.

In the center of the concrete floor surrounded by empty space, four young men sat at large cubicle-style workstations packed with monitors, radios, and computers. Thick cables snaked along the floor. Held up by skinny columns, a lightweight prefab ceiling sheltered them and their equipment from the elements.

At the nearest workstation, a Black man in a CTS-style uniform clacked on a keyboard. Screens displayed maps of various areas of operations within Mosul. Another showed an overhead thermal image of men standing around a truck. The man's eyes shined, his mouth hanging open as if he were deep in a video game.

He noticed the major standing over him. "Be right with you, Major Haddad." Judging by his accent, he was on loan from the British Army.

"When you are ready," Haddad told him.

Coop realized this was a joint tactical air controller operations center, seemingly thrown together from spare parts and a mix of military and civilian technology. It was like watching a high school computer club manage a kill chain that ended in airstrikes.

A video game played with real bombs.

The screen flared to instant whiteout. The brightness faded to reveal the truck and men replaced by a hot, smoking crater rendered in shades of gray.

The young British soldier swiveled his chair to fix the officer in a wide, cheerful smile. "Now, how may I be of service to you, my good major?"

Coop couldn't help but marvel at the violent apparatus on display.

Out in Mosul, the Iraqi Army applied brute force, feeding thousands of bodies and vehicles into a meat grinder until the grinder broke. Here, a handful of young JTACs conducted hundreds of surgical airstrikes every day in a rapid kill chain that extended across the region, possibly the world.

No wonder the operators didn't want him around. The Iraqis allowed brass and press to walk in and out at will. If this were an American-run operation, military police would be tackling him right now, assuming he'd somehow made it this far.

Major Haddad checked his phone and then bent to point out a little rooftop on one of the map screens.

"You're sure about the target?" the soldier asked.

The CTS officer pursed his lips and said nothing.

"All right, then, I'll run it through. Don't you worry, mate. We'll hit it."

"*Inshallah,*" the major said automatically, as if mildly scolding.

The soldier typed. "Wait and see, it's going to be *smashing.*" Apparently, a catchphrase. The humor seemed to go over the taciturn CTS officer's head.

An overhead view of a Mosul street popped onto the screen. A building with an L-shaped rooftop dominated the view.

With a satisfied grunt, Major Haddad walked away toward the sandbags.

Coop trailed after him. "Don't you want to see, Major?"

"Come, come. Not everything in life happens on a screen." The major reached one of the ladders and started climbing.

Coop scuttled up the other. At the top, he rested his elbows against the top of the sandbag wall and gazed out at East Mosul. Haddad picked up a pair of binoculars someone else had left and aimed them into the city.

Coop had expected things to look better from up here on the hilltop, sanitized by elevation. If anything, the place looked even worse. Entire buildings had been hollowed out to skeletons, while others stood with miraculously intact apartments exposed by an outer wall that had been sheared off by heavy ordnance.

Accustomed to limited counter-terrorism operations, the Golden Division was being used as shock infantry here. They were well trained, well equipped, and relentless. They'd taken Fallujah back from ISIS in a month, Ramadi in eighteen, and then they'd slowly ground their way up Highway 1 to Mosul. Coop could see the progress they'd made blasting into the city block by block, leaving buildings emptied of life and standing as broken, barren shells.

At the bottom of the hill, refugees toiled across a cemetery, searching for sanctuary from the horrific violence. Coop glanced behind him and saw the roof of the little JTAC ops center visible from up here. The topside of the ceiling panels were large blow-up photos of rubble designed to camouflage the center from the prying cameras and bombs of jihadist drones.

"Tell me what brings you to Mosul," Haddad said.

"I served here from 2003 to 2005. At the base by the airfield."

"I remember it. It was called..."

"Marez."

"Yes. It is gone, you know? Daesh. They tore every bit of the old base apart with their bare hands. There is nothing left of it. Not even a single grain of dust that might have come from America. Daesh knows how to hate."

"I didn't know that." Coop didn't really care, but he felt a little shiver anyway. ISIS had erased a part of his past. "My sergeant was helping out with Knightingale—"

The major lowered his binoculars with a scowl. "*Ya haram*, Daesh captured him. I have heard about this. Sadly, you will not find him."

"Well, that's the thing," Coop said, sick of hearing this thrown in his face, even if it was very probably true. "We came a long way, and we're going to try."

Haddad grunted. "Admirable. I understand loyalty."

"You've been in the Army a long time?"

"Ha!" He ran his hand over his stubbled face. "I am forty-eight years old. My first war was against Iran, the one that made us a poor country before the sanctions made us even poorer. Almost everyone in my generation served. Then Kuwait and then America. Death from the sky. A very bad night on the Highway of Death. Twelve years later, I fought America again." The man let out a derisive snort. "This is my fifth war. But I meant I am loyal to Mosul. This is *my* city. My home. I have come to take it back from Daesh."

"Is the exhibition hall your post?"

"My regiment is down there in the city, advancing into Bakir. I command a company. Once the Daesh strongpoint in our way is destroyed by your planes, I will return to them, *inshallah*."

Coop heard a succession of martial bangs in the distance. At the limit of the CTS advance, smoke plumes sprang into the gray sky. Small arms crackled. In urban warfare, a battle, even one as big as this, was rarely seen but always heard.

"We're heading that way ourselves," he said. "Perhaps we might join you for a while, if you don't mind."

Back to glassing Mosul's blocky horizon, Haddad shrugged. "Go as you like to the front. Do not go. That is up to you."

"I'll ask my people about it."

"You will be safe with my boys. You will like them. They are good boys."

"If we were to find out where our man is and it's close to your positions, would you be willing to stage a rescue?"

The man cast him a sideways glance. *Don't be stupid*, it said.

The major's mouth said, "If such a thing were possible, then certainly we might be able to assist you."

Definitely maybe, the Iraqi way of saying *no*.

A jet passed overhead in lazy aerosol roar. Haddad turned away to hunch behind the binoculars.

Moments later, a powerful *boom* punched the atmosphere as debris flew up from a distant part of the city. Smoke and dust mushroomed over the rooftops.

"Allah akbar," the man said softly. Whether in celebration or regret, Coop couldn't be sure. "This time, *I* have the power."

They exchanged WhatsApp information, which incorporated Coop into the major's military communications network. Haddad disappeared down the ladder. Coop lingered for a few minutes with the binoculars.

He swept the brown and tan buildings looking for landmarks, anything he might recognize from his deployment in Mosul. Nothing came to him. He'd spent almost all his time on the western side, and even then, most of the city had all looked the same to him.

"Coop," Stuckey called from below.

"LT." He stepped down the ladder. "Did you find out anything?"

"I did," the lieutenant answered. "I learned the local operators all know Ramos was captured but don't know where he is and can't do anything about it."

"Not exactly helpful."

"Oh, and I learned the operators aren't babysitters and that if we get captured ourselves, it's basically our problem."

"I'll bet they were really respectful about it."

Stuckey chuckled at the sarcasm. "Yeah, it's kid gloves all the way with those guys. What about you?"

Coop told him about the bizarre afterschool Scotch-tape-and-GPS-satellites project that was the anti-ISIS coalition's JTAC team and that it looked pretty damn effective. He then described his meeting Major Haddad.

"He won't help us if we figure out where Ramos is, but he's an ally," he added. "At the very least, he's going the same direction we are. I'm supposed to text him, and then he'll send us his posit."

"You did better than me," Stuckey said. "My guy basically told me I was stepping on his unit's ops just by being here."

"Well, the Iraqis are pretty loose about things. LT, listen…"

They'd left the building and stood outside now. The major and his black Humvee with its fierce eagle emblem were gone. The heavy overcast had finally decided to launch its own offensive, and a light rain was falling.

The dry soil soaked the moisture like a sponge. Free of the ever present dust and with no fires burning nearby, the air smelled clean and clear.

If the rain kept coming, they'd have to add mud to the city's mounting hazards they had to contend with. Right now, however, it felt pure and cleansing.

"I'm listening," Stuckey said. "Send it."

"I'm starting to wonder, maybe those operators are right? We're in the way here? Look, I'm not trying to be a downer. I'm just saying we've got nothing to work with. Nobody knows anything about where Ramos is, and even if they did, nobody will rescue him. We're totally on our own."

"Okay, Coop. I hear you. I'm feeling discouraged too. But it's only been two days. We're leaving in five. Why not ride it out? You never know. We might get a lucky break."

Coop thought about it. "I guess we could ask around among the refugees. See if any of them know where ISIS is keeping prisoners."

"There you go," Stuckey said. "We came all this way, right? We might as well give it the full college try until it's time to go back."

They started walking back to their vehicle. Coop cast a sidelong glance at his old platoon commander, who'd worn a determined but glum face since last night.

"Is, uh, everything okay with the Household Six, LT?"

The man sighed. "Carol doesn't understand. She thinks I'm choosing the Army over my family. She doesn't understand I'm not choosing at all. I know I'll have my work cut out for me making this up to her when I get home."

"I'm sure you'll figure—"

"It's about time," Horvath called from the Pathfinder. "Get over here, you two."

They hustled back to the vehicle, where Doc and Sazan stood close to Horvath, who held out his phone like some prize he'd won at a fair.

"What's this?" Stuckey asked.

Horvath grinned. "We know where Daesh is keeping Sergeant Ramos."

Golden Division

It was ISIS itself that tipped them off.

Horvath played the latest Amaq video posted to the Islamic State website.

Close up of Ramos's blanched face. Running sweat has turned the NO GOD BUT GOD painted on his forehead into a harsh smear.

The camera pans as he is marched to the edge of a flat roof and forced to his knees. Small arms fire pops in the distance. Pillars of smoke pour into the sky from artillery strikes.

Coop absorbed every detail. This was the front line as seen by ISIS.

A black-garbed captor shouts in Arabic. The same very tall, skinny man who'd appeared in the first video.

"He will gaze upon our might before he meets God," Sazan murmured.

The man shoots his pistol toward his distant enemy. He pivots to press the barrel against Ramos's head and pull the trigger. The gun clicks, empty.

He speaks again.

"He will watch the apostates and puppets of the Jews and Americans die."

The ISIS torturer slaps a fresh magazine into the pistol and repeats the process, shooting into the blurry, shattered landscape before swinging the barrel to Ramos.

Again, the gun clicks.

"And then he will join them."

A final shout before the video cuts.

"God is the greatest," Sazan translated. "His enemies are powerless."

"Blah, blah, blah," said Horvath.

To him, it was all just cheap, empty theater for psychopaths. Coop saw an art in it. A method and purpose.

Ramos gave no confessions nor praise for his captors and their cause. In each video, he'd simply suffered silently without any agency at all.

And that was the point, he believed. ISIS had mastered the art of oversimplification essential to good propaganda. Everything it did was to demonstrate its own power operating on a righteous and separate moral plane.

This time, Ramos's brutal captors did it fearlessly, right out in the open. To them, their American prisoner didn't have a name or a voice and therefore wasn't even human. He was there to bear witness to the triumph of the caliphate.

The message to the faithful: *We have the power, and you can stand with us and live or kneel with him and die.*

The main message Coop received was his old sergeant was still alive.

"So what's his posit?" he said.

"He's in Mosul, bro!" Horvath said. "And not that far from the front line."

"Play it again," Stuckey said. "Everybody, look for a landmark."

They watched the video on repeat. Doc opened a map on his phone so they had a reference.

No one could fix a posit, even Sazan, who'd visited Mosul in better times but didn't know the city intimately.

"I'd put him in East Mosul," Doc said. "The only place where the Iraqi Army is that deep into the city is right here."

Stuckey shot Coop a smile that said, *And there's our lucky break.*

It didn't solve all their problems, not even close. But it put them far ahead of where they'd been only this morning.

ISIS had shown themselves in order to flaunt their prisoner in the face of the enemy. What they hadn't counted on was a small team of Americans was coming for him. Not quite as fanatical but possibly just as crazy.

"I know a guy who might know that ground," Coop told the group. He explained his meeting Major Haddad.

Stuckey inspected his team and cataloged a spectrum of hope and fear. "It's a break, and I think we should explore it. Suggestions?"

Horvath raised his hand. "You're in charge, LT. Give the order."

"Well. I say we go."

"Mount up, y'all," said Horvath. "We're Oscar Mike."

The lieutenant eyed Doc's sour expression but said nothing. This was their best lead, he wanted to see where it went, and the best time to do it was now. At the same time, he didn't want to force anyone to do anything they didn't want to do.

He'd also promised they'd stay behind the front line at all times, a promise he was now breaking.

Doc got back into the Pathfinder without protest, which settled the issue. Stuckey sank into his seat behind the wheel, looking far from settled himself.

He turned to Sazan. "A hundred a day."

The Kurdish woman nodded. The extra money didn't matter to her at this point. He simply wanted her to know that he understood what he was asking. He appreciated that she was still on the team when they needed her most.

Stuckey shifted into gear and maneuvered the Pathfinder onto the little road that dumped them back on the westbound lanes of Highway 2. They drove with windows down, rifles out, and windshield wipers scraping drizzle and dust.

They passed the burned-out skeletons of vehicles, an enormous truck-sized crater torn out by a VBIED, and cosmetic ads on billboards with women's faces blacked out by religious fanatics with spray paint cans. An artillery barrage filled the air with rapid thunder, the horizon throbbing with dust, the city trembling at the bursts.

Everywhere they looked, there were apocalyptic portents and signs they were driving into Hell's closest analogy on Earth.

At an electric substation, their GPS guided them off the highway into a network of narrow, muddy streets barely wider than alleys. They were still behind the front line, but assumptions were like landmines in Mosul, especially where the front line was concerned.

Communication between CTS units was sketchy. To avoid friendly fire on their flanks, they gave each other a wide berth, resulting in large gaps in the line. At any time, ISIS could be almost anywhere.

Coop took cold comfort in the view of houses crumbling with smashed-in roofs and pockmarked walls, which indicated CTS recently had pounded through this neighborhood. Led by a donkey-drawn wagon piled high with what appeared to be an entire house worth of possessions, a family slowly trudged east in search of safety. A heavy bulldozer had plowed and heaped all the broken pieces onto the roadsides. An abandoned Humvee, taken out by rocket fire, sat wedged against a house at the end of a trail of broken armor plates. Beyond it, the dead body of a civilian lay curled on the ground. A woman keened and wailed from a rooftop.

Again, he processed these images as normal and moved on.

All around, gunfire boomed in pouty fits and sudden avalanches, desultory but general. Covering his sector, Coop automatically translated the noise into useful intel. If you knew how to listen, gunfire told you a story, every dice-cup rattle and popcorn pop and angry, snapping drum roll. It told him where the combatants were, how disciplined they were, and what weapon types were in play.

Right now, he heard ISIS probing and testing the CTS positions for weakness while the CTS boys unloaded with everything they had probably just because they could. The steadily increasing volume told him they were getting close.

At the sight of Humvees and hulking MRAPs in the road ahead, Stuckey let off the gas pedal to proceed at an even slower speed while Sazan reached out the window to wave the white flag they'd fashioned from a stick and a torn bedsheet.

A black-uniformed CTS soldier motioned them forward while screaming in Arabic, his M4 carbine planted against his shoulder ready to shoot.

"Slow," Sazan breathed. "Very slow."

This was a war where a car could take out an entire platoon and where Iraqi soldiers took zero chances.

Stuckey parked behind the rear vehicle, a black Humvee with an Iraqi flag hanging from the pole atop the rear and a heavy machine gun mounted in the turret. Coop finally remembered to breathe. He looped his rifle around his neck and got out with his hands in the air.

Word spread Americans had arrived, and soldiers streamed down the line of Humvees. As they approached with grins and cries of *Ameriki!*, Coop was struck by how different each looked, a stark contrast with his own Army's standardized and regulated appearance in the field. He spotted flak jackets and simple fleece pullovers, black uniforms and long-sleeved tan shirts with digital camo sleeves, patrol caps and Adidas winter tuques and helmets, keffiyehs and scarves, sweatshirts and jackets, and every manner of chest rig.

This fierce if motley army was the best the Iraqi government had, and they'd gone head to head against ISIS for the past two years. Suffering a horrific casualty rate, most of these hardy survivors likely had been wounded more than once.

Coop and his team had found the CTS, the Golden Division.

"*Yalla, yalla,*" the company's burly sergeant major shouted.

The soldiers parted at the barked command. Trailed by an entourage of wolfish fighters cradling M4 carbines, Major Haddad emerged from the throng. Coming to a halt, he fixed Coop with his piercing eyes and the briefest tug of a smile.

"My IT specialist," he said.

Coop placed his hand over his heart. "*Salaam alaikum,* Major Haddad."

"*Alaikum salaam,* Mr. Coop."

Coop introduced the members of his team. Haddad greeted each with a curt *salaam* then regarded Sazan with a respectful if wary final glance that said, *Nice to be on the same side, huh? I wonder if I'll be shooting at you next when all this is over.*

He swiveled his piercing gaze back to Coop. "You have come to search for your friend?"

"I think we may have found him, Major."

He showed the man the Amaq video on Horvath's phone.

"*Al'ama,*" Haddad swore.

"Do you know where that rooftop is?"

"Yes, of course. They were looking almost right at us."

A soldier cried a warning, and the company began to scatter toward the sides of the garbage-strewn street.

Haddad frowned. "We will find cover now."

Fleeting mosquito buzz.

Coop's eyes jerked up to identify the source of the strange whirring sound.

Sazan yanked at his sleeve. *"Run."*

Soldiers ventured back onto the road, their M4s aimed at the sky and clacking. Coop and the others hustled into the ruins of a house to join Haddad, who stooped to peer out from a firing slit that an ISIS fighter had chiseled through the family room's outer wall. The ISIS fighter lay dead on the floor, shoved like garbage into the corner and half covered in a rug.

Haddad barked an order into his radio and then turned to Coop.

"Drone," the major said.

A heart-stopping *bang*. Shrapnel violently crackled against the wall, which trembled and shed a layer of paint dust.

Down the road, a second loud crash sounded.

"I see a nice house here," Haddad said.

Coop looked around, wondering what the Iraqi saw that he didn't. The house was barely standing.

In the aftermath of the blast, every seam groaned under the strain. Plaster covered the floor. Rain puddled where it dripped through the porous ceiling. The furnishings and possessions that made a home for a family lay strewn about like garbage. The ISIS fighter lay at the end of a smear of dark blood.

The major scooped a copy of the Quran from the floor, blew dust and ash from the cover, and gently returned it to its shelf.

Next to the shelves, a succession of holes bored through walls offered a circular view into every house down the block. ISIS had done this so its fighters could move between firing positions and escape while under cover. It was a tiny subset of a vast network of such passageways and underground tunnels that allowed them to move around the city and emerge to attack almost anywhere.

"When we rebuild," the major added. "A family will make a home here and live in peace."

Coop wanted to say something, but only platitudes came to mind, not a single one authentic. The truth was it would take generations to rebuild what ISIS had degraded and the Iraqi Army was now destroying. The truth was many Moslawis would return to find their homes crushed in mountains of rubble entombing the dead, and they would live in the ruins with the ghost of a once great city.

"Mosul will rise again," he said anyway. Whether it was true or not, Haddad obviously needed to believe it.

"*Bismallah*," the major said, declaring it in the name of Allah. "Mosul will be green and full of life." He fixed the pale, still body half covered by the rug with a cold stare, as if regarding a dead cockroach. "When we finally destroy Daesh."

"Where did you live when you lived here?"

"Near the university. My family…" His green eyes flashed inward to some horrific idea before smoldering outward again with hate.

Outside, the shooting petered out.

"*Aman,*" soldiers called the all-clear.

Haddad shook his head free of bad memories.

"Normally, I am not the first to take cover," he said. "I must remind the boys how to be brave by my example. But the drones have been targeting me for days, and I cannot lead them against Daesh if I am dead."

Yes, stay alive, thought Coop, who'd taken a liking to the major. *You do that.*

He left the house grateful to be free of the dead body and found another unsettling sight, which was the smoking pothole the grenade had produced almost exactly where he'd just been standing.

Down the street, a blazing Humvee pumped thick coils of oily black smoke across the street. A group of soldiers huddled around a body lying on the road, their hands raised in prayer.

ISIS had built its own air force from off-the-shelf parts and a little ingenuity with signals and switches. Most were quadcopters modified to drop mortar shells or grenades. Others carrying a small C4 payload plummeted with mosquito whine to kamikaze against a target. The drone pilot who attacked the Humvee down the road was either very good or very lucky; he'd guided it right into the turret.

Coop shuddered. He'd read about ISIS's use of drones. Reading was one thing. Surviving an attack by one was another. His ears still rang from the blast.

"I'm glad they didn't have those back in the day," Stuckey said.

"No kidding," said Coop.

It would have been another virtually invisible source of sudden death to add to IEDs and mortars in his Sandbox deployment's pantheon of terrors.

Outside, Haddad gloomily received a sitrep from the sergeant major and walked down the column to join the men praying over their dead comrade.

"So he says Ramos was looking almost right at the CTS," Stuckey said. "If we climb up onto a roof, we might even see the building he was on."

"It's a wide front, Hud," Doc reminded him. "A whole division is here."

The lieutenant scowled at Coop. "Does he know Ramos's posit or not?"

"I think we're about to find that out. Here he comes."

Major Haddad returned with his usual long, determined strides. He removed a tablet from a pocket in his rig and shared it for inspection.

It was an app showing eastern Mosul overlaid with colored geometric shapes indicating degrees of Iraqi Army control by district. Coop took in the sizable gray area to the west, streets and structures stacked to the Tigris and beyond across West Mosul, terra incognita of a sorts, a landscape that on ancient maps might bear the warning: *Here be monsters.*

"We are here," the Iraqi said. "And here is our lead platoon out front. I am not absolutely certain, but I believe Daesh took the video of your friend here."

Stuckey gasped. "Wait. Major, you know the actual *building*?"

"Na'am." Arabic for *yes*.

"What? How?" Horvath sputtered. To his eyes, the background scenery in the video had offered no distinctive landmarks as clues.

"At the end of this road ahead of us, there is a police station just to the north," Haddad said. "It is distinct in that it was built with an observation tower. This tower is about four meters across, which matches what you see in the video."

Doc chuckled in admiration at the simple puzzle solving. The solution wasn't in the scenery but the roof itself.

As for Coop, he couldn't help but grin. This was good news, a miracle, in fact. They had good odds that they'd found their needle in the seventy-square-mile haystack, and it was a little over two kilometers distant. He'd feared Ramos was being held in the main ISIS command and control apparatus at Mosul University, which was on the right side of the city but on the banks of the Tigris, deceptively close on a map but currently about as accessible as the moon.

The question now was how to reach him.

Again, the major had the solution.

"We are attacking again tomorrow," he said. "Still pushing west."

Horvath glanced at Stuckey, who set his jaw and nodded. Smiling, the sergeant offered the Iraqi commander one of his Marlboros and lit it for him.

He said, "What do you say to us riding along?"

War Stories

The Iraqi soldiers lounged on colorful blankets they'd hauled from their vehicles and spread across the floor of the family room of an abandoned but relatively intact house. This was 2nd Squad, 3rd Platoon in Major Haddad's four-platoon company now standing at roughly a hundred men.

Tomorrow, Coop and his team would be sharing an MRAP troop carrier with them during the assault. MRAP stood for *mine-resistant ambush protection*, the Army's answer to IEDs. Coop didn't mind a bit.

Basically a massive, blocky truck that had the stout look of a zombie apocalypse vehicle or a Humvee on steroids, its V-shaped hull deflected bomb blasts for greater survivability against many types of IEDs. The model they'd be riding in was a Cougar variant that could fit up to ten riders and their gear.

By the light of an electric lantern, their evening prayers completed, the soldiers watched videos or called home on their phones, joked with each other, and cooked supper in pots set over propane stoves while slamming Tiger energy drinks.

Having lived in their boots, Coop could tell they were scared, and he didn't blame them. Not in any war but particularly this one, the kind of darkness even General Sherman hadn't imagined when he'd famously uttered that *war is hell.*

On the plus side, these men had a clear and powerful mission: defeating a malevolent enemy that was as evil as the Nazis. Coop envied them for such stark purpose, which had slowly died for him during his deployment.

The last time he'd been in this country, he'd worked with men like these, whom he typically regarded as unreliable at worst and a nuisance at best as soldiers. It was strange to see Iraqis fighting their own war and probably similarly regarding him as being in the way.

Coop expected the cold shoulder from them, but Iraq's famous hospitality extended even here onto the battlefield.

A heavily stubbled, tough-looking specimen who appeared to be a fireteam leader introduced himself as Sergeant Hammadi. While sharing plates of rice and plastic bags of khubz with the Americans, he pointed out his boys.

Azim, whose name meant "defender," was a giant SAW gunner, fearless in combat. Mohamad, the pious one fighting his own jihad, was called the "alarm clock" by the squad for his daily nagging to observe salat. The quiet one cleaning his rifle was Omar, who hated Daesh more than anyone and got a sick joy from watching bootlegged videos of Daesh prisoners being tortured by security forces.

Azim spoke to Sergeant Hammadi, who translated, "He wants to know if you are soldiers."

"Yes, we were." Coop opened his plastic bag and let the steam pour out.

"No longer?"

"No." He studied the big SAW gunner. "How old was he in 2004?"

"Azim was ten when the Americans came," the sergeant answered.

"So he was the one throwing rocks at me," Horvath said.

Tittering, Hammadi translated this for his team. The Iraqis howled with laughter. Horvath, who'd been glowering, suddenly broke into a chuckle.

"Yeah, go ahead and laugh it up," he said.

The past was over. Whatever horrible history the two nations shared over twenty years, two wars and crippling economic sanctions, these Iraqis didn't seem to care. America, it appeared, remained a respected frenemy, a bizarre and magical place of unlimited wealth and power.

Only Sazan seemed to weird them out, a Peshmerga and a woman to boot.

"Now we are all on the same side," Hammadi grinned. "Now we fight the evil of Daesh. Now we fight for Iraq and Mosul."

"Fuck Daesh," Omar spat. "Fuck Mosul."

"Omar thinks the Moslawis who stayed support Daesh. Many of the soldiers do. He hates everybody."

Horvath glanced at Coop, who nodded: *They sound like us twelve years ago.* Back when everyone in this city felt like the enemy.

The sergeant added, "But that is not who we are now. Major Haddad is right: We are here for all Iraq. Sunni, Shia, Kurds, everyone, all our brothers now. This is where the war ends. This is where all the wars end. This is where history ends."

Most of the people here were Sunni Muslims, but the Army was predominantly Shia and had a history of oppression in Mosul that had created support for ISIS.

Now the Iraqi generals were taking pains to defeat ISIS while respecting the local population. To end the war, it was not enough to capture Mosul and destroy the Islamic State. Peace rested on stopping the cycle of hate that had created it.

Forty thousand civilians had died so far in the civil war. As for the survivors, they remained as ever caught between a rock and an even bigger rock—stuck in the crossfire between the Iraqi Army, ISIS, Shia Popular Mobilization Forces militias, the Peshmerga, and coalition artillery and airstrikes.

At some point, their only choice was to pick a side and join the fighting themselves.

Something had to stop it.

"Bismallah," Coop replied to Sergeant Hammadi, meaning it.

"Bismallah," the Iraqi echoed. "Now we eat."

Coop dug into his rice and khubz, which was quite good. Their meals finished, the Iraqis lit American cigarettes from a pack Horvath shared with them. Azim dragged over a TV set and plugged it in. The building had no power, however, so he traded his SAW for an oud, a short-necked lute, and began strumming a song. Mohammad unwrapped a hookah and lit the coals. Omar turned his back to Sazan and stripped off his layered shirts for a quick bottle shower. The pale scraps of an old shrapnel wound curled along his shoulder.

All the while, the men joshed back and forth, and Coop chuckled as he recognized colorful phrases that Basam, his old platoon interpreter, had taught him. Insults like *tozz feek, kol khara,* and *telhas teeze,* which respectively meant *piss off, eat shit,* and *kiss my ass.*

The familiar rough, brotherly talk of soldiers.

"Your English is very good," he told Sergeant Hammadi.

"Mashallah," the man answered automatically, warding off bad luck and the evil eye by giving God the credit for anything good about him. "I grew up under Saddam, back when everybody went to school. These dumb boys grew up in civil war. Most of what they know they learned on the street and the internet. Half of them do not know history from conspiracy theories."

"Why don't you guys wear your PPE?" Horvath asked.

Hammadi frowned. "This word I do not know."

"If it was *my* squad, I'd make sure—"

"Personal protective equipment," Coop cut in before his friend insulted their hosts. "He is curious why your guys don't wear helmets and flak jackets."

Sergeant Hammadi translated, and the Iraqis laughed again at the earnest but clueless Americans.

"We fight until we die," the man answered with a grin. "It is, you might say, in our contract. We might as well do it comfortable."

"Come on," Horvath said. "The PPE—"

"It is war," Hammadi growled, all mirth gone.

In war, men got hit and they died.

And when it was your turn, it was your turn. Period.

Coop said nothing. He figured that after years of fighting ISIS, these men had earned their fatalism.

Azim smirked at Horvath and barked something in Arabic.

"He is curious to know why you brought AKs," Hammadi translated.

The Iraqi Special Operations Forces used M4s and looked down on the Kalashnikovs as cheap garbage.

"I equipped with a shotgun," Horvath sputtered, but it was too late, as the Iraqis were all laughing again.

Stuckey probably figured the butt-sniffing and bonding was either over or in a lull, and so he jumped into business.

"What kind of resistance do you think we'll be facing tomorrow?" he asked.

Sergeant Hammad's face again flipped from mirth to grim.

"Daesh came to Mosul to die," he said, his voice a mix of disgust and grudging respect. "They will fight us for every step. They will attack us nonstop."

"What the hell are we doing here," Doc muttered to himself.

The lieutenant asked about friendly assets, enemy tactics, the CTS approach to responding to ambushes. Tomorrow morning, he learned, the company planned to recon to contact, part of a battalion-sized push to move the front line.

Sergeant Hammadi spoke reverently of Major Haddad, who'd led them since Fallujah. Whatever Daesh planned, he said, old Haddad would meet them head on.

Then he looked at his buzzing phone and hissed an entreaty to Allah. Hearing it, his fireteam cackled and shouted, *Yumma! Yumma! Ahebech, Yumma!*

"I have to accept this call," he said, turning scarlet. "It is my mother. She calls five times a day to see that I am okay." He shrugged.

The sergeant went outside speaking softly into his phone.

Horvath turned to Doc and said, "What we're doing here is finishing our mission to save Sergeant Ramos. Reporters embed with these guys all the time. If a goddamn liberal media reporter can do it, you can do it."

"He's not wrong, Doc," Coop said.

"I *know*," Doc growled back. "Just let me bitch."

Omar sat up on his blanket and glared at them. "You help us kill Daesh tomorrow, yes, *Ameriki*?"

"You speak English," Stuckey said.

"A little. All CTS learn a little from *Ameriki* instructors. I also learn at Tikrit Air Academy. I was senior cadet when Tikrit fall."

"Oh, shit," said Doc, who knew what was coming.

"What?" said Horvath. "What happened?"

"When we were here, it was Camp Speicher. It's not a happy story."

Omar stared at Horvath. "You should know it."

Doc sighed but said nothing.

"When Daesh capture Tikrit, many commanders run," Omar told them. "We do not know what to do. No weapons we had. No defending ourselves. We hear if we go home, we not harmed, so why not go? We put on civilian clothes and walk. On the road, Daesh round us up in trucks. They take all Shias and tell us march into holes. They shoot us one by one by one. They make us say, 'Long live Islamic State' before killed. Human sacrifice to filthy state. Seventeen hundred, all dead."

Coop gasped. "How did you survive?"

"My friend killed next to me. My brother. When he shot, it was like I shot too. I fall with him. I wear his blood. Daesh laugh and say, 'Let him bleed until dead.' At night, I escape. You see what they are? Daesh is plague on world. Disease. The only cure is bullet in brain."

The Americans said nothing. For Coop, not even a polite if ineffectual platitude came to mind as it had with Major Haddad. Seventeen hundred cadets, blindfolded and bound, shot in the back of the dead and dumped in mass graves. Omar had survived a literal hell, and he was still fighting his way through it.

No wonder he hated ISIS as much as he did.

"We help you find friend," Omar added tersely. "That is your fight. You help kill Daesh. That is our fight. That is human fight."

As if sensing the souring mood, Azim began to sing as he played his oud. The CTS soldiers quieted to listen. Coop didn't know the words, but he understood the emotion. It was the same song sung by soldiers throughout time.

A young man leaves home to go to war, and he wonders if he'll ever see it again. A young wife waits for him in a cold bed, wondering if her love will survive to return.

Stuckey hissed, "It looks we might be in the shit tomorrow."

"We'll be all right," Horvath said. "Hell, after hearing that story, I wouldn't mind plugging a few Daesh myself."

Coop nodded, driven by a restless burning in his chest. He was feeling pretty pissed off and murderous himself. The Islamic State may not have been Hitler's Third Reich in scale, but its genocidal brutality sure looked familiar.

He wondered if this was what had drawn Ramos to return. That Omar was right, and this was a fight not for Iraq but for humanity.

"That's not our mission," the lieutenant reminded them. "We're here for Ramos, and we're all getting home."

"Amen," said Doc.

"If bullets start flying, we hunker down and wait it out. When we get to Ramos, that's when we'll need to step up. We'll have to go guns free on target until he's good to move."

"That's not the hard part," Doc said.

"I know," said Stuckey.

"Wait." Horvath frowned. "What's the hard part?"

Doc said, "When ISIS sees CTS getting close to its little torture dungeon, they're going to either ship out or kill their prisoners. That's assuming CTS doesn't call in an arty strike and blow up the building first."

Horvath grunted. "So we bound ahead of the column when we're close. We get in there quick and clear it with the violence of action."

"That's how to do it," Coop said glumly.

All their efforts were going to end in a suicidal rush.

Stuckey saw it too. "Let's see how it goes. We may end up with another lucky break and have the opportunity to go in quick and stealthy. All I'm saying is we might have to be prepared to do some shooting ourselves."

Few plans survived contact with the enemy. Considering their meager assets, *let's see how it goes* struck Coop as the only plan that made sense at this point.

Stuckey turned to Sazan. "Now's the time to quit if you're quitting."

She stared at him. "I want to see Daesh destroyed. This is my fight too."

The Peshmerga glanced at Horvath, who turned away suppressing a proud smile. Stuckey stood and dusted his pants.

"All right then." He offered up a wan smile. "I guess it's time to load our nuts."

"Hooah," Horvath said.

"Where are you going?" Doc asked the lieutenant.

"If it comes to a fight at the end, we could use more muscle. I'm going to call Colonel Reynolds and tell him that we found the door."

"I'll come with, LT," said Coop. "I could use the air."

Outside, Stuckey walked off to make his satphone call. Having grown accustomed to the constant gunfire until it had become mere background noise, Coop again listened to its story. What it told him was ISIS lay entrenched ahead of them in strength, and there would be heavy fighting tomorrow.

For now, he was safe. On the road, soldiers passed between the vehicles and buildings on their martial errands. The silhouettes of buildings appeared inky black against the dull red glow of dying fires. In the cold distant dark, an AC-130 gunship rained hell on an ISIS target in streaming tracers.

Coop's war was long over, but Iraq's had never ended.
This wasn't his war, but it also was.
In a sense, it always had been.
And to fulfill his mission, he'd have to go to the next level.
Tomorrow, he knew, he would no longer be a tourist.

Winning

December 2004.

One month after the Battle of Mosul, which lasted eight days—

Fourteen months into Coop's deployment—

Three days before his second Christmas in-country—

On a broad stretch of wet ground offering a dull view of Quonset huts in neat rows, 1st Squad was getting its ass handed to them by the Iraqi National Guard.

Orange traffic cones marked the boundaries of the pitch, with striped cones delineating the centerline and goal posts. Gasping and sweating in the brisk air in his tee and shorts, Coop punted the soccer ball past the centerline and chased after it as a laughing ING dude huffed after him.

He poured his heart into it, allowing his feet to act on their own accord, juggling leather to keep control. Only he had nowhere to go. The laughing ING guy seemed to be everywhere, waiting for Coop to make a mistake.

He couldn't keep this up. He had to pass the ball, and now.

Reyes, the team forward, wasn't in position.

Then Thompson came flying.

The midfielder soared at the diagonal on huge strides, positioning himself to deliver a direct kick that would put Team America back in this game.

Past him, Coop glimpsed the soldiers and ING who'd gathered along the sideline to spectate the match. Ramos stood among them with his arms crossed.

Coop wasted a precious second beaming at this father figure, hoping to see pride and encouragement reflected back at him. All he received was the usual amused smirk that said when it came to human nature, the sergeant had cataloged every species of bullshit there was, and Coop hadn't surprised him yet.

Giggling, the ING dude darted in and almost took the ball from him.

This was it. Now or never.

After a year in a war zone, Coop had developed a sixth sense for detail and vectors. In an instant, he spotted Thompson flying into position, Reyes hoofing it to get anywhere useful, the Iraqis defenders guarding their husky goalie.

The geometry of the goal sang in his subconscious. Coop feinted and then leaned back in to give his all to produce a beautiful crossing pass.

The ball rolled exactly where he wanted it.

Legs pumping, Thompson zeroed on it with a breathless cry.

"Watch me *zoom*."

Only he flubbed it.

The kid's leg swept forward too soon to bunt the ball in a weak plop so comically tragic that even the Iraqis hesitated before rushing toward it. Thompson kept going on momentum into a skidding slide as if stealing home, disappearing in a spray of mud.

An ING midfielder took the ball. Team Iraq's forward raced past him in an overlap, accepted the pass, and proceeded to dominate Team America's defense. After a weaving psych-out, this Iraqi David Beckham deftly kicked the ball between Sergeant Murray's lead feet in a move colorfully termed a *nutmet*, and then he drove it home with nothing but open field between him and Horvath at the goal.

Bouncing on his feet, Horvath braced himself to meet the kick. He dove into a faceplant as the ball sailed past him.

While the ING cheered, Murray waved his arms. "No goal!"

Lacking proper goal posts and nets, they'd all agreed if the ball went over the line at a height taller than the goalie could reach, it wasn't a legit score.

The teams converged at the center. Gasping for air, Coop hustled over to join his red-faced teammates. They were all close to being smoked.

"It was too high," Murray said. "Basam, get your ass over here!"

With an irritated sigh, 2nd Platoon's grizzled Iraqi interpreter jogged over from the sideline to mediate. Given the rate at which terps disappeared, it was something of a miracle he was still alive after six months with the Americans.

Basam translated for the Iraqis, who tossed their hands in annoyance.

The ING sergeant acting as Team Iraq's captain patted his chest several times, a local gesture that meant, *Thank you, I've had enough.*

"*Khalas, khalas,*" he muttered. *Okay, okay, you can stop now.* He turned to his men and gestured at the Americans, barking in Arabic.

Coop caught a term that had the ING guys sneering.

"Basam, what's that word mean, *yahud*?"

"Jews," the terp answered. "He said you are Jews."

"What? Why?"

"He means you are cheating. Israel is not a popular country here."

So much for boosting allied relations. Coop suppressed a groan. Fraternizing with the Iraqis had marked them for ribbing by other units, but these guys, part of an ING platoon that had rotated in for training, had stepped up and done their part during the Battle of Mosul the month before. They'd fought hard while thousands of Mosul's police officers had simply fled.

Murray thought a friendly soccer game would do some good, doing his part for COIN, winning hearts and minds and all that. The only problem was Alpha's team leader hadn't accounted for a drubbing.

The Iraqis pretty much started soccer in the crib, and before joining the Guard, their team's forward had been something of a local star at the sport. 1st Squad's idea of a ringer, meanwhile, was Thompson, who knew the lingo like when to shout *golazo* and otherwise claimed to be a soccer legend at his old high school, but who otherwise sucked.

"This is embarrassing," Coop said.

"This is America," Murray replied. "Game on!"

This is America. They could be wrong, but they weren't allowed to lose.

Only they did. The ING guys plowed them over to score another goal and cinch their victory. Cheering, they swarmed Iraqi

David Beckham, who'd scored the winning goal. The Iraqi spectators rushed from the sideline to join in.

"God damn," Coop said. "Even cheating, we can't win."

1st Squad moped over to Ramos and flopped panting onto the muddy ground while the American spectators chuckled at their misery.

"Impressive game, Gamblers," a guy from 1st Platoon called out to laughter. "I was taking notes."

"Well," Murray said. "That whole idea backfired."

Ramos snorted, *backfired* being a bit of an understatement.

"Come on, guys," said Coop. He was cold and miserable and wanted hot chow and a shower. "Let them have it. The hajjis have to be good at something."

Iraqi David Beckham yelled out something from the crowd. Coop looked over at Basam to translate.

"Sometimes, it is better not to know," the terp said dryly.

"Even the hajjis are laughing at us," Murray gloomed.

For months, Coop's platoon had driven around in their Strykers chased by laughing children looking for candy and flashing the Americans a determined thumbs up as they drove away. *They really love us*, he'd thought. Then Basam ruined it by explaining that in Iraq, the gesture meant *Up yours*.

The squad pulled on blouses and pants over their PT clothes, slung weapons, squared their patrol caps. The jerky rhythm of Arabic song wafted from the Iraqi side of the playing field. Plucking qanoun, trilling nai flute, pounding drums. Both teams had brought boomboxes so that they'd enter the pitch with a theatrical flair.

Holding hands, the ING team broke into celebratory chobi line dancing while their comrades raised their rifles toward the sky with a shout.

"They're rubbing it in our faces," Reyes groused. "We'll never live this down."

Ramos let out a rumbling chuckle.

"You're not wrong," he said.

Murray bleakly watched them gloat. "So what can we do?"

The rumbling stopped. "You walk over there and shake their hands like men."

Reyes set his jaw. "I got a better idea, Sarnt."

"I am sure you do not," Ramos said.

The SAW gunner wasn't listening. "Watch me, boys. And follow my lead."

"Wait," Coop said. "What are we doing?"

Reyes was back on his feet. "We're gonna show hajji how it's *done*, Specialist." Recognizing Coop's newly minted bump in rank from PFC.

With that, the SAW gunner picked up his own boombox and hoisted it onto his shoulder like the proverbial chip.

They all looked at Ramos, whose customary smirk turned into one that was slightly more impressed. Finally, his boys had managed to surprise him with a new brand of bullshit.

"Victoria o muerte," the sergeant said in growling Spanish.

Victory or death, it meant.

Coop jumped to his feet and joined the others in repeating the words as a martial shout.

Grinning, Reyes forwarded through his dance mix CD and pressed PLAY. "Gamblers, stand by to represent! Here we go, get funky!"

The pulsing bass of Mr. C's "Cha Cha Slide" boomed from the speakers. Clapping in time, 1st Squad swaggered over to the Iraqis and formed a line.

A slide to the left, to the right. A hop and stomp.

Then, for the cha-cha, Coop and his squad mates put it out there and poured it on full funk—Reyes riffing a merengue, Horvath going for a bump and grind, Murray whipping through the Macarena, Thompson bouncing at the Running Man, Coop pumping his arms while waggling his legs Charleston style.

Some of the Iraqis regarded the Americans with incredulous looks. The soccer team let out defiant war cries as they continued their chobi.

Then Iraqi David Beckham shook off their hands and strode up to the Americans.

And did a slide to the right. Two hops and stomps.

The rest of the ING team joined in for the swishing cha-cha, laughing. The other Americans and Iraqis crowded around, egging them all on.

When the song ended, everyone cheered. Reyes took out the CD, returned it gently to its jewel case, and presented it as a gift to the grinning ING sergeant.

"Shookran," the sergeant said.

No translation needed this time. It meant *thank you*.

"Good game, guys," Murray said.

1st Squad swaggered back to Ramos with their heads held high.

"I don't know if I'd call that victory," Ramos said, "but it looked like peace with honor." In short, they'd saved some face. "Go get your chow, boys."

The Iraqis were already flowing toward the D-Fac, the steel frame over the door decorated with festive red and green bunting for the upcoming holiday. Another lame Christmas in Iraq. The Americans trudged wearily after.

Suddenly famished, Coop looked forward to anything the cooks wanted to sling him today.

"You got to *be* the ball," Thompson was saying.

"I thought you were supposed to be a high school soccer legend," Horvath said.

"It's like a *mindset*."

"Dog, you were all like, 'Dude! Dude! I could have gone pro'—"

Thompson wasn't listening. "That one ING guy was phenomenal. I'll bet he could even teach me a thing or two. I'm gonna go shake his hand. Good sportsmanship is everything."

He took off.

"And you guys suck shitty dicks!" he called over his shoulder.

Too depleted to react, Coop and his squad mates watched him run.

"He's like the Energizer Bunny," Reyes said. "Me, I am smoked."

Thompson caught up to the ING guys and started pumping hands. An Iraqi in a regular army uniform joined them and was surprised to get his hand pumped as well. They all disappeared into the D-Fac laughing.

Murray shook his head. "Force of nature is more like it."

Thompson seemed to have his own reality and logic that governed it.

"You know, this was a good day," Coop said.

In forty-five days and a wakeup, he was going home. It'd all be over. He wouldn't miss most of it, but he'd miss this, the times when the deployment felt like endless summer camp.

He hoped his last day would feel like this one.

Horvath smiled. "Yeah. Sometimes, it feels like we're winning."

The dining tent erupted with a colossal *bang* that shook the ground and struck Coop with a shock wave that felt like a staggering punch to the solar plexus. Something tugged at his side and left a fiery itch.

The white canvas forming a section of roof rippled and waved, smoldering pieces of it flying up before collapsing. Smoke wafted out of the building through a score of newly created vents.

Then the screams poured out. Screams and frantic shouting.

Something too horrific to grasp had just happened.

Reyes took a rasping breath. "What the...?"

Horvath gasped. "Gimp! Thompson!"

He broke into a sprint. Coop raced after him.

Inside, he confronted the horror.

The dead lay like broken dolls. Body parts were everywhere among splintered chairs and splashes of blood and people's dinners. The dazed survivors were already loading screaming casualties onto tabletops and anything else that could be used as a stretcher. Doc was there, blood pouring down his face from a hastily gauzed scalp wound, applying a tourniquet onto the arm of a crying woman whose hand squirted red and hung at a grotesque angle from its wrist.

Horvath looked around. His face turned green. "Thompson?"

"They're *gone*," Murray said.

There was almost nothing left of him and Team Iraq.

The suicide bomber had nearly vaporized them.

The dude in the Iraqi Army uniform, Coop thought.

The man had found a way to infiltrate the base and had just walked right in here wearing a suicide vest under his blouse.

The angry itch in his side continued to burn. He looked down and fingered the rags of his own blouse. A piece of shrapnel had pierced straight through and shredded it. He probed again and this time, his finger came out bloody. He raised his blouse and stared at the nasty grazing cut across the flesh above his waist.

Holy shit, I was hit.

He pulled it back down. He wasn't even going to tell Sergeant Ramos about it. He did not want another Purple Heart. Not for this.

Instead, Coop rolled up his sleeves, approached the nearest officer he could find, and asked what 1st Squad could do to help.

Another Day in Mosul

Iraq's blazing sunrise remained hidden behind drifting smoke and clouds.

In the weak dawn light, Iraqi Special Forces clanking in battle rattle formed up in squads and fireteams next to their vehicles. The column lay stretched along three hundred meters of muddy, trash-strewn road. Eighteen vehicles, Humvees mostly along with a few MRAPs and trucks, a massive bulldozer on point.

Ahead, gunshots echoed through the cold, damp air like two-by-fours being slapped together. An airstrike thudded like the single stroke of a massive bass drum. Coop ignored it all to gaze east, back the way they'd come.

In the constant black-and-gray landscape of broken concrete glistening with overnight drizzle, soldiers fidgeted and smoked, each looking scared or resigned or working on his war face. The gunners loaded the trucks' turret weapons. Men walked along the hoods washing the windshields with little watering cans.

Civilians emerged from a few houses to offer them hot tea and fruit; happy to be appreciated, the soldiers gave them cigarettes, winning hearts and minds.

No sign of the Knightingale Commandos, however.

Reynolds hadn't come.

Stuckey had told Coop that Knightingale was in the field supporting a 9th Armored offensive but would arrive in force as soon as possible.

At this point, however, *soon* was looking like *too late*.

"The Iraqis take their time about everything," Horvath said. "We might have hours before this show gets on the road."

Stuckey blew a relieved sigh. "I think they're here."

A black Humvee drove down the column at fast speed. The soldiers stepped aside to let it pass. Stuckey's smile faded as it splashed through the mud. The vehicle bore the painted inscription ISOF for Iraqi Special Operations Forces and the CTS eagle emblem. A driver, passenger, and gunner crewed it.

In the backseat, bright colors darted behind metal mesh as it passed.

Horvath turned to Coop as the Humvee ground past. "Bird cages?"

Coop shrugged. These men certainly weren't the Knightingale guys.

The company sergeant major flagged the Humvee, which pulled over to park. A portly Iraqi general sporting a Saddam mustache exited the passenger side, coolly lit a cigar, and entered the house Major Haddad was using as his headquarters. Soldiers crowded the Humvee for a look at the general's pet parrots.

"I love you, man," Horvath said.

Coop started. Then he remembered.

OP Applejack, the night of the counter mortar mission. The squad brooding over the D-Fac bombing. They'd talked about the end of their deployment and what it all meant to them. The insurgent crawled through the reeds.

"It's about goddamn time you said it," he said.

Horvath chuckled and let it rest.

Clad in his fleece pullover, flak jacket, and winter cap, Doc shivered either from the chill or his electrifying nerves. He held his Zastava rifle loosely in one hand like a burden he couldn't seem to get rid of.

"Reynolds isn't going to show," he said. "We're going without him."

"Take a page from Coop, Doc," Horvath told him. "Hang loose."

"I'll work on that." Doc had never seemed the type who knew how.

"The number one rule of Mosul is *inshallah*. Well, God put the sarnt almost right in our laps. It don't get more *inshallah* than that. We're getting him back."

"If you say so." Doc wasn't the type who believed in fate either.

"We will," said Coop, thinking of Reynolds walking through mortar fire. He remembered Doc running through a hail of bullets to reach a burning Stryker.

Their experiences in Iraq. Their return to rescue Ramos, which led them here at the start of an offensive with the sergeant only a mile or so distant.

Maybe some things were meant to be.

A 101st Airborne veteran once told him the best way to remain effective in combat was to believe you were already dead. Coop no longer believed that. He was starting to think the best way to keep your head was to believe in your story.

They'd come to get Ramos. In a bonafide miracle, they'd actually found him. To free him, they had to believe they would with so much conviction that it became a self-fulfilling prophecy.

You got to be the ball, as weird little Thompson had once said.

"You know what else, Doc?" Horvath said, and Coop braced himself to have to listen to the inevitable ragging. "I love you too, brother."

Doc blinked behind his glasses. "Okay."

Horvath turned to Stuckey. "And you too, LT. I mean it."

The lieutenant's anxious face broke into a smile. "Thank you, Joe. I have no regrets about being here, and I'm sure damned glad that you're with me."

Horvath next looked at Sazan, who paused her munching on an apple to fix him with her own pursed smile, one that challenged him to *do go on*.

He waggled his eyebrows clownishly and grinned, and she laughed.

The general left Haddad's HQ and got into his Humvee, which executed a three-point turn and sped out of sight back down the road. The CTS soldiers stared at the house expectantly.

The major walked out and twirled his finger over his shoulder.

"Yalla, yalla," he said.

Let's go, let's go, the Arabic version of, *We're Oscar Mike*.

The order echoed down the line. The steel column revved to life. Soldiers tossed back tea, crammed bread into their mouths, and took final drags on smokes before flicking them onto the wet road. They hustled to mount their vehicles, which idled in a throaty grumble, spewing exhaust into the brisk air.

"It's showtime," Stuckey said. "Let's mount up."

The fifteen-ton MRAP stood with its back doors flung wide and a helmeted gunner standing behind the big turret gun. With its bulk and desert-tan paintjob, it stood out from the muddy black column like a sore thumb.

Coop piled into the back with the Iraqi squad. The troop compartment was a mess of blankets, gear, soldiers, and body odor. In the cab, the driver waited with a hand draped over the wheel while Staff Sergeant Ghazi talked into an ICOM radio.

Sergeant Hammadi smiled. "You are soldiers again."

"Fuck Daesh," Horvath replied, which made all the Iraqis grin.

Propelled by its 330 HP diesel engine, the MRAP surged forward. The shock absorbers creaked as the heavy vehicle humped a toppled traffic light.

Still amped they were getting moving, Horvath smiled at Doc. "What are you so glum about? You want to be a doctor, right? Look at all the doctoring you're getting to do."

"I want to help people," Doc said. "I want to save lives. I just hate getting shot at while I'm doing it."

"Hell, that's the fun part."

Coop turned to look out the observation window with its shielding of protective metal slats. A storefront with a crumpled security gate glided past. Then a wall pitted by gunfire and graffitied with some revolutionary message. Then a tangle of downed power lines and exposed rebar jutting like monstrous teeth from shorn concrete. And then burning tires, part of a roadblock ISIS had set ablaze to block their path and the bulldozer had made short work of.

A never-ending dreary, shattered landscape.

Black smoke billowed to obscure his view, and he turned back toward his crew. Americans and Iraqis alike stared at nothing with wide eyes. Azim breathed heavily through his nose while chewing gum. Omar took out his phone and eyed it blankly. Mohamad checked and rechecked his M4. Sergeant Hammadi listened to observation reports from the truck commanders bleating over his handheld radio.

Horvath caught Coop's eye and pulled an anxious face. They'd been driving too long without anything happening, not even a single shot.

Coop nodded in agreement. He had a bad feeling himself, and if Horvath had it too, then it was serious.

Somewhere ahead, a heavy crash made them all stiffen to alertness. Coop heard splashes of small arms fire. The voices on Hammadi's radio grew louder.

"One of our gun trucks was hit by a rocket," the sergeant said as the column ground to a halt. "The lead platoon is engaging."

"Complex ambush," said Horvath.

"Are we dismounting?" Coop asked.

A round cracked against the windshield in front of the MRAP driver's face, splashing a fractured pattern in the ballistic glass.

Hammadi stared at the impact. "I have no orders."

Another bullet thumped against the driver's door. The driver yelled in frustrated Arabic, most likely, *Cut it out, leave me alone, stop shooting at me!*

The MRAP rumbled forward only to stop again. A second later, the vehicle rocked with a deafening boom. The vibrations rippled through Coop's mind and blanked out rational thought better than any meditation.

The vehicle's gunner ducked down cursing and patting himself for wounds.

"Qathifa," he snarled.

"RPG," Horvath translated. "We're okay."

Coop could only answer with a weak, sickly nod as his body processed a flood of adrenaline and his war genie assaulted him with threat information. Next to him, Doc hugged his ribs with gritted teeth. Stuckey looked at the Iraqis as if wondering whether he should be saying or doing something.

Omar sneered at them. "Another day in Mosul."

Outside, the small arms fire intensified. The gunner returned to his post and opened up with the 7.62 machine gun as the turret slowly spun with the metallic clunk of heavy moving parts. Hot shell casings rang along the floor.

A round pinged off the turret armor. Another cobwebbed the windshield.

Then a mind-numbing *BANG* filled the world, followed by a roar like the sound of every wave in the ocean compressed to a single crash. The very earth under the heavy MRAP rippled with a lurching jolt.

Sizzling shards of metal clattered onto the street around them. The gunner dropped pale and gasping into the compartment, shouting again in Arabic. Coop didn't have to speak the lingo to know the man was close to losing his shit.

"We're hit!" Doc shouted into the noise. "Were we hit?"

"Car bomb," said Horvath, as if marking a card playing terrorist bingo. "My guess is they took out one of the last vehicles in the column to box us in."

The compartment grew hot and suffocating. This heavily armored box on wheels appeared safe, only it was a giant rocket magnet.

It was only a matter of time before they were hit again. A rocket boring straight through the thick armor and shredding them all in a dancing meat grinder.

Horvath knew it as well. Next to him, Sazan stood ramrod straight in her seat, her hand digging her nails into his leg. He didn't seem to notice. Air slowly hissed from one of the MRAP's tires.

"Sir," he said with the pure calm of a seasoned combat veteran, "I recommend we exit this vehicle and establish a security perimeter."

Stuckey gaped at him, his eyes wild.

"You're in command now," he said.

"Roger that. Sergeant Ham—"

In the cab, Sergeant Ghazi flung his ICOM radio against the small dash and turned in his seat as two more rounds splashed the windshield near his head.

"Yalla, yalla, yalla!"

The back doors yawned wide. Hammadi let his M4's bolt clack forward to deliver a round into the firing chamber ready to shoot.

"Yalla!" he joined in.

"Wait," said Doc.

"Time to help, Doc," Coop said. "We got this."

The Iraqis jumped out.

"Another day in Mosul!" Horvath called out as he followed.

Coop set his RK62's selector from safe to shoot and rushed out of the MRAP to take cover in its shadow with the other Americans. Tunnel visioning from a fresh shot of adrenaline, he focused on his breathing.

In with the good, out with the bad.

Stay alert, be prepared.

With no immediate threats, his brain clawed at situational awareness. To the west, a scorched Humvee listed on the road, fire extinguisher chemicals wafting like a departing ghost from the empty turret. Other vehicles jockeyed for position around their fireteams, who used the vehicles as cover.

In the intersection, a Humvee had driven along a patch of rubble shoved aside by the bulldozer and ensnarled, whining with engine strain. Clumps of Iraqi soldiers gestured at each other to point out targets.

A SAW gunner leaned around a corner to fire in bursts of gun smoke. Coop's eyes darted to see what he was shooting at, but buildings blocked his view. Accustomed to the fog of war, he just had to trust all this chaos had a purpose.

Standing by his command vehicle, Major Haddad greeted an elderly couple who emerged from a house. They fell to their knees crying and reaching to kiss their liberator's hand. He bent to speak to them.

Mother, Uncle, Coop imagined him saying, his voice as always firm and loaded with authority. *It is not safe. Please go home.*

Horvath stood over him. "Why aren't you guys in a security perimeter?"

A round cracked through the air to puff against a nearby building.

Doc glared back. "Are you kidding?"

"I'm gaining situational awareness," said Stuckey, who appeared confused.

Coop said, "Joe. *Joe.*"

"*What?*"

"Stay low. The Iraqis have this. We'll pitch in when we're needed."

Coop hoped the CTS units would wear down the militants, consolidate their vehicles, and get back on the move. As for him and his comrades, they'd come to save Sergeant Ramos, not fight a civil war.

"Suit yourself then." Horvath glowered as he scanned windows and rooftops.

The battle proceeded in fits and starts until the hours took on a sleepy, dreamlike quality. An ISIS fighter would pop up shooting from a window somewhere, soldiers would unload on him, the fighter would break contact, and then the soldiers would wait again. As if reacting to some mysterious prearranged signal, at seemingly random times the turret guns would start rocking all at once.

The tall and slim mushroom cloud that marked the VBIED detonation at the column's rear slowly dissipated. Carrying trays of tea for the soldiers, civilians crept from their homes like groundhogs wary of their own shadow. Squads stood around smoking until a round snapped past their ears, and then they scurried back to cover asking each other if they'd seen where the round had come from.

They all tensed even further as word passed down the line another VBIED was coming. Following a monstrous roar, a smoke cloud billowed over the distant rooftops. *We got him*, the soldiers grinned. *Took him out with an AT4.*

Another hill on the emotional rollercoaster that was combat.

All the while, Coop sat with his back against one of the MRAP's big tires and then stood to scan windows with his aimpoint red dot optic and then sat again. He fired his rifle twice at movement, hoping he was in fact shooting at legit targets. Then he sat again for a while fuming he was doing something he'd sworn never to do again, regardless of how badly a part of him wanted to murder all ISIS.

He cycled through this shooting and resting until a sharp bang yanked him back to alertness from a catnap. Stuckey and Sazan still sat on the ground next to him, but Doc was gone.

Horvath blew a stream of smoke and flicked away his unfinished cig. "They're dropping grenades on us from the rooftops now."

The jihadists were getting scarily close. Coop looked up at the roof's edge overhead and wondered if a grenade was about to sail straight into his lap.

"Why aren't we moving?" he asked.

"My guess is too many vehicles are disabled," Stuckey put in.

He was right. The ISIS fighters were prioritizing knocking out the vehicles, which provided mobility and mounted the company's big guns.

"Hammadi said they hit the bulldozer," Horvath said. "We might be trapped."

"If I was in command, I'd be calling for backup," the lieutenant said.

The jihadists were too near for close air support. *Danger close*, the military called it. Even a smart bomb would be landing practically on top of the company's heads. Stuckey was talking about reinforcements or exfilling via a QRF.

Horvath scowled at the houses. "If we're staying put, we'll need to start securing these buildings. Push out a perimeter."

"Haddad knows what he's doing," Coop said. "I think."

Pinned by the ambush, the commander could either attack his way out of it or strongpoint his position and wait for reinforcements. Haddad hadn't decided yet, though Horvath was right. The major was running out of time.

Coop looked to the west and spotted him again. As always, the lanky commander paced fearlessly out in the open while he barked into a handheld radio. His radioman paced with him, holding out a phone.

A woman in a bulky abaya crept toward him, weeping and visibly shaking, arms raised as if surrendering or pleading.

Haddad glanced up at her and raised his hand. *I am sorry to make you wait, Mother, but I am in a battle at the moment.*

Then she exploded in a blinding flash.

"Jesus Christ," Coop swore.

"What's wrong?" Stuckey asked. "What was that explosion?"

"The usual." He winced at the edge of tears. "We're still good here."

Enemy Kalashnikovs rattled as if in triumph. Soldiers rushed to where Major Haddad lay in a motionless heap by his radioman, who sprawled facedown nearby, the bulky radio on his back smoking. Several of them opened fire on the nearby house.

The jihadists had strapped a backpack full of explosives onto the woman under her cloak and sent her out to die.

Sergeant Ghazi hadn't seen it. He barked orders at his squad. Sergeant Hammadi called to the Americans.

"*Ameriki!* We are taking these two houses. *Yalla.*"

"Doc!" Horvath roared at the combat medic, who was wrapping a man's leg in bandaging at the next vehicle. "We're Oscar Mike!"

Doc jogged back, med kit flapping at his hip. "We need to set up a casualty collection point!"

"Later," Hammadi said.

The Iraqi squad split into two fireteams, kicked in doors, and poured into the houses rifles first. Shotgun planted against his shoulder, Horvath went with them.

"Aman!" they called out as they cleared rooms. *"Aman!"*

Coop went in with Stuckey, Doc, and Sazan, passing a foyer to enter a spacious family room that led to a kitchen, bedrooms, and a pleasantly green courtyard.

At a glance, he knew ISIS fighters had been here and recently. Empty water bottles and breadcrusts littered the floor. All of the furniture in the house, it seemed, had been piled into one of its corners as an Alamo fighting position.

He tapped Stuckey's shoulder and signaled. The lieutenant nodded. Rifles at the ready, they advanced to make sure no one was hiding behind the mess.

They found enough space for several men to hide, but no one was there.

Then Coop looked down.

Oh, shit.

He signaled again. Stuckey aimed his rifle at the little carpet that appeared to sink into the floor.

Coop yanked it back.

And found a chiseled, square-shaped manhole leading down into the earth.

Alamo

At night, the jihadists started yelling from the house across the street.

Raising his head where he lay on the cold floor, Coop glanced over at the manhole that he and the lieutenant had covered with a credenza. The hole that led down into the ISIS tunnel network.

Nothing moved over there in the darkness. Next to him, the others stirred. Sazan remained curled around her weapon, though her eyes were open and alert.

Coop shifted his rifle to aim through the foyer toward the front door, ear cocked for the tramp of feet signaling the jihadists were coming to finish it.

"What is it?" Doc said, his voice edged with anxiety. "What are they saying?"

Among the Americans, he'd seen the most action that day, roaming up and down the street to treat wounds. He hadn't fired his weapon once; when it came to shooting, Doc dithered and froze.

As always, however, he proved utterly fearless as a medic.

"They are saying what they are going to do to us," Sergeant Hammadi said gloomily in the dark. "After they capture us."

"Smack talk," Stuckey said. "Just ignore it."

All day, the jihadists had chipped away at the company's vehicles, then its command structure, and then its men. Reinforced by fresh squads, CTS's enemies seemed to multiply as the day wore on. As night fell, the front line moved up, and ISIS fighters now had the exhausted company more or less surrounded.

On the CTS side, most of the vehicles had been disabled. Eight men were dead. Thirty were wounded, most of these still in the fight but running low on ammunition and water like everyone else.

Now the jihadists were trying to wear down what was left of their morale.

Coop lowered his rifle, though he was still bristling.

"I'd give my left nut for a pair of lousy NVGs," Horvath growled.

A soldier came down the stairs and crossed the room toward one of the windows, where Azim stood watch with his SAW. Judging by his limp, it was Omar, who'd caught a ricochet in his thigh during the rooftop fighting that broke out after the short unspoken truce for evening salat.

The man hobbled to the gated window, pulled the curtain a few inches to the side, and shouted back a long, withering stream of Arabic so colorful that Azim and Hammadi burst out laughing.

"He's going to get us killed," muttered Horvath.

Azim crouched and moved quietly to the other side of the room, where he'd bored a firing hole through the wall with a hammer and chisel earlier in the day. Sergeant Hammadi hustled over and patted him on the shoulder.

The gunner gently inserted the barrel of his SAW through the hole and waited.

Finishing his tirade, Omar ducked down.

A voice called out: *"Allah akbar!"*

Muzzle flashes erupted across the street, the rounds chewing the outer wall and sparking off the MRAP still parked outside. Azim shifted aim and let off several controlled bursts.

The shooting stopped.

Hammadi exchanged a grinning high-five with the big SAW gunner while Omar started yelling again in triumph, using Haddad's name.

This time, Coop could easily guess what he hurled at ISIS.

Fuck you, Daesh, you sons of whores! That was for Haddad!

The reaction was instant and general.

Rifles rattled in windows and across the flat roofs and cracked against walls and parapets. The gated window strobed in tracer light as Omar emptied his M4. A grenade burst in the courtyard behind Coop.

Stuckey shifted to cover the rear while Coop and Horvath aimed their weapons at the front door. In an instant, they achieved three-sixty-degree security.

A man on the roof cried for a medic. Doc jumped to his feet and banged up the stairs with his med kit.

The battle raged for another minute before petering out with a final RPG burst near the roof that shook the house.

The ensuing silence rang in their ears.

"Guys," Stuckey said in a solemn, thoughtful tone.

"No," said Horvath.

"I'm starting to think we won't—"

"Shut up, sir," he growled. "Don't even think it."

But they did think it.

Reaching Ramos at this point had become impossible.

Less than a few hundred yards from where they believed the sergeant was being held prisoner, Mosul's war had stopped them cold.

"We're definitely going to think about it," Coop told Horvath and then added to Stuckey, "But not yet, LT. We may get another lucky break."

Stuckey sighed. "Shit. I really miss my kids."

They were shivering and miserable and scared. By the minute, Erbil and its comforts sounded better and better.

Sazan whispered, "There is a way..."

"A way? What do you mean? A way we can reach Ramos?"

"Let her talk," said Horvath. "Go ahead..."

Sergeant Ghazi lumbered sideways down the stairs, hauling a groaning man in a fireman's carry.

"Doc's upstairs," Coop said.

Grim-faced, the squad leader gently placed the wounded man on the ground.

Stuckey gasped. "Oh, no."

Doc's face glowed white in the gloom, a drooling rictus of pain. Shrapnel had riddled his left leg, which he'd apparently tourniqueted himself.

Drawing his knife, Coop sawed away the pantleg. Stuckey ransacked the med kit for supplies. Sazan gently lifted Doc's head to insert a pillow.

Wincing at the edge of tears, Horvath remained frozen.

"Damn it, Doc," he groaned.

Ghazi removed his own canteen and placed it on Doc's chest. *"Shookran."*

Thanking Doc for mending his boys today. This done, the hulking sergeant got back to his feet and trudged back up the stairs.

Coop hesitated. *Doc's a good man. One of the truly good ones. He didn't deserve this. He just wanted to help people.*

He compartmentalized it and got back to work.

Working by penlight, he tweezered pieces of metal from the pale and purpled flesh. Stuckey packed sterile gauze into the larger wounds and then taped thick padded bandages over them.

The lieutenant sighed with relief. "It missed his femoral artery."

They removed the tourniquet and gave him another thorough inspection. It was looking good. There was a solid chance to save the man and the leg as well.

Doc's eyes, however, had turned glassy.

At last, Horvath moved. He took the man's hand and gripped it.

"Stay with us, Doc," he said. "We're going to get you out. You'll be back to lecturing us dumb shits in no time."

Doc smiled weakly and nodded.

"All we brought is Ibuprofen," Coop said, reaching for the bottle.

"Ghazi gave me a shot," Doc said dreamily. "I'm feeling fine. You did good, Coop. You and the LT. You guys should have been medics."

Utterly drained, Coop sat back and replied with a single numb nod. Now that he had nothing to do, he was exhausted.

"Joe's right," he said. "As soon as relief arrives, we'll get you out."

"No," said Doc.

Coop exchanged a worried glance with Stuckey. "You're *gonna* be okay."

"The mission."

"Don't worry about that," Stuckey told him. "We're done. I'm sorry, Doc. This was a mistake, and it's on me. I never should have talked you guys into—'"

"It wasn't your decision, Hud."

The lieutenant chewed his lip and said nothing.

"Get Ramos, if you're still willing," Doc murmured. "I don't want to hear he's gonna die because I got hit. If there's still a chance you can do it, take it."

"We have to see what our options are," Coop said. "If there's a way forward, then maybe. If there isn't, it's not on you, okay?"

"Promise me. You'll drive on."

Coop took his other hand and squeezed it. "We promise, Doc. If it's possible, we'll do it."

The man didn't hear it. For a while, they listened to his slow and steady breathing.

"He's asleep," Horvath said.

The lieutenant took a deep, ragged breath.

"All right. This is it. I…"

He froze, stricken with guilt and indecision. His movie-thriller plan to rescue Ramos, so audacious that it conveyed a strange and compelling plausibility, had nearly killed one of the men for whom he felt responsible.

A man to whom he'd promised they wouldn't be looking for trouble.

What good was saving Ramos if one of them was lost—maybe two, maybe all of them? What if he himself were killed, and his boys grew up without a father?

He knew why he'd come, and he'd done that.

How far did he have to go?

The gravity of it seemed to weigh on him until he could barely breathe.

He started again. "I…"

"Yeah. What are we doing?" Horvath wondered aloud.

Coop turned to Sazan. "Is there a way or not?"

The Peshmerga pointed toward the furniture piled in the corner.

The tunnel.

Coop said nothing. No one did.

Nothing needed saying.

The way led into a tunnel network possibly crawling with ISIS fighters. Through a dark passage that would take them deep into enemy territory.

They'd be going alone, without any backup, and if they were captured, they'd be tortured and murdered on jihadist TV.

Another lucky break that only offered another open path to even greater danger. An option so horrible that they hadn't even considered it.

Burying themselves alive.

That was the only way forward.

And it was either that or go back to Erbil and await Ramos's beheading.

Coop bowed his head in quick meditation, though his thoughts fired on full cyclic. The philosophy that kept him straight back in the real world allowed him to act or not act here, as long as it was without desire, but that wasn't possible.

But even desire chewed him up with indecision. He desired to rescue Ramos. He also desired that no more of his friends get hurt. He wanted these equally.

Then he pictured himself going home. Climbing back into his old familiar truck and driving around America. Always restless, never home.

"I'll go," Coop said. "I'll do it alone."

He wasn't giving up yet, not while he had purpose and a viable path.

"Hang on a minute," Stuckey said.

"You heard Doc, LT. It was your idea, but it's not your decision. It never was."

The lieutenant scowled at him. "Okay. My turn this time. What's the plan? How are you going to get in and out?"

"I'll follow the tunnel and egress as close to the police station as I can, hole up somewhere until dark, and then go in with surprise and the violence of action."

Horvath chuckled. "Goddamn, Coop. I never heard anything so stupid and so awesome in my life. I'm in."

Coop didn't know whether to be relieved or horrified. "Are you sure?"

"What else am I gonna do? Go home and find some dead-end job, pay bills, argue with my bank? And while I'm golfing, I can think about the time I walked away when I had the chance to save Ramos's life? All or nothing, brother. I'm in."

"Shit," said Stuckey, who looked like he'd just been asked to eat some.

The lieutenant had come here out of a romantic ideal for his military days born from restless middle age. A longing for adventure and meaning. What he'd gotten was way more than he'd bargained. Their mission had completely changed from pushing someone to save Ramos to saving Ramos themselves.

In the end, Carol was right. He had to make a choice what was more important to him. This should have been easy for him, but it wasn't.

Not at all.

"Go home to your family, LT," Coop said. "We'll take it from here. Whatever happens, if it's good, it's your win too. We wouldn't be here if it weren't for you. If it's bad, then, well, it's on us. We're making this call."

"You and Sazan can make sure Doc gets back safe," Horvath put in.

Sazan frowned. "You are deciding for me?"

"I just thought—"

"*I* decide for me, *Ameriki*. And I am going."

"You know where we're going."

"Yes."

"Then why the hell would you want to?"

"I told you. Daesh is my problem too. This is our fight."

Horvath let out an exasperated sigh. "Then why not do it with the Peshmerga?"

"Your Ramos is a good man. He came to help the people of Iraq. He deserves better. He deserves someone to help him. You are willing to risk your life to do it. You deserve someone to help you. I am here. So I will go."

"Well. Okay, then." He didn't like it, but he respected it.

"Okay, then," said Sazan.

"The same goes for me," Stuckey said. "I guess I'm coming too. I don't think I'd be able to live with myself if I let you all go without me."

Sergeant Hammadi slowly got to his feet and stomped over to the credenza. Heaving, he hauled it scraping across the floor and set it back down.

"If you go, then go," he said. "Captain Jaafar is in command now. When the relief column comes, he will make you return with us."

Coop looked down at Doc. "Somebody should stay with him."

The sergeant placed his hand over his heart. "He took care of us. We will take care of him." Making it an oath, he raised his hand and added, *"Wallah."*

Coop looked at Horvath and Stuckey, who nodded. Sergeant Hammadi was a good man and would honor his word.

He patted Doc's shoulder. "I'm glad you're not coming for this part, brother."

Horvath said, "See you on the other side, Doc."

Stuckey finished scribbling a note and crouched to put it in the man's shirt pocket. A note for his wife, Coop knew. Just in case.

The lieutenant stood with a sigh. "Okay, we're Oscar Mike."

They gathered around the manhole, where Hammadi offered Coop a final gift, which was a hand grenade. Knowing the man was dangerously low on ammunition, Coop gave him one of his rifle magazines. He now had two left, hopefully enough for what he had in mind.

The Iraqi extended his hand. "May Allah guide you, *Ameriki*."

Coop shook it warmly. "*Shookran*, Sergeant. For keeping us safe today."

He passed the grenade on to Horvath, who would know exactly when and how it should be used. Then he attached his flashlight to his RK62 and aimed the powerful beam down the length of a ladder, where the darkness swallowed it.

He'd made the call to keep going. He should go first. He took a deep breath, expecting another bout of jingling nerves.

Instead, he felt surprisingly steady.

"Well," he said. "Here goes nothing."

He descended into darkness.

I Love You

January 2005.
    Fifteen months into Coop's deployment—
    Twenty-two days and a wakeup before he redeployed home—
    Oh-dark-thirty, the waning moon having set hours ago—
    Counter mortar mission at OP Applejack.
    On a promontory overlooking the Tigris River, near a cluster of half-built, unfinished houses, 1st Squad gazed out across the waters toward East Mosul. Parts of it glittered with lights, the rest dark due to electricity shortages.
    Kalashnikovs rattled in the distance, which set a pack of local stray dogs living near the hill braying and howling. Tracers lazily streamed into the sky to wink out before they reached the stars.
    "You break it, you own it," Horvath said.
    "Word," Reyes agreed.
    "Once you give a war, you can't take it back."
    "Word to the max."
    The hill was in a marshy area, surrounded by tall reeds. Out in the dark, the river, livened by the winter rains, gurgled past with force. The soldiers shivered, though they didn't mind the chilly night. In the summer, mosquitoes and other feasting bugs came out in multitudes, and the river carried a fishy outhouse smell.
    Camp Courage, the other major American forward operating base in Mosul, lay situated across the river in one of Saddam's old palaces. In keeping with the Iraqi dictator's penchant for the grandiose, it had been named the Palace of Swords. Now it housed American infantry and task force administrative personnel.
    The Gamblers had come here to wait for it to get mortared again. If the mortars were fired from their side of the river, they'd

mount up, rush out to place of origin, and do some half-hearted ghost hunting that hopefully didn't involve them getting wacked in an ambush.

Long gone were the days when even this night shift job carried any sense of adventure. It hadn't taken long to recognize it for what it was, a mind-numbingly boring tasking. So close to the end of their deployment, it was now excruciating.

Coop's fireteam hadn't gotten through the last fifteen months without a scratch, but they had gotten through it. They were alive and in one piece. The Bravo half of the squad hadn't been so lucky, with Sergeant Franks convalescing at Rammstein Air Base in Germany and Jerry Thompson blown to bits on their own turf.

In the home stretch, with the end in sight, Ramos had quietly replaced the old standing order of engaging the enemy with a new one: "Nobody gets hurt."

No heroics, no risks.

They'd already been there, done that for almost a year and a half.

Following that order would be no easy task, however. Mosul was becoming more dangerous by the day, particularly with the historic Iraqi election coming up.

To Coop, the political rivalry splitting the country was absurd even for the Middle East. He'd arrived in-country believing Sunnis and Shias had fundamental religious differences akin to Catholics and Baptists, but he'd learned it was based almost entirely on a political dispute fourteen hundred years ago.

After Mohammad died in 632 AD, a debate erupted over who would succeed him. One side believed it should be someone in Mohammad's bloodline; they eventually became the Shias. The other side believed it could be any pious man who would follow the same path as the Prophet; they became the Sunnis. Otherwise, they worshipped the same God in almost the exact same way.

Shias constituted a majority in only four Muslim countries, two of which were Iran and Iraq. Under Saddam, the Sunnis dominated the country, but Saddam was gone, and with democratic elections coming up, the Sunnis knew they were going to lose. As far as they were concerned, not only their power and wealth but even their survival was on the line.

They'd go on fighting.

The Gamblers, meanwhile, would continue patrolling and raiding outside the wire as security conditions steadily worsened.

Six months earlier, American forces across the entire city had seen maybe three or four enemy contacts a day. Now it averaged thirty—often sustained, toe-to-toe firefights like the one they'd survived at Yarmouk Traffic Circle. After the Christmas D-Fac bombing, they'd rolled out to engage the enemy in a cold fury, but that fury was spent, a baton passed to the unit replacing theirs.

The men glumly eyed Camp Courage standing among a hateful city.

"Welp," Murray said, looking at the city he'd hoped to love, developed indifference toward, and finally grew to hate. "Nobody can say we didn't try."

Over a year ago, they'd come to a freshly liberated Iraq to keep the peace while it transitioned into a free and prosperous country, all of it sounding great in their ears. They were the tip of democracy's spear. They'd come to make things better.

From where they stood now, however, things only looked worse.

"Our country called us," Ramos set them all straight. "We answered. At the end of the day, that's all you boys need to know."

Our country called us. We answered.

Coop thought of the silence after the platoon sergeant called for Thompson at roll call. Three times he called, each time answered only by silence, producing a fresh bout of mourning in the platoon.

The previous day, the crowded memorial service for the victims of the D-Fac bombing had similarly been powerful and moving for Coop and his comrades. More than twenty battle crosses—boots, upright rifles, helmets, and dog tags—stood in a line.

And the chaplain read from Psalms:

"'Praise the Lord, who is my rock. He trains my hands for war and gives my fingers skill for battle... May our sons flourish in their youth like well-nurtured plants. May our daughters be like graceful pillars, carved to beautify a palace. May our barns be filled with crops of every kind. May the flocks in our fields multiply by the thousands, even tens of thousands, and may our oxen be loaded down with produce. May there be no enemy breaking through our walls, no going into captivity, no cries of alarm in our

town squares. Yes, joyful are those who live like this! Joyful indeed are those whose God is the Lord.'"

By the time the bugler played Taps, almost everyone was weeping.

Thompson was a freak. No one in the squad really liked him. But he'd died in the line of duty. Regardless of who he was in life, in death he became one of the war's true heroes.

His famous last words, *You got to be the ball*, became a catchphrase across the platoon. And they could picture him wearing his annoying smile and saying, *You were never better than me. Why did you get to live?*

Standing in the miserable cold on a hilltop in Mosul, Coop didn't want to wait until someone died to let them know how much he'd depended on them to get him through this.

"I love you guys," he said. "I just thought you should know that."

The squad smiled back at him, disarmed for the moment but no doubt pondering how best to ride his ass for expressing such an earnest sentiment.

"It warms my heart," Ramos said. "Since you're all feeling the love, I think it's time to talk about re-upping."

The boys laughed.

"No need to go that far, Sarnt," Horvath said.

"I'll re-up if Bush and Cheney enlist," Reyes said. "All that *bring it on* tough talk. If they make it through boot and last a month out here, I'll become a lifer."

"Sad to hear it, you guys," said Murray, who'd decided to make a career of military service. "You're gonna miss the party."

"I *might* re-up if the staff sarnt tells me he loves me," Horvath said, unable to resist poking the bear. "Since Coop was man enough to share his feelings."

Ramos snorted. "If you—"

Lieutenant Stuckey popped onto their radios. "Gamblers Six to 2-1."

Ramos keyed his mike. "This is 2-1. Send it, sir."

"Location, status?"

"We're on the grassy knoll overlooking the river, putting eyes on Camp Courage."

"Be advised 2-2 spotted an Iraqi individual approaching the hill from the south. They lost him in the reeds. No positive ID as an insurgent."

"Appreciate the heads up, Six. We'll take care of it."

Coop pulled his NVGs into place and took a knee while Ramos placed most of his shooters in the small clearing facing south, Coop and Horvath facing west, and Reyes on rear guard pointed north.

The minutes dragged by in silence.

At last, they heard rustling in the reeds at the base of the hill. Coop couldn't help but glance over in that direction. A man stood at the bottom of the slope and looked around to orient himself. He carried a Kalashnikov rifle.

The squad opened up on him in strobing flashes and a murderous roar, venting their bottled stress and rage for a furious full mag each.

Ramos waved his hand. "Cease fire. Cease fire!"

"Yeah, he's down," Murray said.

Gambino, Bravo's SAW gunner, chuckled. "And then some—"

"GRENADE!" Ramos hurled himself into the tall grass.

Coop dove with a clatter of gear as Reyes unleashed a withering blast into the reeds to the north and then hunkered down himself against the expected blast.

For a half-minute, the squad lay in the cold, dewy grass.

"Status," they heard over the radio. "Sitrep."

Coop sat up and looked around. The rest of his squad did the same.

The hill was quiet.

"What happened?" Horvath asked.

"The sarnt called out a grenade," Murray said. "Only it wasn't."

Sometimes, the insurgents threw rocks to try to flush American soldiers out of their fighting positions into fields of fire.

"And then I lit that fucker up," Reyes boasted. "He's down."

"If there had been a grenade, we'd all be dead," Horvath put in.

Murray glared at Reyes. "He got close enough to toss rocks at us? You were sightseeing the firefight, you asshole. You weren't covering your sector."

"Don't be so hard, Sarnt M. It all worked out, didn't it?"

Coop gaped at Ramos's prostrate form still lying where he'd fallen. "Sergeant?"

Their squad leader didn't move.

"Is he hit?" Horvath reached to give his shoulder a little shake. "He's breathing steady, but he's stiff as a board. Something isn't right."

Murray radioed the lieutenant a sitrep and asked for Doc, who came flying through the reeds so fast they almost shot him.

Doc plunged to his knees next to Ramos and started feeling for wounds. "Are you sure he was hit?"

Coop exchanged a worried glance with Horvath. Anxious, the others shrugged. They weren't sure of anything.

"Sergeant Murray, help me turn him over," Doc said. "Gently."

Murray helped him flip Ramos onto his back.

The man looked fine, only he wasn't.

He wasn't fine at all.

He was *weeping*.

Something these men had never thought they'd live long enough to see.

Coop started. "Guys…"

He pointed at the ground.

Together, they stared at the old Russian grenade that had failed to explode.

The Tunnel

The earth enveloped him.

Stooping to fit under the low ceiling, Coop aimed his rifle and its flashlight down the passage. The beam weakly illuminated a long and narrow tunnel carved from dirt and rock. Beyond maybe twenty feet, the darkness ate the light.

The air down here felt as thin as a coffin's. The atmosphere was about as foreboding as he'd expected. What in the Army he would have called a *danger zone*. The walls, already confined to single-file marching, appeared to inch closer.

The others came down and tested the air with deep inhalations, breathing in the rich and bitter scents of dirt and minerals.

"Pucker factor on a scale of one to ten," Horvath whispered. "Coop?"

"Eleven," Coop murmured.

Behind them, the credenza slid back into place. If they wanted back out before CTS bugged out, all they had to do was rap a recognized signal.

Still, the hole being covered felt all too much like being entombed.

Horvath tapped his shoulder, and Coop started forward.

After several minutes of walking, he resisted the urge to look back the way he'd come, which he knew would tell him nothing and only disorient him more.

Don't worry about it, he told himself. *The tunnel parallels the east-west road. Every step is taking you closer to the police station.*

The irrational part of his mind was barely listening. It didn't care where the road went. It just wanted out of here. At least part of his rational mind agreed.

The darkness surrounding his light beam was total, giving the impression of floating through a void. Aside from their footfalls and breathing, the quiet was complete. The atmosphere produced a blank slate for loose thoughts and primal fears that gained power the deeper Coop went into the ISIS honeycombs.

What if ISIS fighters were just ahead in the darkness, mouthing their prayers while they waited to jump him?

What if again, that old magic. It not only inspired humans to legendary heroics but paralyzed them with visions of failure.

Coop realized he didn't fear death so much as being captured. Being manhandled and beaten by hateful men who couldn't be reasoned with and who considered inflicting pain on their enemies a sick virtue. Utterly powerless as a punching bag, with no hope of escape or relief except a violent death.

Fighting the darkness now, his legs trembled. His breath turned shallow.

As if sensing his surging dread, Horvath gave his back another gentle pat.

Coop fell back on his training. Not his military but the personal training he'd given himself based on what he took from Buddhism.

Focus on his breath, accept what his eyes told him, and allow his mind to race but refuse to let any single thought take command.

In this way, he stopped living in the future and its worst-case scenarios and accepted he was here, now, and he was okay.

He froze as a deep *whump* overhead produced a short drizzle of dirt crumbs falling from the low ceiling. He guessed they'd reached the head of the embattled CTS column.

From here, the police station stood maybe two or three football fields away.

Horvath blew out a sigh. Coop nodded as if his friend had said something he agreed with, and started forward again.

A bright blob burned like a beacon in the distance. Stuckey's tunnel analogy had manifested as real, and here was its light.

A light meant a way forward or even a way out. It also meant the tunnel ahead was an area more heavily trafficked by fighters, which meant danger.

"They left the lights on for us," said Horvath, as always embracing the Suck.

Coop continued on, marking his steps with a slow, steady tread, rifle planted and ready to shoot. His arms ached from the mounting strain, but he ignored it.

The light steadily grew brighter.

The passage reached a T intersection. Ahead, incandescent bulbs strung along the ceiling illuminated a wider tunnel, marking it as an older and more important artery.

Killing his flashlight, Coop stopped at the intersection while the others stacked behind him. Horvath tapped his shoulder, and they sprang into action with weapons leveled, ready to shoot anything they saw.

The adjoining tunnel, however, lay empty.

Stuckey had gone ahead to cover Coop's flank. He hissed for their attention. Slowly lowering his rifle, Coop walked over to join the others.

Together, they gazed at a limestone relief that was three thousand years old.

The carving depicted a king with a curled beard surrounded by courtiers and winged, muscular protector spirits. The panels continued down the passage, most of them celebrating the military victories of an invincible ancient army.

Archers drew their bows at city walls while sappers tunneled underground. Warriors beheaded, stabbed, and impaled prisoners. Centuries before the internet, the Assyrians had mastered the violent propaganda that ISIS would later perfect.

In the fourteenth century BC, this little kingdom cast off the yoke of Babylon. The Assyrians subsequently expanded into a mighty empire that lasted eight hundred years and stretched from Egypt to the Caucasus, from Persia to eastern Anatolia. Nineveh, buried under modern-day East Mosul, had stood as the rich imperial capital until a Chaldean-Elamite-Median alliance bloodily sacked it.

Coop was looking at history and, in a way, its strange, churning repetition.

ISIS regularly destroyed ancient artifacts like these, claiming they promoted polytheism. By erasing the past, they sought to cleanse the future and safeguard the integrity of the Muslim faith.

For some reason, they'd spared these reliefs.

Perhaps they saw themselves in the Assyrians, who had built a powerful empire through ruthless terror and merciless violence considered brutal even for its period's savage norms. Like the Assyrians, ISIS sought to cleanse the world with its enemies' blood and also faced a coalition that fought to end its scourge.

Stuckey smiled. "Doc would have loved—"

Horvath signaled for silence discipline, and the lieutenant shut it. The sergeant waved them forward, this time taking the lead with the combat shotgun.

Coop followed with his rifle at the low ready, wheeling every five to ten steps to check their six. Next to him, Sazan fell into a rhythm of alternating with him so the team was constantly moving while checking the rear.

The narrow tunnel shrouded in pitch black had been bad enough. This wider, lit passage was even worse.

The hot, bare bulbs producing shadows that flickered in his peripheral vision—

The vast, intimidating size of this underground network—

The vulnerability of maneuvering exposed with no cover or concealment aside from bits of loose trash and the occasional empty crate—

If ISIS fighters showed up now, they'd either have to shoot their way through or run all the way back to the beginning.

The team reached another intersection.

Horvath and Stuckey swung to cover while Coop and Sazan bounded. Then Coop and Sazan covered while the men bounded back to point.

They traveled down the tunnel at a steady brisk pace, acting not as individuals but as a single organism. Coop moved without thought, allowing his old training to revive and assert itself.

Voices ahead.

Two men speaking in Arabic. A side corridor. Someone laughed.

The team froze in place.

Watching the rear, Sazan took a knee. Coop signaled for her to stay there while he turned to find out what Horvath had in mind.

They had three choices. Try to sneak past undetected, engage the unseen enemy, or retreat either to a side passage that led who knew where or all the way back to the beginning.

Horvath ordered Coop to take an overwatch position, and he automatically obeyed. Whatever the sergeant had in mind, now wasn't the time to debate.

Personally, he hoped they'd withdraw. The corridor stretched into the distance front and back. Tactically, this was a horrible position.

One long fatal funnel.

Horvath communicated with Stuckey in an elaborate series of hand signals. The lieutenant blanched but nodded. He understood.

Shit, Coop thought. *We're engaging.*

He wasn't as scared as he thought he'd be. Mostly, he felt a deep relief. Retracing their steps to find a new route would probably only put them in the same predicament with the added risk of traveling even farther from their destination.

Horvath signaled Stuckey again.

Three, two, one—

Horvath swung into the side corridor. His shotgun roared in fierce muzzle flash, high-velocity buckshot flying to pierce and shred flesh. Still blanching, Stuckey hustled into position, braced his feet, and let off two rocking bursts.

"Clear," Horvath said. "Coop, take Sazan across and hold in place."

Coop darted forward. A glance revealed two bodies lying next to weapons. Then they were gone as he passed the corridor.

Taking a knee again, he looked and listened. Nothing happened.

Voices shouted at the end of the hall.

"Dormitory," Sazan said. Crouched behind him, she pointed at a wayfinding sign hanging over the tunnel entrance. "There is a *dormitory down there*."

A lot of jihadists were now wide awake and moving.

Horvath growled as he sized up their situation.

"Okay, the LT and I will hold them here. Coop, you and Sazan go forward, find an exit, and secure—"

Feet stamped in the corridor. The first rounds cracked to puff against the dirt wall.

ISIS fighters were coming. A lot of them.

Everything Horvath said had made sense to Coop. Of course, they'd defend here, where they could use the corners as cover and the enemy would have to pass through a fatal funnel. Naturally, he'd send the element he wasn't using forward to secure a friendly, defendable position ahead.

Still, he hesitated. He hated splitting up.

"Go!" With that, Horvath leaned to deliver another blast.

Coop jumped to his feet and broke into a jog with his RK62 shouldered at the low ready. Sazan panted at his side.

He spared a glance over his shoulder to see Horvath rip the tape off Hammadi's grenade and pull the pin, allowing the spoon to tumble away.

"Frag out!" He tossed it into the corridor as Stuckey ducked down.

BOOM

Billowing dust fumed from the entrance. Horvath popped up again to empty his shotgun into the brown veil.

Then Coop was moving again. The next time he glanced back, his comrades were barely visible, though he heard the shooting well enough.

Sazan yelled something at him. In her excitement, she'd reverted to her native Kurdish, though her meaning was clear enough.

She'd found a little side tunnel.

Heading back into the dark space, he turned on his flashlight, which revealed a ladder going up.

Had they gone far enough? Time and space warped in the tunnel, but he suspected they were closer to the police station than the embattled CTS company.

In the end, it didn't matter. He'd been ordered to egress here, so he'd do it.

The *tuk-tuk-tuk-tuk* of Stuckey's Kalashnikov sounded from down the tunnel. Coop hesitated, pulled by the firefight's gravity.

"We're going up," he said.

He snapped a chemlight and dropped it at his feet to mark the position for the others. This done, he slung his rifle, chambered a round in his Tokarev, and pulled himself up the rungs.

The exit was unblocked. At the top, he stopped to look and listen.

Nothing.

Signaling to Sazan to follow, Coop hauled himself out of the manhole and started clearing rooms. Aside from a few empty plastic water bottles and passageways bored through neighboring homes, he found no sign of ISIS fighters.

The house stood silent and seemingly empty.

Here, the firefight below ground reached him only as distant, muffled booms. He thought he'd hear shooting back from where the CTS was under siege, but either the battle had reached a lull or they'd been rescued by a relief column.

Outside, the sun had risen, its light again filtered gloomy and gray by the overcast sky.

Sazan met him back at the hole. "All rooms are clear. What now?"

"I'm going back to help Joe and the LT bound out of there. You wait here."

She nodded.

The atmosphere overhead tore open with a breathless wail. A moment later, the house across the street burst and crumbled in an avalanche of masonry.

At the first bright flash, Coop understood.

The CTS hauled ass and called in an artillery strike.

He gripped Sazan's arm. "Back down the ladder!"

They clambered down as the artillery barrage pounded the area. *This is not good.* With big shells raining topside, their exit was effectively cut off.

At the bottom, he shouted: "Wait here!"

Coop dashed back toward Horvath and Stuckey while the barrage tore the neighborhood apart over his head. The deafening booms shook the tunnel. The lights danced crazily on their wires until the power died. Clods of dirt crumbled and poured from the dissolving ceiling and down the walls.

Muzzle flashes burst like sparks in the distance and then disappeared.

"Joe!"

Staggering, he turned on his flashlight but saw nothing beyond a thick veil of dust that already had him choking.

Another shell landed close overhead, the sound alone making him stumble, his head vibrating with reverberations.

"LT! *Shit!*"

BOOM BOOM BOOM

The close succession of heavy impacts drove him to his knees.

The tunnel around him dissolved. Dirt avalanched across the floor. Chunks of ceiling plummeted in his flashlight's grainy, dying beam.

Pieces thumped across his head and shoulders. A shard of concrete struck his neck with a sharp pain.

In the cascading roar, Coop thought he heard Stuckey scream something. He lurched forward only to stop as his anxious worries about his comrades shifted into blind terror that he himself was about to die.

Bolting back down the corridor pelted by falling rocks and dirt, he found Sazan quaking at the base of the ladder.

He wrapped his arms around her and surrendered himself to fate.

This is it—

The Crucible

With a final heavy thud, the barrage stopped.

Slowly, reluctantly, Coop uncoiled.

The walls around him had held. Through shifting swarms of dust particles, daylight feebly glowed in the manhole above.

"Are you okay?" he heard himself asking, though his voice sounded muffled and distant in his ears, as if someone else were talking.

Unable to speak, the Peshmerga's head jerked in a nod.

He stood and dusted himself off as best he could, leaving dry smears. Slowly, methodically, he checked himself and his weapons. He felt along his aching neck, but his hand came away bloodless.

Still fit, Coop thought. *Now back on point.*

Wary of another collapse, he crept back into the tunnel.

And found the way sealed by tons of earth and rock.

Sazan finally found her voice, which came out tinny and faraway: "They…"

Coop shook his head, which produced a wince of pain, and returned to climb the ladder again. At the top, he found the house still standing, though every single object in it had been rattled and tossed like peanuts in a jar.

Nothing stirred except waves of dust still settling from the bombardment.

He similarly spotted no movement in the passageways exposing the neighboring homes. The one leading east ran through a single house before terminating in smoking wreckage. The final hit that had stoved in the tunnel.

The passage running west appeared more or less clear. Across the street, all the houses in view had been pounded into skeletal masonry and rubble.

He removed a water bottle from its pouch, swished a mouthful, and spat. He handed the bottle to Sazan and fumbled in another pouch until he palmed his cellphone.

No Wi-Fi here, and no cellular service either, it seemed. But phones didn't need either for GPS.

Inspecting the map glowing in his hand, he rasped: "We're real close."

His voice still sounded muffled over the loud, grating ring in his ears.

Taking a long drink, Sazan eyed him for any sign of emotion.

Coop readied his rifle and tramped west, stooping through the holes to enter new houses. In the third, he found a family cowering under the stairs and ignored them. In the fourth, dead bodies that stank of rot.

He proceeded this way until he reached the end of the block, where he checked his phone again. Putting it away, he pulled aside a window curtain and peered out.

The police station was within view, its walls pitted but intact.

A black ISIS flag hung from a pole over the door.

He turned to find Sazan gaping back at him with wild eyes.

"It's on me now," Coop told her. "We wait until dark, and then I'm going to go rescue Ramos. That's the plan. Understood?"

She studied him again with her probing stare. "I am coming too."

He shrugged. So numb he didn't care either way.

A long day of waiting lay ahead of him. He sat under the window with his back against the wall and closed his eyes for a moment. He thought about scarfing an MRE for the calories but couldn't summon an appetite. He found a pack of cigarettes in his pockets and lit one, only to hand it off to the woman after a single drag. He set out his cleaning kit and started field stripping his weapon.

Coop removed the magazine and cleared the rifle. Then he removed the parts: dustcover, recoil spring, bolt carrier group and connected piston, and the bolt.

"Load your nuts," he muttered. "And drive on."

Believing these words would empower him like more soldier magic, he'd said them with determination.

Instead, something inside him broke.

The lieutenant screaming during the collapse, which Coop realized now had been a simple repetition: *Jeremy! Jeremy!*

He let out a choking sob. The metal parts in his lap dissolved in a hot blur.

I failed. I should have kept going to reach them.

If you did, you'd be dead. Buried in that tunnel.

I could have helped. I missed something. Something important.

It was out of your hands. Man up and deal with it.

Sazan crouched in front of him and gave his shoulder a shove. He barely felt it. His ears rang even louder. She hissed scolding words in Kurdish, as if too upset to use English, though he understood her well enough.

Get your shit together. Get it together or we're dead.

He nodded but kept on sobbing, his face a mess of tears and snot. A stricken expression crossed the woman's face, and then she was crying too.

In a motherly gesture, she took his bowed head and cradled it against her chest, her cheek hot against the back of his head.

In this way, they mourned Horvath and Stuckey together.

Coop steeled himself with a shudder. "I'm not giving up. I'm just hurting."

Whether it was my fault or not doesn't matter, he thought. *I can do right by them and finish the mission.*

Make it all mean something.

Even now, he was trying to recreate the story he needed to go on.

"I was wrong," she murmured. "Grief arrives in a ton and leaves by the pound. Take your time. Take your time, and then be strong for us again."

He remembered another proverb the Peshmerga had shared as a warning during that first day's long drive into the war zone: *Every bad has its worse.*

He had believed in his story hard enough he'd thought it was real, but this had only been another illusion. War made a mockery of stories, creating and destroying them at its fickle whim without any regard for karma or any other moral balance.

Take your time, Sazan had told him. He didn't have time. Focusing on his breathing, his body calmed. Shunning his racing thoughts, he compartmentalized again.

He didn't move, however. Whatever his feelings, he took strength from Sazan's embrace, while he knew he was helping her mourn. This he had time for.

Outside, a rising wind whistled through the ruins. The light dimmed.

A storm was coming.

And when it arrived only minutes later, the wind suddenly raged in a fury, splattering Mosul not with nourishing rain but scouring sands.

The sky turned tan then pink and finally a bright, angry red.

Shamal, the Iraqis called it. A gale.

Out west, a thunderstorm sucked air into it until collapsing, its rain evaporating in the arid air to accelerate the downdraft, which blew gusting winds in all directions but strongest in its easterly travel path.

Striking the desert, these winds swept tons of dust into a raging, moving wall reaching as high as ten thousand feet.

Grand and terrifying, the *shamal* now swept over Mosul.

Headlights blazing in the swirling dust, a truck rumbled over wreckage outside, grinding gears as it shifted. Sazan stood to gaze out the window, using her keffiyeh to shield her face against the stinging sands.

The truck stopped and idled.

Coop hurriedly lubricated, scrubbed, and wiped his rifle's internal parts as needed and reassembled them. He checked the mag and slapped it into its well.

"Trouble?" he asked.

He hadn't expected anyone to be moving in this sandstorm, but of course ISIS would make the best of it. The *shamal* allowed them to move freely without being targeted by planes, which were grounded on their airfields for the duration.

"Come," Sazan breathed. "Come see."

Raising his own keffiyeh around his face, he squinted into boiling dust that rustled against the buildings in billions of tiny impacts.

He couldn't see much of anything. It was like looking at the street through reddish tan TV static. As his eyes adjusted, he made out the dark hulk of the truck parked in front of the police station under the snapping black flag.

A huddle of figures moved into the building.

"Was that…"

"A man being dragged inside," Sazan said. "I believe so. That was the second man they brought in."

"Stuckey and Horvath might be alive," said Coop.

One of the figures stayed outside. Even through the seething dust, across the distance, he knew who it was.

The tall, gaunt ISIS torturer.

Ramos's captor.

The man remained standing, as if suspicious of something.

Coop felt the man looking right at him.

Not at *him*, but the building.

He shivered, knowing he was being somehow sensed.

The torturer didn't act any further on his instincts, however. The man slowly turned and walked into the police station on his long legs. The truck rumbled away and disappeared in the shifting sands.

Coop's story clicked into place.

"They *are* alive," he amended his earlier statement.

Needing it to be true.

The horror he'd witnessed in the tunnel had confirmed the worldview he'd accumulated since his homecoming. Life was suffering, and suffering was an illusion. To free oneself of suffering, one had to free himself from desire first.

Let it all go.

He rejected the idea now. In a sense, ISIS had taken a vital part of him in the tunnel, and the only way to get it back was in that building.

He needed it back. He needed to save his friends. More than anything.

His own personal sense of karma demanded it. What made him a man.

Coop had become a creature of desire. He seethed with it. Right now, he *was* desire.

He had intended to wait for night to attempt to rescue Ramos, but then the *shamal* arrived like a sign of providence. One last lucky break.

The storm might last minutes, maybe hours. It would work to conceal their escape as well as darkness.

"I'm going now, Sazan," he said.

Coop checked his weapon's action and chambered a round. The selector lever was set to fire. Yes, now. He had to do it now, while he was still fueled by desire. If he didn't, he would freeze up. He'd stay until it was too late, and then he'd leave.

"Wait," Sazan said.

"I can't."

"Wait," she said again, making it an order. "One moment only."

She disappeared into a back room of the home and returned with an abaya, a head-to-toe cloak many Iraqi women wore as a veil in public and took off at home or in the company of other women to reveal a brightly colored dress.

"Take off your hat," she told him.

Coop removed his filthy visored cap and stuffed it in his back pocket.

The Peshmerga tore a length of the abaya into strips and began wrapping it around his head. He accepted her winding in silence, as if this were some local ritual anointing him for war.

By the time she'd finished, he wore a black head covering similar to a turban that many Iraqi men wore. Black being the Islamic color of radicalism, ISIS's team color.

Coop soaked his keffiyeh with bottled water and wrapped it until it covered his face except for a slit for his eyes. It now served both as a filter against the dusty air and as a disguise.

Between the head covering and keffiyeh, he hoped any fighters in the police station would regard him as one of their own until he was ready to act.

"I'm going to walk in there and get as close to them before they start trying to talk to me," Coop said. "Then I'm going to kill them all."

"Once I hear shooting, I will then come inside and kill the rest," Sazan said.

"Good plan." He suspected anything more sophisticated than that wouldn't work. Underneath the keffiyeh, he put on his war face. "Are you ready?"

She sprayed a generous amount of gun oil into a slot under her Kalashnikov's dust cover and cycled the bolt back and forth. Then she chambered a round and wrapped the weapon in another length of the abaya.

Coop did the same, wrapping his RK62 in cloth to shield it from the dust.

"Now we are ready," she said.

"Before you met us, had you actually seen any combat?"

"No. I told you, I am driver."

"Well." Coop wasn't sure what to say. "Thank you for helping us. But if you want to sit this one out, you—"

"Daesh killed my husband," she told him. "Now you know."

"What?"

"Two years ago. He was Peshmerga. They cut off his hands and feet and left him for the dogs."

"I'm sorry. I didn't know." He didn't know what else to say.

"It is why I joined Peshmerga. I joined to avenge him. I joined to defend my country from them. But KDP does not allow women to fight."

Coop absorbed all this. "I guess we're in this together."

"During the ambush, I did not fire my weapon once," Sazan said. "I was too afraid. Not anymore. If you want to go back, go. I am going."

He knew all about the heavy burden of debts and honor.

"Then let's go," he said.

Gripping his rifle, Coop went out into the blasting storm. The winds and flying dust raged against him like a living thing.

Bracing his feet, he marched steadily across the street until a shuttered storefront appeared. Behind him, Sazan was invisible in the swirling murk. Then she appeared, a ghostly dark shape that steadily gained form as it neared.

He started forward, one hand on the wall, the other hugging his weapon. At the doors of the police station, he unwrapped the rifle and tossed the rag into the wind. The snapping ISIS flag broke free of its pole and fluttered after it to disappear.

Testing one of the doors, he found it unlocked.

He went in alone.

The security vestibule lay empty, the metal detector powered down. Beyond it, the public reception desk and its teller windows stood empty. Coop wound his way through these obstacles into a large open office area surrounded by private offices, kitchen, and records room that appeared to have been ransacked.

His heart quickened at the sight of ISIS fighters staring back at him in the gloomy light of a handful of electric lanterns.

Time slowed as his awareness expanded.

They lounged around the open office area. Young men with old eyes and bearded faces. They wore black hoodies or short, baggy kaftans that reached the thighs of blue jeans, desert camo, or olive-green cargo pants. They sat in office chairs or on cushions arranged on the floor.

In an instant, Coop registered that none of them had a weapon in his hands, though their rifles all rested within easy reach. Their chest rigs hung from chairbacks. One looked up from a tattered copy of *Penthouse*. Their body language was relaxed but curious, a little wary.

Maybe twenty men in all. The tall man wasn't here. A concern, but he had bigger things to think about right now.

He had thirty rounds in his rifle.

His awareness tunneled as adrenaline poured through his veins. The top of his head felt like it was detaching to float somewhere above him. He imagined bullets thudding into him, ripping his organs apart in fiery trails, snapping blood vessels.

A man barked in angry Arabic on a radio, likely the ISIS FM radio station. Coop felt his legs weaken in the heavy atmosphere of hate. These men hated him for being American. Hated him down to his bones. They wanted to destroy him, his country, the entire world they believed they owned.

A burly ISIS fighter was talking to him.

This is the guy, Coop thought.

The guy who dropped mortars on him for a year and a half and almost killed him. Shot Sergeant Franks and murdered Thompson and twenty-two others at the D-Fac. Ordered suicide bombers to murder innocents in countries around the world. Bled Mosul like a plague. Killed Major Haddad and wounded Doc.

This was the guy who'd captured his friends and would soon behead them in a snuff film posted on the internet to inspire the ISIS faithful.

The fighter squinted at him with growing suspicion. Coop stood only several yards away now, too close to miss.

He blinked, and the man was still there.

"*Salaam,*" Coop said.

And fired a single round from the hip.

The bullet struck the man in the chest, spinning him until the chair wobbled and spilled onto the ground.

The other men shouted. Coop let out a cathartic gasp.

Then he shouldered the rifle and opened up on the rest.

The warm gun bucked like an animal in his hands, spitting flame and smoke and empty shell casings. The rounds splashed across the scrambling shapes and punched holes in walls and filing cabinets. Survivors ran or snatched weapons.

His rifle ran black, clicking on an empty chamber.

Screaming, an ISIS fighter fired a burst with wobbling aim. The rounds snapped past Coop's ears as he dropped the mag and fumbled for another.

Then the man shrugged in a spray of blood as a Kalashnikov started firing from the right. Sazan marched into the room, draining her own mag on full cyclic and putting another two men on the ground in a bloody spray.

This took only five seconds, an instant or forever in Coop's distorted perception, but it was long enough for him to reload.

Another round whined past his ear like a supersonic bee. He started firing again, all his terror channeling into an enraged and sublime joy. Bodies banged and tumbled to the floor or across desks.

The rifle clicked empty again. No more mags.

He dropped the weapon and snatched his Tokarev from where it rested against his thigh. No threats in sight.

The wounded writhed and screamed under a drifting pall of gun smoke. Coop looked at Sazan, who panted over her smoking rifle wearing her own fierce expression of either joy or horror, he couldn't tell.

He turned to drill a round into a squirming body. The body went still. Sazan fired several shots. The police station went quiet.

Turning on his flashlight, he advanced deeper into the building with his Tokarev ready to shoot.

As he turned the corner, a shape lunged at him. Coop emptied his magazine into the man's chest. The body slid down the wall in a red smear.

Reaching for another pistol mag, he froze.

An open door yawned in front of him, revealing a room the Iraqi police had used as an interrogation room but ISIS had converted into a chamber of horrors.

On a wide red stain, a single steel chair stood in front of a video camera mounted on a tripod. Hanging from nails in the walls, leather straps, pliers, chains, hammers, drills, machetes, saws, and a large scimitar rested within easy reach for televised torture and murder.

The tall man stood in the shadows.

"Allah akbar," he murmured.

And surged forward with a flash of steel.

Coop backpedaled, raising his empty pistol in an automatic if feeble gesture of defense. Behind him, Sazan screamed in Kurdish.

The machete rang against the Tokarev and sent an agonizing shock up his arm. The blade snapped inches over his head.

Acting either on training or reflex, Coop lashed out with the mangled pistol and struck the man in the face, ripping into his cheekbone.

With a snarl, the ISIS torturer sized up his odds.

And bolted down the hall.

If the man escaped, he'd come back with his friends, and Coop and his friends would never leave Mosul alive.

Still stunned, Coop raced into hot pursuit.

Feet slamming the dusty carpet, he reached the detention cells, where the torturer struggled to open a locked door.

The man started to turn as Coop hurled himself at him.

Coop yanked the man's shirt to put him off balance and stay behind him. The man was surprisingly strong, Coop exhausted. He thrashed wildly against Coop's efforts to wrap an arm around his throat and choke him out.

An elbow lashed into his face with a painful jolt. His arm felt strange and weak from the shock it received during the machete attack.

The man squirmed, almost free.

Pulling again on the man's shirt, Coop thrust one leg forward and allowed the ISIS torturer to haul him upright again.

The man went down in a faceplant.

Gasping, Coop reached for his knife only to pinion an elbow, all his focus and strength needed simply to keep the bucking fighter under him.

Then Sazan slid to her knees next to him. She gripped one of the man's arms and twisted, hissing in Arabic, telling him he was going to die like a filthy dog.

Coop yanked the knife from his belt. He held it high to strike.

Under him, the straining man shrieked in panic.

Coop turned away with a wince to see Ramos staring back at him, his face a mask of terror and despair behind iron bars.

Kneeling on the floor, the sergeant nodded.

It must be done.

The knife skidded sickeningly along the man's ribs, producing an even louder shriek. The second thrust found its mark and sank to the hilt.

Blood fountained from the wound. A killing stroke.

The man groaned. The groan became a sigh.

The sigh stretched until his body went still.

In combat, every kill was an intimate act. Like a sacred ritual. Coop did not ponder it now, but he would. At heart, every soldier was a theologian. A cosmic trade had taken place. He'd gained his life, but the dead man had taken a little piece of his soul with him.

He'd taken the man's life, but the torturer would live on in him forever.

Again, Coop intuited but didn't think about any of this.

Instead, he thought, *I'm alive. I'm alive. I'm alive.*

The Mosul Mile

The American and Iraqi prisoners stared at him hungrily as he unlocked the door. The lock clunked. The great iron door slid to the side.

Wearing a smile so pained it morphed into a deathly grimace, Horvath limped out first and patted Coop's shoulder. Stuckey emerged next nursing his left arm, a battle of relief and agony raging on his own wincing face.

Then Sergeant Ramos, who grabbed Coop and hugged him.

"You're either the craziest or the luckiest son of a bitch I ever met," the man rasped. "And that's counting John Reynolds."

"Hooah, Sarnt," said Coop, agreeing to either.

The words didn't matter. The tight grip they kept on each other's shoulders conveyed all the meaning they intended.

The man felt skeletal and shaky under his hands, and Coop wondered what they'd done to him.

At the same time, he wasn't sure he wanted to know.

Ramos broke free with one hand to pull in Horvath and Stuckey. Together, the four men huddled as if holding each other up.

That *band of brothers* line was written for moments like this, because it wasn't about killing or victory or proving one's courage. It was about survival.

"I thought I was dead," Stuckey gasped. "I thought…"

"We *were* dead," Horvath said. "But then… Christ, Coop. What was that? I didn't know you had it in you."

Coop said nothing.

His training had taken over, but that wasn't all of it. He'd reverted to something else, an older animal part of him that had known exactly what to do.

Do what had to be done.

Right now, he only felt numb. He sensed he'd compartmentalized enough he could spend a lifetime exploring everything he'd locked away.

But not now. First, they had to get home.

Horvath freed an arm to welcome Sazan into the huddle.

"Thank you," he said.

Coop nodded. *Thank you, Sazan.*

The dazed woman said nothing. She shivered against them. Then she broke away to vomit noisily in the corner.

Today, she'd avenged her dead husband and truly earned her place in the Peshmerga, those who faced death.

They were all Peshmerga today.

The Iraqi prisoners turned out to be captured soldiers from 9th Division. An older sergeant spoke enough English to ask where the relief column was.

"We're the relief column," Coop said.

"So we walk."

"We walk. Gather up weapons. There was a *shamal* outside when we came in. If it's still happening, we'll use it as cover. Do you understand?"

The sergeant said, "Enough."

"Gather up weapons, ammo, water. Whatever you need."

The ISIS torturer had hurt Ramos in a variety of ways the man refused to detail, and overall the sergeant looked shaky, but he said he was mobile. Both Horvath and Stuckey had taken shrapnel in their arms and legs, and Coop treated them as best as he could from his med kit.

Horvath dry swallowed Ibuprofen. "Gimme a goddamn rifle, anything."

When they reached the open office, Stuckey blanched as if he regretted everything about this crazy mission even though it had miraculously succeeded. He had the look of a man who'd fought way above his weight and now realized how lucky he was to still be standing. Realized everything he'd very nearly lost.

Gritting his teeth at his wounds, Horvath managed a grin. "Christ, Coop. You cleaned house."

Coop looked around at the carnage. Dead bodies lay everywhere in pools of blood. He knew every second of the fight had permanently imprinted itself in his memory, but right now, he could only recall it as fragments.

Shooting the first man in the chest. The chair spinning. Shooting another shocked man in the face while he still held his open issue of *Penthouse*.

"The lady did her share," Coop said.

"The lady might just get a marriage proposal."

Hearing this, Sazan, who still looked green, laughed out loud, which sounded both macabre and surprisingly pleasant in this slaughterhouse.

"Laugh it up," Horvath said. "Don't be surprised, that's all."

"Big American talk," she shot back.

"I can't shoot a rifle," Stuckey said.

The man's left arm was a swollen mess, but it was more than that. Coop guessed Stuckey would be selling his gun collection when he got home. The man looked at the scattered weaponry as if they were a batch of live snakes.

"Find a pistol," said Coop.

The man winced again.

Coop added, "Sorry, LT. Everybody fights until we're home. After that, we can make our own choices again."

"Yeah. Okay." The lieutenant's face hardened as he remembered who was depending on him and who was waiting for him back home. "I'll fight until then."

Together, the Americans and Iraqis pulled chest rigs, weapons, and ammo from the human wreckage. Coop retrieved his RK62 and scavenged fresh ammo for it. His arm no longer tingled and had begun to ache. He ignored the pain.

Lurching like a zombie on his weak legs, Ramos carried the torture devices into the room and planted them one by one in the ISIS fighters' dead hands.

A message that they'd reaped what they'd sown? A message for the ISIS guys who would discover these bodies?

Coop didn't ask. It was more soldier juju.

He resoaked his keffiyeh, wrapped it again around his face, and opened the police station's door.

A part of him thought all of ISIS would be waiting for him outside in pickups bristling with snapping black flags. A tragic but strangely fitting end to his story, karma clearing every obstacle to bring him here but then righting the scales.

Instead, the street lay veiled behind the swirling dust, seemingly empty.

Too bad, Coop thought.

At nine men, they were now a full-strength rifle squad. If ISIS *was* here, he would have put real money on his side coming out ahead.

The squad marched into the boiling dust.

Ramos staggered along next to him. Malnourished and tortured, he seemed to be held together by Scotch tape and willpower. Coop again wanted to ask what they did to him but knew it wasn't the right question.

Instead, he asked, "Are you gonna be okay, Sergeant?"

"I've died before," Ramos said.

OP Applejack. The night of the counter mortar mission.

"You didn't die, though."

"That's true. You could say I was reborn."

"Is that why you came back to Iraq?"

Ramos didn't answer for a while. The winds buffeted him forward. Every step seemed to hurt him as he marched in a steady gait powered seemingly by determination alone.

The man was still the definition of *tough* that Coop remembered. He wanted to help but knew the sergeant wouldn't accept it.

"A man can do good things for a bad cause, or he can do bad things for a good cause," Ramos said finally. "Tell me which is better."

"I guess it'd be the one that does the most good and the least harm," Coop said.

The sergeant nodded. "There's your answer."

Coop nodded. It wasn't so different than the choices he'd made after coming home. The war had propelled each of them to some moral imperative.

Only in Ramos's case, it had hurled him toward fresh purpose and a different kind of service, while Coop had run from it altogether.

Sand pelted his back while he kept moving. His throat was hoarse from combat dehydration and yelling over the gale. If they made it out of here, he knew he'd be coughing dust from his aching lungs for days.

"Your turn," Ramos said.

"Sergeant?"

"Why did *you* come back? You must have known there was a snowball's chance in hell of saving me. I don't know whether to name my firstborn after you guys or kick your lucky, dumb asses for being this stupid."

"I owed you something."

The man snorted. "You didn't—"

"I owed you, and that's it," Coop said firmly.

Ramos had jumped on a grenade and showed Coop what love was. The purest kind of love that existed, the kind where you died for someone else.

Ramos had taken that love and turned it into a love for humanity. Already dead in a sense, he'd transformed himself into a being of service. Inspired by it, Coop had returned to Iraq with a sense of purpose he'd lacked for a decade.

All of them had been shaped not only by their war but by that one fateful night on the banks of the Tigris. The grenade hadn't gone off. Instead, a psychic bomb had exploded, and it had given them all a moral injury.

Horvath had stayed in the service, and Coop understood why now. He remembered how his friend had made a joking promise to do it if his tough-as-nails squad leader told him he loved him.

Instead of saying it aloud, Ramos had showed him the real thing.

Then there was Doc. He'd been there too. Until Marjorie gave him new purpose, the man had been rendered rudderless by the fact Ramos had nearly sacrificed his life—for his men, true, but ultimately for a pointless war.

As for Reyes, his failure to cover his sector, which resulted in his sergeant's psychic death, had chewed him up until he'd eaten a bullet. Sergeant Murray had caught an itch he couldn't scratch and drank himself into a car accident.

And then there was Coop and his wandering, ever vigilant to threat and searching for something that might earn his own sacrifice.

"We all had our reasons for saying yes to the LT's crazy plan," Coop said. "But you were the catalyst, Sergeant. We owed you. What you did took a piece of me that I wanted back, and I had to give something to get it."

Ramos nodded. This he understood.

"It's yours again?" he asked.

"All of it," Coop told him.

People appeared in the dust ahead. They were refugees, propelled from their homes by the same idea of using the storm to escape the nightmare their city had become. Coop's ad hoc squad joined the rear of the throng as it flowed around dark, hulking shapes that appeared next on the road. These were the damaged CTS vehicles, which now stood derelict and broken into pieces.

"Do you think you'll ever go home?" Coop asked his old sergeant.

"Home isn't what's familiar. It's where your soul finds rest."

Coop nodded at this and wondered where his own restless soul might finally call home. He wanted to ask more questions, though he wasn't sure where to start. Sergeant Ramos had always seemed a mystery to him.

He wondered whether the man was happy with Knightingale living so close to the devil he knew. Whether he still sang in karaoke bars.

As if anticipating a lot of sharing he didn't want to do, Ramos reached out and pounded Coop's shoulder. "You did good, troop."

"It was Lieutenant Stuckey's... It was all of us together, Sergeant."

The Mosul mile was almost over. They were nearly at the finish line—the CTS positions Major Haddad's company had assaulted from twenty-four hours earlier.

Supported by Sazan, Horvath hobbled to catch up to him on his other side.

"I guess I owe *you* now," he said. "You dick."

Coop said, "You can pay me back by getting your head out of your ass."

Horvath laughed. "That's asking a lot."

Coop turned to make sure Stuckey was still behind them. The man stumbled along, nursing his hastily bandaged arm.

"Hang tough, LT," he said. "We're almost home."

"Careful what you wish for, huh?" said the lieutenant.

Even with the keffiyeh covering the man's face, Coop could tell it might take a long time before Stuckey accepted that he had in fact survived.

"You succeeded, sir," Ramos said. "And you're alive. Just leave it at that."

After a pause, Stuckey said, "He's already setting me straight."

Coop smiled. Even after everything that happened and the bizarre landscape he now traveled, this all felt familiar enough to be comforting.

Figures materialized in the dust around them. A voice called out in Arabic to halt and drop their weapons.

Coop blinked into the dim red light and spotted rifles.

He raised his RK62, ready to shoot—

"Stand down," another voice roared. "Stand down!"

The strangers lowered their weapons.

One of the figures strode forward to hug Ramos. Stepping back, he pulled down his keffiyeh to reveal a bright grin.

"Praise the Lord," said John Reynolds.

Coop smiled back and thought, *I've arrived.*

Within the next days, Coop and the others will visit Doc in an Erbil hospital and share the good news. By the end of the week, Coop and Horvath will see Lieutenant Stuckey off at the airport.

The LT will return home to Carol and the kids and work hard, with great humility, to repair his marriage. He will finish writing his book around the time Doc is finally healed enough to head home himself, feeling whole in both mind and body for the first time since the war. Doc will later go to med school and set up a comfortable life for himself in peace—both the external and the inner kind—though he and Marjorie will return to hotspots in the Middle East and Africa as members of Doctors Without Borders multiple times before the birth of their daughter. Long before then, while the Battle of Mosul is still raging, Horvath will marry Sazan in a hybrid Christian-Muslim wedding, and as he'd once idly imagined by a hotel poolside, he does in fact stay in Kurdistan, becoming a military adviser to the Peshmerga.

Coop will never understand how, exactly, going back to Iraq on a wild rescue mission solved the problems these men had brought home from Iraq, but that is war. That is life.

All the while, he has decided to stay in Iraq. He helps Stuckey prepare to go home and visits Doc in the hospital. He attends Horvath's wedding. During this time, he returns to Mosul and looks up the Knightingale Commandos. John Reynolds accepts him with little fanfare. Ramos welcomes him with a knowing nod. Working with these men, Coop updates and levels up his combat medic skills and is soon applying them to Iraqi soldiers and civilians wounded by the monsters in human form that are the men of ISIS. In return, he teaches his tough comrades meditation, yoga, and the art of letting go.

He'd once fought for this country while hating everyone in it. But that war was over, and his new war, saving lives as a soldier for humanity, delivers a sense of sacred purpose, something at last worthy of living and if needed dying for.

In July 2017, the Battle of Mosul will be all but over, though sporadic fighting and arrests of ISIS leaders will go on for months. At the end, every district will have received at least some damage, with six almost utterly destroyed. More than five thousand buildings will be damaged in all. Estimates of casualties will range from ten to twenty-five thousand ISIS fighters killed, a thousand Iraqi soldiers killed and five thousand wounded, and anywhere from twenty-five hundred to up to forty thousand civilians killed, with more than nine hundred thousand displaced.

Coop will celebrate Iraq's victory with Knightingale's hardened Hospitallers at a wrecked military base that was once FOB Marez. That night, he understands his war never owned him, though he owned it and it was a part of him just as he was a part of it, a brief chapter in Iraq's violent history. In a sense, he belongs here, now. Taking a page from Doc's book, he finds the right time and place to be.

Coop also knows that history has a way of repeating itself. Iraq and Mosul once were the birthplace of civilization and the nexus of empires. Major Haddad died for an idea that Coop will believe with all his heart is true and correct. That Mosul may take generations to rebuild, but it will be strong and green again.

A month after the liberation of Mosul, he is told the Iraqi Army will launch a fresh offensive to retake Tal Afar, one of the last ISIS strongholds in the country. It will take the rest of the year to destroy ISIS and drive its remnants underground, but that is still in the future.

Coop immediately packs his kit. He will go wherever he is needed. Where he can do the most good until the day arrives when at last he will be ready to go home.

About the Author

Craig DiLouie is an American-Canadian author of military and speculative fiction. His published novels span WW2 and other military fiction to horror and other speculative fiction; his most notable works include *Episode Thirteen* (Redhook/Hachette, 2023), *The Children of Red Peak* (Redhook/Hachette, 2020), *Our War* (Orbit/Hachette, 2019), *One of Us* (Orbit/Hachette, 2018), and *Suffer the Children* (Gallery Books/Simon & Schuster, 2014). He is a member of International Thriller Writers. Learn more at CraigDiLouie.com.

Printed in Great Britain
by Amazon